# JUROR #3

A complete list of books by James Patterson is at the back of this book. For previews of upcoming books and information about the author, visit JamesPatterson.com, or find him on Facebook or at your app store.

# JUROR #3

## JAMES PATTERSON
### AND NANCY ALLEN

Little, Brown and Company
New York   Boston   London

Copyright © 2018 by James Patterson

Hachette Book Group supports the right to free expression and the value of copyright. The purpose of copyright is to encourage writers and artists to produce the creative works that enrich our culture.

The scanning, uploading, and distribution of this book without permission is a theft of the author's intellectual property. If you would like permission to use material from the book (other than for review purposes), please contact permissions@hbgusa.com. Thank you for your support of the author's rights.

Little, Brown and Company
Hachette Book Group
1290 Avenue of the Americas, New York, NY 10104
littlebrown.com

First Edition: September 2018

Little, Brown and Company is a division of Hachette Book Group, Inc. The Little, Brown name and logo are trademarks of Hachette Book Group, Inc.

The publisher is not responsible for websites (or their content) that are not owned by the publisher.

The Hachette Speakers Bureau provides a wide range of authors for speaking events. To find out more, go to hachettespeakersbureau.com or call (866) 376-6591.

ISBN 978-0-316-47412-2 (hardcover) / 978-0-316-41985-7 (large print)

LCCN 2018943825

10 9 8 7 6 5 4 3 2 1

LSC-H

Printed in the United States of America

*To Randy, Ben, and Martha*

# PROLOGUE

# ONE

BALANCING A TRAY loaded with dirty glassware, Darrien Summers dodged the masked men and women in evening dress as he made his way through the dining room. The annual Mardi Gras ball at the country club in Williams County, Mississippi, was in full swing, the dance floor so crowded that many guests swayed to the jazz band in the narrow spaces between the tables.

Darrien shouldered his way through the door into the kitchen. As it swung shut, the heavy door caught his bad knee. He grimaced and dropped his tray on a metal counter by the dishwasher. Limping over to a chair, he sat to massage the knee with both hands.

A white-haired waiter stood by the back door, blowing cigarette smoke into the outside air. He pointed the cigarette at Darrien. "That football knee still hurting you?"

Darrien nodded with a rueful laugh. "Sometimes it sure does."

"You played at Alabama? Or was it Arkansas?"

"Arkansas," Darrien said. He added, "Arkansas State. Not good enough for U of A."

The flare-up in his knee was a painful reminder. He'd been a strong player at the high school level—maybe not enough of a star for Ole Miss or the Crimson Tide of Alabama or University of Arkansas, but he'd been signed for a full ride at Arkansas State, not far across the state line from Mississippi.

"Bet your daddy was proud. You going back in the fall? When your knee gets better?"

"No," Darrien said, and turned away to discourage further conversation. He'd been answering that question since he was sidelined with a knee injury back in his sophomore year. He'd needed to remain on the team to get his degree, but shortly after, he'd been busted at a campus party in possession of a joint. They'd pulled the scholarship, and here he was.

Darrien's phone buzzed in his pocket, and he reached for it under his white waiter's jacket. Reading the text, Darrien smiled, whispering "Sheeiitt" under his breath.

The club manager, Bert Owens, came into the kitchen, pushing the door open with a bang. Darrien rose from the chair, and the other waiter pitched the cigarette out the back door. Owens marched over, tilting his head back to look Darrien in the eye.

"Summers, you get paid by the hour. I want you working all sixty minutes of it, not sitting on your ass and playing with your phone."

Darrien slipped his phone into the pocket of his jacket.

"Mr. Owens, can I go on break now? Sir? I haven't had a break all night."

The manager pointed a finger at Darrien's chest. "Twenty minutes. Then I want you back on the floor."

Before Darrien could make his exit, the swinging door

opened wide and a man in a black tuxedo stepped into the kitchen. His hair was parted on the side with razor-like precision, so that Darrien could see the white skin of his scalp. The man leaned against the door frame, crossing his arms on his chest.

"Damn, Owens. Have to chase you into the kitchen to get a word with you."

The manager wheeled around, snatched a towel, and wiped his right hand before extending it.

"Mr. Greene, sir. We're mighty happy to have you here tonight. What do you think of our shindig?"

Owens was grinning so hard, it looked like his face might crack.

Greene accepted Owens's hand and gave it a brief shake. "Y'all put on a fine Mardi Gras party, that's for sure. But I just heard that the band will stop playing at midnight. Owens, we can't have that."

As if on cue, the whine of a saxophone drifted into the kitchen.

"Mr. Greene, the band's got a contract."

"Is that so?" Greene's blue eyes fixed on Owens. "Well, I do know a thing or two about contracts."

"Yes, sir. You should, working with the finest law firm in Jackson."

"And I didn't come all the way from Jackson to go home at midnight, not at Mardi Gras. No, sir."

Beads of perspiration shone on Owens's forehead. "Mr. Greene, if the band plays past midnight, we got to pay them extra."

Mr. Greene's face broke into a smile. "Well, if that's all." He pulled a wallet from his pocket. He folded several bills and slipped the money into the manager's hand, then pushed the door and walked out, with Owens at his heels.

Seizing the opening, Darrien slipped through the back exit out onto the patio, then walked toward the swimming pool at a brisk pace. The pool was drained, the lounge chairs and snack tables locked up until Memorial Day weekend. A dozen cabanas made a semicircle beside the women's dressing room—and the door to cabana 6 was ajar.

Jewel Shaw would be waiting for him inside.

# TWO

SHE WAS BAD news, he knew that. At twenty-eight, she was seven years older than Darrien; and as the only daughter of one of the club's founding members, Jewel Shaw was forbidden fruit. Even in the twenty-first century, rich white women usually didn't mix with the black waitstaff at the country club. Not in Rosedale, Mississippi.

But Jewel was a wild child.

He pushed open the door to cabana 6 and slipped inside. It was dark, but Darrien knew from experience there was a light switch somewhere on the wall. Feeling for it with his fingers, he bumped against a table—with his good knee, thank Jesus. He found a lamp and switched it on.

He saw Jewel lying on the chaise lounge near the far wall of the small space. Her left arm dangled off the side, and it looked like her purple dress had stains all over it.

He hesitated. Maybe he ought to turn around and head back to the kitchen. If Jewel was passed out—and that had happened before—he was in no position to deal with it.

But he reconsidered. It wouldn't be right to leave her like that. He'd best check on her, make sure she was okay. He approached carefully in the dim lamplight.

"Jewel?" he whispered. "What you doing, baby?"

When he got to the lounge, Darrien muffled a groan.

Blood was seeping through slits in the fabric of her purple dress, where she had been slashed in her chest, abdomen, and side. The green and gold Mardi Gras beads at her neck were wet, and blood matted her blond hair where it fell past her shoulders.

Her eyes were open and her chest heaved.

Darrien squatted on the floor beside her, barely noting the pain that knifed through his knee. "Oh, Jesus." He picked up her limp wrist and, not feeling a pulse, pressed his ear to her chest to try to listen to her heart, smelling the coppery odor of Jewel's blood.

Nothing. Her chest didn't move again. Leaning over her, he lifted her head and spoke her name. "Jewel." Then louder: "Jewel?"

Dropping her head back onto the chaise, Darrien squeezed his eyes shut, trying to think what he should do. He pressed his hands onto her chest, trying to revive her with CPR. It didn't help. He reached into his pocket for his phone, registering with panic that his hands were bloody, and his white jacket was smeared with blood.

He would dial 911. But his hands shook so violently, he couldn't enter the passcode.

Footsteps sounded on the cement outside the cabana and he heard men's voices. Darrien tried to shout "Hey!" but it came out like a squawk.

As he held the phone, a flashlight beam cut into the dim room. Darrien dropped the phone and said, "Oh, my God."

# THREE

THE CLUB SECURITY guard, a reserve deputy for Williams County, tackled him to the floor. Bert Owens trained the flashlight on Jewel, then turned the light into Darrien's face. "What have you done?"

Darrien shook his head, pinned beneath the deputy, trying to frame the words: I tried to help her. Owens said to the deputy, "Stand him up."

The man pulled Darrien to his feet and with the help of another security guard pinned his arms behind him. Owens swung the flashlight and smashed it into the side of Darrien's head. "Boy, what have you done to Miss Shaw?"

"I didn't—"

Owens punched him. Darrien felt his lip split over his teeth and tasted blood.

The reserve deputy said in a doubtful tone, "Read him his rights, you reckon?"

Owens said, "Fuck that." He swung the flashlight again, hitting Darrien's scalp near his left eye. His knees sagged, but the security guards held him upright.

Owens held the flashlight so that the beam shone straight into Darrien's eyes. "What did you do? Talk, boy."

Darrien struggled to catch his breath, then said in a hoarse whisper, "I want a lawyer."

# PART ONE

# FOUR WEEKS LATER

# CHAPTER 1

I TOLD MY client not to bring her kids to court.

It wasn't that I was unsympathetic to her situation. My mom was a single mother, too. But Darla Lamar should have been sitting next to me at the counsel table, to present a united front while I made the case to the judge about her gripes against her slumlord. Instead, she was seated in the back row of the Williams County courtroom, wrestling four-year-old JimBob and his little sister Lily.

The judge said, "Miss Bozarth, are you ready to give your closing argument?"

When I rose from my seat, I heard an ear-splitting whine coming from the back of the courtroom. The judge peered at me over his eyeglasses.

Turning around, I gave Darla a pleading look. She slapped a hand over Lily's mouth.

As I walked around the counsel table to address the judge, I tried to look supremely confident, like a woman who'd been practicing law for decades. In fact, I'd been at it for eight short months, since I graduated from Ole Miss and passed the Mississippi Bar Exam, and I held my yellow legal pad in a sweaty grip. But in this case I knew I had the facts and the law on my side.

Standing up straight, I fastened the jacket of my suit, purchased the week before at Goodwill. The button popped off into my hand.

Shit.

I slipped the button in my pocket, trying to look like having my buttons pop was totally cool.

"Your Honor, we've established by a preponderance of the evidence that my client's landlord has violated the implied warranty of habitability." I scooped up photos from the counsel table. "Defendant's Exhibit One proves that, despite repeated requests from my client, Darla Lamar, her landlord has failed and refused to exterminate the vermin that inhabit the apartment: cockroach infestations throughout the property, as well as rats. *Rats,* Your Honor."

I placed the photographs on the bench, so the judge would be sure to give them a second look. One showed roaches crawling from a kitchen cabinet; the other caught the image of a rat peeking into a crib. A picture really is worth a thousand words.

"And those conditions can adversely affect the health of her young children."

At the mention of Darla's kids, I heard JimBob cry "Mama!" I gave the judge a nod, as if having the children fuss in court was all a part of my master plan.

At least Darla didn't bring her infant. The judge was looking testier by the moment.

I faced him with what I hoped was a steely look, steadying my voice. "The case is clear, Your Honor. For all the reasons stated, I urge you to enter a judgment in defendant's favor, in both plaintiff's action for rent and our countersuit for damages."

I smiled, turned, and sat at the counsel table with an expectant air, waiting for him to announce our victory. We were sure to win; it was a textbook case, straight out of my landlord/tenant law class at Ole Miss. From the moment Darla Lamar had walked into my office with her three kids and her tale of woe, gripping a fistful of rat pictures, my gut had told me that this case was a winner—money in the bank.

The judge flipped open the file, lifted his pen, and announced, "Court rules in favor of the plaintiff."

My jaw dropped. *How could he?*

I could feel my temper flushing a shade of pink up my neck. *How could I have lost this?*

I had clawed through law school on the belief that my gut instincts were generally right. Growing up poor in small Mississippi towns, I had learned at an early age to anticipate other people's reactions.

And when my gut failed me, I had my fists. Too bad I couldn't throw a punch at the county judge.

Darla Lamar was at my elbow, tugging on my secondhand jacket. I gingerly pulled away, afraid the fabric would pop a seam.

"What does he mean?" Darla asked in a frightened whisper.

Keeping my voice low, I said, "Darla, we lost. The judge found in favor of your landlord."

Darla's face contorted. "Where does that leave me? And my kids? You said we was going to win."

Oh, no, I had *not* said that. My trial practice prof had beat that into our heads: Never guarantee victory. With an effort, I kept my voice patient. "Darla, what I said was that the law was on our side, and it surely is. But you still have the right to appeal."

Darla started to cry. She pulled her enormous black purse up onto her shoulder with such a violent jerk, it smacked me in the chest.

"I don't get it. This ain't right." She turned to the gallery. "JimBob, get your sister over here!" Fixing a glare in the judge's direction, she wiped her eyes and said, "I gotta go pick up the baby, and now I'm out ten bucks for the sitter this morning. This ain't right."

I picked up the Darla Lamar file and tucked it into my Coach briefcase. Darla watched me zip it up.

"Fancy purse," she said.

She was eyeing the bag with resentment. Darla said, "Must be nice, buying things like that."

"It was a gift," I said—which was the truth. "It's a briefcase," I added, as if explaining the bag's purpose might make a difference to her.

Apparently not. She turned her back to me without further comment, gathered her children by the hand, and led them out of the courtroom. Watching them go, I felt sick to my stomach. Darla was right to be upset with the judgment, but I was pretty unhappy, too. I'd taken the case on a contingent fee basis. In other words: "No fee unless you win!" But it looked like I'd be eating Kraft macaroni and cheese for supper.

Again.

"Ruby Bozarth?"

When I heard my name, I looked around. The circuit judge's clerk stood in the courtroom doorway.

"Yes, ma'am?" I said.

"Ruby? Judge Baylor wants to see you in his chambers."

Well, that was weird. I didn't have anything pending in Judge Baylor's court. Baylor handled the big cases: felonies, big-money civil matters. Looking at the clerk, I shook my head and said, "Me? Are you sure?"

The clerk nodded and pointed at the hallway. "He's waiting. It's about your murder case."

Huh? I didn't have a murder case.

How could I? I'd never handled anything bigger than a country roads DWI. And I'd lost that case, too.

# CHAPTER 2

I DIDN'T WANT the judge to spy the dangling threads hanging off my suit, so I tucked the side of my jacket behind my back and entered the office with my hand on my hip, like a Salvation Army fashion model walking the runway.

"Miss Bozarth here to see you, Judge," said the clerk.

"Good! Excellent! Take a seat, ma'am."

Two leather wingback chairs faced his mammoth walnut desk. I set my shiny briefcase beside the one nearest the door.

"No, not over there. Sit here."

He pointed to a small wooden library chair to the right of his desk. I got the message, loud and clear. I wasn't important enough to sit in the fancy chair. My jaw clenched as I picked up the briefcase.

Settling on the hard edge of the chair, I smoothed my skirt and primly crossed my ankles.

"Judge Baylor," I began, but he cut me off.

"So you're a grad of Ole Miss law school?"

I nodded. "Yes, Your Honor. I graduated last May." Should I tell him my class rank? Because it was pretty damned good.

"Did you know, I graduated from Ole Miss, too—class of 1976."

I smiled politely. Life had been good to the judge. By his appearance, with salt-and-pepper hair and a trim physique, I'd thought he was younger than that.

He smiled back. "Got my undergrad degree there, too. Oxford is a grand old town. Beautiful campus."

"Beautiful," I echoed.

"I was a Sigma Nu, back in undergrad. How about you, Miss Bozarth? Which sorority did you pledge?"

Was there a murder case, or had he called me in to take a trip down memory lane?

God, I wanted a piece of Nicorette. My hand itched to reach down and dig for the box inside my briefcase.

I said, "No sorority. Not my scene. Your Honor, your clerk said—"

He tilted back in his chair and propped his feet on the shiny desktop. "How'd you happen to come to Rosedale to hang your shingle?"

I answered by rote. "I like small towns, sir. Grew up in them."

Actually, one of the places I'd lived as a kid was right here in Rosedale. But I wasn't inclined to tell him the whole story.

I also did not confide that I'd had a cushy job lined up after graduation at a big law firm in Jackson. A generous offer that disappeared when I broke off my engagement with my ex-fiancé, Lee Greene, whose family knew a whole lot of people in Mississippi.

It still gave me satisfaction to recall the shocked look he wore when I threw the diamond ring in his face. The Coach briefcase he gave me, though, was another matter. A woman has to be practical.

"Whereabouts?"

"Sir?"

"Where'd you grow up?"

Was he digging, or just being polite? Was there a chance that he knew I'd spent time in Rosedale? I shifted my weight in the uncomfortable chair. "All over. We moved around Mississippi. Even spent a while across the river in Arkansas."

I fell silent but tried to send him a telepathic message: *Don't you dare ask me what my daddy did for a living.* Because the fact was, I didn't know. I was the product of a one-night stand following a concert. Mom was taken with my biological father because she thought he kinda looked like Garth Brooks. "That's where you get your shiny brown hair," she'd say, and kiss the top of my head.

"Well, Miss Bozarth, y'all being new to town puts you in a prime position for the Summers case. You'll be more comfortable handling the defense, since you don't have a history with the victim and her family." He shook his head, his mouth turned down in an expression of deep regret. "Jewel Shaw was a Kappa at Ole Miss."

Finally. "Exactly what kind of case are you talking about, Your Honor?"

"State v. Darrien Summers. He's been charged with the murder of Jewel Shaw. It happened over at the country club, if you can believe it."

I was poised so close to the edge of my wooden seat that I was in danger of falling onto the floor.

"But Judge Baylor, what's this got to do with me?" When he frowned, I added hastily, "Sir, I don't mean to sound impertinent. But I don't represent Mr. Summers."

"Oh, yes you do." He dropped his feet back onto the floor. "I appointed you this morning."

A wave of panic washed over me and I let out a nervous laugh.

"Your Honor, I'm not qualified. I've only tried one case before a jury—it was a misdemeanor. I've never handled a felony defense."

While I spoke, he began to smile at me. "I'm surprised to hear you say that. My clerk tells me you've been begging for appointments."

It was true. I had—but not appointments like this. "For guardianships. I told your clerk I wanted to serve as guardian ad litem in family law matters."

"In fact, Grace told me you'd been complaining about it, saying it was downright unfair that I hadn't given you an appointment yet. Now I am." He smirked.

I should have known that his clerk would repeat my rash words. But I'd been angling for GAL work for months, and he kept handing the guardianships to the same two lawyers. "Judge, if you have a guardianship, I'm more than ready to take it on. But not a murder. I don't have any background in that kind of case."

"Miss Bozarth, if you want to learn how to swim, you're going to have to jump in the water." His tone was benevolent.

My heart beat so fast, it was hard to breathe. "I have to decline. Respectfully. I respectfully decline."

The kindly expression disappeared. "You, ma'am, are a member of the Mississippi Bar. And when you became a member, you swore an oath." He tossed a file at me. "I expect you to honor your obligations as an attorney licensed to practice law in this state."

I picked up the file with a shaking hand. Opening it, I skimmed through the judge's docket sheet.

"Your Honor, it says here that Darrien Summers is represented by the public defender."

"Was. Was represented. The public defender withdrew. Look at the most recent docket entry. The defendant is represented by you, Miss Bozarth." The judge turned to the phone on his desk and pushed a button. "I'm ready for my next appointment, Grace. We're all wrapped up here."

Clearly, I was dismissed. I stood, my briefcase in one hand, the file in the other. Judge Baylor gestured toward the file I held. "You can keep that copy. It'll bring you up to date."

As I tottered toward his office door, a thought struck me. I turned around.

"Beg pardon, Your Honor, but why did the public defender withdraw?"

"Oooooh," he sighed. "Well, the defendant took a swing at him the last time they appeared in court. Tried to punch him out. The attorney could hardly be expected to continue representation, under the circumstances."

Judge Baylor winked at me. "Y'all be careful, now. Watch your back."

# CHAPTER 3

A MURDER CASE. I had a murder case.

I walked out of the judge's office in a fog, heading for the courthouse stairway. I grasped the banister at the top of the stairs with a sweaty palm.

*Get a grip.*

I was going to have to pull it together. Gotta deal.

Directly across the hall from Judge Baylor's chambers was a door painted in bold black letters: THOMAS LAFAYETTE, DISTRICT ATTORNEY. I left the stairway and headed for that door.

Because if this was really happening, and I was actually representing a man charged with murder, I needed to know the evidence the state had against him. Lifting my chin, I walked into the DA's office.

"I need to see Mr. Lafayette."

The receptionist gave me a glance as she clicked her computer mouse. "He's got a tight schedule this week. If you email him directly, he might be able to squeeze you in."

"I need to see him today. I've been appointed to represent Darrien Summers."

Her eyebrows shot up as she looked up from the computer screen, picked up the phone, and pushed a button. "Tom, there's a woman out here, says she represents Darrien Summers."

The door to his inner office flew open. A forty-year-old man in a pinstriped suit with a deep dimple in his chin leaned in the door frame, looking me up and down.

He laughed. "Well, get on in here, and let's get acquainted."

In his office, I took a seat facing his desk and sat up straight, trying to look professional.

"Mr. Lafayette, I'm Ruby Bozarth."

"Call me Tom." He plucked a business card from a brass display on his desk and handed it to me. I checked my pockets, hoping to find a card of my own to offer in return, but I only found the button.

"So, Ruby, you set up shop across from the courthouse, right? In the old Ben Franklin store? I can't believe we haven't met."

Lafayette had a speech impediment, just a slight emphasis on the letter S—a tendency to hiss.

"I haven't done too much criminal litigation." Did I imagine it, or were his eyes unusually wide set?

He picked up a fountain pen, twirling it in his fingers. "I didn't think Baylor would find anyone fool enough to take this on. Do you realize we're set for trial in two weeks?"

My stomach did a flop. I had a spasm of such intense nausea, I was afraid I might vomit on his carpet.

I swallowed. "I'll get a continuance."

He laughed again. My hand itched to punch his dimpled chin.

"Well, I guess you can ask Baylor for a continuance. But asking ain't getting. The judge doesn't intend to let this case languish on the docket. Summers won't plead, and the community wants justice." He set the pen down. "How much are they paying you?"

I opened my mouth and clamped it shut, astounded to realize that I had no clue. I hadn't thought to ask the judge.

Lafayette said, "The last time the public defender conflicted out, a lawyer that Baylor appointed tried to bill the county a fortune for his time. But they cut him back. You should know that up front. You'll only get paid eighty dollars an hour for in-court time, fifty dollars an hour for your out-of-court time."

I blinked. That sounded like a fortune. I'd been wrangling small fees from clients who couldn't afford to pay for their groceries. I started doing math to calculate how many hours I'd rack up for a jury trial.

I could pay my rent at the Ben Franklin.

Lafayette reached over to the credenza behind his chair, picked up a file, and tossed it across the desk at me. "There's your discovery: it's the contents of our Darrien Summers file."

I opened the file and flipped through it. Skimming the pages, I tried to play it cool.

"Tom, what do you see as the core evidence you have against my client?"

"It's all right there, in the sheriff's report. Summers was found with Jewel Shaw's body in a cabana out by the pool at the Williams County country club on the night of the Mardi Gras ball. She had thirteen stab wounds, inflicted by an instrument consistent with a butcher knife."

When he talked about the deceased's injuries, he rolled the words on his tongue: *ssstab woundsss inflicted by an inssstrument.*

"What was my client doing at the club?"

"Summers was on staff at the club—a waiter."

I had the sheriff's report in hand, skimming through it as fast as I could. "I don't see anything about a murder weapon. Where is it?"

"Damn shame—they looked for it. Never found it."

I looked up from the report and tried to read his reaction. "No murder weapon? What did he do, eat it? And no eyewitness? Your evidence is circumstantial. My client sounds like a bystander, a guy who stumbled into the wrong place at the wrong time."

Lafayette laughed at me—for the third time. "Keep digging in that file, Ruby. They found Jewel Shaw's cell phone at the scene. And the last activity on her phone was a text message to the defendant, telling him to meet her at the cabana."

"I don't get it. She's texting the waiter? What—she wants another dessert? This is totally arbitrary. What's the motive?"

"Keep turning the pages, ma'am."

I did. When I came upon photocopies of selfies of a blond woman and a tall black man engaged in a variety of sexual positions, I almost dropped the file.

"Oh, my Lord."

"Yep. Looks like Miss Shaw didn't delete her photos too often."

Something about the name of the deceased rang a bell, but I couldn't quite place it. "Jewel Shaw," I repeated.

Lafayette nodded. "Jewel was cut down in her prime. We'll never know how he got rid of that knife—but he didn't get rid of those phone pictures. And those pictures there are going to get your client the death penalty."

*The death penalty.* Bile rose up in my throat again. I grabbed the file and my briefcase and made a run for the women's restroom.

# CHAPTER 4

I'D NEVER SEEN the inside of a jail before.

The smell hit me first: an unhappy combination of dirty feet and school cafeteria food. I dug into my briefcase, palmed a Nicorette tablet, and chewed down hard.

As the jailer led me into the inmate interview area, he pointed to a phone receiver on the wall, next to a foggy pane of security glass. "You'll talk through that."

"Okay," I said, and pulled out a folding chair that faced the glass. When the jailer left, the electronic door slammed shut behind him, locking me in. I shuddered.

While I waited for Darrien Summers to appear on the other side of the cubicle, I pulled out my legal pad, turned to a fresh page, and tapped my pen on the paper in a nervous rhythm. I started to wonder whether the gum chewing would make me look like an immature kid.

He wouldn't know I was trying to kick the Marlboro habit I'd started in high school, when I used to filch cigarettes from my mom's purse. I quit in college; it was a habit I could ill afford. But I picked it up again in law school from my ex, Lee Greene. Somehow, his overblown confidence made the vice look genteel. Those were the bad old days.

But I was done with tobacco, and done with my false southern knight, Lee. The Nicorette was a handy panacea, but my client might think I was chawing down on a lump of bubble gum. I tore off a piece of paper from the legal pad and spat the gum onto the paper just as my client walked through the door on the other side of the glass.

The fuzzy selfies I'd seen of Darrien Summers didn't do him justice. He was well over six feet tall, dwarfing the jailer who led him in, and his muscled biceps and forearms looked like those of a DC superhero. His hair was buzzed close to his head, enhancing his sculpted cheekbones and strong jaw. He was dressed in orange jail scrubs, his hands shackled behind him.

I waved at Summers through the glass. As soon as the jailer unlocked the cuffs and made his exit, I picked up the phone.

Darrien Summers stared at me with disbelief. I pointed at the phone receiver in my hand. "Pick up."

Shaking his head, he dropped into his chair. Slowly, he picked up the phone on his side of the glass and held it to his ear.

"Who are you?"

Smiling, I said, "Mr. Summers, I'm Ruby Bozarth. May I call you Darrien?"

"What do you want?"

"Judge Baylor just appointed me to represent you in your criminal case. You can call me Ruby. Sir, can I call you Darrien?"

"Well, shit."

Through the glass, I could see his eyes rove over my long hair, my face, the worn business suit. After a long silence, he spoke again. "How old are you?"

I dropped the grin. It was a fair question, and there was no point in trying to dodge it. "Twenty-six." Hastily, as if it would boost my credibility, I added, "I'll be twenty-seven in two months."

Summers dropped the phone. It made a metallic whine when it hit the counter. The noise hurt my ear, and I winced.

His head rolled back on his neck, with his eyes focused on the ceiling. Then his eyes closed, and he gave a deep exhale.

Gripping the phone, I spoke loudly into the receiver. "Darrien? Mr. Summers? Pick up the phone, please."

He ignored me. Turning sideways in his chair, he faced the blank cinder-block wall.

I shouted into the receiver. "We have got to talk. You're going to trial in two weeks. Two weeks!"

Summers rose from the seat. Turning his back to me, he took a step to the locked door inside his cubicle and knocked on it.

My face hot, I rapped on the security glass. "Darrien, I need your help. You have to assist in your defense." The phone was wet from the sweat in my hand.

He began to pound on the door with a closed fist. I didn't need the phone to hear what he was saying on his side of the glass.

"Out! Get me out of here!"

The door on his side of the cubicle opened abruptly, and the short jailer's face appeared, wearing a bemused expression. "What the hell?"

"I'm done here. I want to go back to my cell."

As the jailer shackled his wrists, I tried again. "You need me. Come back! Talk to me." I was ashamed to hear the whine in my voice. I beat on the glass. "I'm all you've got."

Darrien Summers left the interview room without a backward look. As the door clicked shut behind him, I slammed the plastic telephone into its base. To the empty space, I announced:

"I quit."

# CHAPTER 5

MY MAMA DIDN'T raise no quitter.

I repeated the thought like a mantra the next morning as I rose from my sofa bed at the office, showered, and brushed my teeth. I pulled on jeans and a loose sweater. I was heading back to the jail for another shot with Darrien Summers, and I figured I might as well be comfortable. My courtroom suit hadn't impressed my new client the previous afternoon.

*No quitter no quitter no quitter.*

If the sun had been shining, I might have headed straight for the jail. But it was gray and overcast, with a blustery wind. A cup of coffee would give me a lift, and I hadn't had a drop that morning. The Maxwell House can at my office was empty.

A diner sat on the south side of the square, around the corner from my office. As I hurried down the sidewalk, I checked out the exterior to make sure it was open for business.

A neon sign sparkled in vintage glory, blinking an outline of a pan of eggs and bacon in yellow and hot pink. Above the blinking pan, SHORTY'S was spelled out in sparkling white bulbs.

A brass bell hanging from the door jingled to announce my entry. I'd only frequented Shorty's diner a few times since I'd moved to town. In the storage room behind my office, I had a microwave, a hot plate, and an ancient refrigerator; since I was counting pennies, I made do.

I surveyed the booths, upholstered in bright orange vinyl, but since I was eating alone, I sidled up to the counter and sat on an old-fashioned bar stool.

I swiveled on the stool like a schoolkid, taking in the surroundings. A waitress delivered a breakfast plate to a man down the counter from me: pigs in a blanket. Steam rose from the pancakes.

*Oh, Lord, have mercy.*

A man wearing a white apron walked up with a mug and a coffeepot. "Coffee, ma'am?"

"Yes, please."

As he poured, I stared at the apron. Over his heart, in bold black stitches, it read SHORTY. I'd swear he was six foot four. I snorted.

He pointed an accusatory finger. "Just what are you laughing at, ma'am?"

"I beg pardon, I don't mean to laugh. It's your apron."

"It's clean." He brushed the front of it, looking down. "What about my apron?"

"It says Shorty."

He stood tall: six foot four, for certain. Extending his hand, he said, "Yes ma'am, it sure does. Shorty Morgan, damn glad to meet you."

I shook his hand. He squeezed it just right: a friendly grip, not too tight. "I'm Ruby. Ruby Bozarth."

"Ruby from the Ben Franklin!"

"Yep, that's me."

"Well, then, this is a special pleasure. That old dime store was sitting vacant for too long. Just looking at it made me blue. Everybody was awful glad to see the lights turned back on in there."

I nodded, stealing another glance at the breakfast plate nearby.

"Ruby, you're giving Jeb's pancakes and sausage links the eye. You want me to order them up for you?"

I checked the prices on the menu. "Short stack, please. Butter and syrup."

He wrote "SS" on a pad and disappeared into the kitchen. I sipped my coffee and pondered the best way to approach Darrien Summers.

Shorty was back in a New York minute, carrying a steaming plate of pancakes. A magazine sat on the counter near me, a copy of *Foreign Affairs*. He nudged it out of the way to make room for the syrup pitcher.

As I poured syrup on my pancakes, he marked a page inside the magazine with a paper napkin and set it beside the coffee station.

"So you're doing some light reading this morning?" I said. The pancakes were making me feel sociable.

Shorty smiled. "Just trying to keep abreast of what's going on in the world."

I was curious about his reading choice, but my fellow customer at the counter interrupted. "Shorty! Your coffee's weak this morning!"

"Jeb, hush your mouth." He grabbed the pot and refilled the man's mug.

"Just look there. Like a cup of weak tea."

Jeb swung around on his stool and called to a dark-haired man sitting alone in one of the orange booths. "Hey, Troy? How you like the coffee today?"

The lone diner looked up from a newspaper he'd been studying. He looked to be older than me—maybe in his thirties. A port-wine stain birthmark covered one side of his face.

The man with the newspaper said, "I didn't order any coffee."

His tone was so chilly, I'd swear it lowered the temperature of the diner by ten degrees.

Jeb turned to me. "How about yours, honey?"

I sipped my coffee and said, "I like it." It was true. I didn't care for those hip coffee places where baristas gave you the caffeine shakes with a single cup.

Shorty set the pot on its coil and smiled at me. To Jeb, he said, "Hear that? A satisfied customer. And she's a lawyer, so she knows what she's talking about."

Feeling a little self-conscious, I dug into the pancakes. As I mopped up syrup with my last bite, Shorty refilled my coffee and asked, "How's the murder case going?"

I almost dropped my fork. "How did you know?"

"Oh, come on, now. We get the courthouse crowd at lunch and dinner. You were the main topic of conversation yesterday."

"Oh, Jesus," I said under my breath.

"Hey, you're famous now. So how's it going?"

"No comment. Attorney-client privilege." I gave him a wink. Because he was really pretty cute. I dug into my wallet and pulled out some bills to pay the check. As he rang it up on the cash register, Shorty said, "You going over to the jail today?"

I nodded. My counter companion, Jeb, shook his head. "Sure better hope it goes better for you than yesterday."

Oh, my God. Rosedale was a goldfish bowl. Even the man with the port-wine mark was staring at me; his scrutiny made me uncomfortable. I kept my mouth shut, but I must not have been wearing a poker face, because Shorty called to me as I walked away. "Come back for lunch. Bet you'll have a whole new attitude by noon."

"That right?" I said over my shoulder.

"I can feel it. And I have great gut instincts."

I laughed at that. It sounded like something I used to say, before I was tripped up by my own misguided instincts. As the bell on the door jingled over my head, Shorty called out.

"Lunch is on the house, Ruby. You're good for business. See you at noon."

"See you at noon," Jeb echoed.

I looked over my shoulder to reply. The port-wine man was smiling. But not in what you'd call a friendly way.

# CHAPTER 6

BACK IN THE interview room at the county jail, an overhead vent blasted hot air at me. I pushed the sleeves of my sweater up past my elbows.

The door on the other side of the cubicle opened. I tensed, waiting to see Darrien Summers's reaction to my reappearance. I withheld the toothy grin I had displayed on my first visit.

They repeated the procedures from the day before. The jailer unlocked Darrien's cuffs. Darrien sat down in the chair. I picked up the phone receiver.

As he stared through the glass, I wished I could see what was going on in his head. Though I itched to break the silence, I was determined to make him speak first.

He picked up and said, "Yesterday, we had fourteen days to do this. Now we're down to thirteen."

In a guarded tone, I said, "That's right."

"How can a woman who doesn't know what she's doing handle my defense?"

I bristled, though the question was justified. "How do you know I don't know what I'm doing?"

Darrien smiled—a beautiful smile, though there was no humor in it. "You know what the inmates are calling you in lockup? Jailtime Ruby. Some of them are calling you Execution Ruby. Have you heard that?"

The revelation made me want to wince, but I kept a dogged face. "Why'd you try to punch out your last lawyer?"

His cynical expression slipped away, replaced by anger. "They brought me into court to see that dude—the public defender. I'd met him, what? Like, twice before? He says he's got a deal for me, I'm going to plead guilty to capital murder, get life without parole."

I listened. Kept my mouth shut.

Darrien gripped the receiver and edged closer to the glass panel. "I told him—like I'd told him before—I didn't do it. He said he was trying to save my life."

At that, he paused.

"Then what?" I asked.

"He said it was a done deal. I'd plead or they'd convict me, give me the death penalty. Because of the pictures. The fucking pictures." His voice cracked, and I was struck by how young he looked at that moment. Barely old enough to buy a six-pack of beer.

"I lost it. I swung at him. I didn't hurt him. If I'd wanted to hurt him, I could've. But I'm not like that."

I locked eyes with him as I spoke into the phone. "I don't know what they call me at the jail, and I don't give a shit. But here's one thing I promise: I'd never advise a client of mine to plead to a crime he didn't commit."

He breathed out. It sounded like a sigh.

"Okay," he said. "Okay. That's a start."

I uncapped my pen. "I've got the prosecutor's file; I know their point of view on the case. I need to hear from you. What happened that night?"

He started at the beginning: the Mardi Gras ball, the masked country club members, the party that lingered on into the night. Jewel Shaw was there, wearing a glittery green mask with purple feathers. Though she ignored him in the early part of the evening, she started giving him the eye and flirting as the party dragged on.

"You had a relationship with Jewel; I'm aware of that. I saw the pictures. How long had it been going on?"

They had kept it secret, he told me. He would have been fired for certain, might have faced worse consequences. "Things haven't changed all that much in Mississippi. You know that."

I nodded.

"Me and Jewel, we got together whenever she felt like it. Almost always at the club. The first time, we were in the women's restroom."

"When was that?"

He stared off to the side as he tried to remember. "Six months ago, maybe? I'd been working at the club for a while, couple of months."

"Were your meetings always at the club?"

"Sure. What were we going to do, walk into a movie together? In February, when it warmed up some, we started going to her daddy's cabana by the pool. More private." He grimaced, then said in a defensive tone, "It was casual. Just a woman having fun. I didn't mind."

Oh, my Lord. There was in fact a sexual harassment angle to the tale, but I didn't think I could sell it to a Mississippi jury.

"So the relationship was casual—you mean, it was strictly physical? Not a romance?"

"A romance? No, nothing like that. You don't think she wanted to end up with me? Take me home to the family? That's crazy."

"But it was her idea? For you to hook up?"

"Always. I never pushed it. Shit—never."

I was still trying to get my head around their dynamic; they were a mismatched pair, for sure, by Mississippi standards. "So she wanted sex. Okay—what was in it for you?"

He gave me a look of disbelief. "Have you seen what she looked like?"

I had. In her lifetime, she was a 9.5, at least.

"And she had that charm thing going on. You know."

I knew what he was talking about. I'd been taken in by the "charm thing," too.

I asked: "So how'd you end up in the cabana the night of the Mardi Gras ball?"

"She texted me. I asked to go on break. Once I got into the cabana and saw her lying there, I thought maybe she was drunk."

"Was that a possibility?"

"Oh, yeah. But then I got closer. And I saw the blood."

I made a note; the blood was an issue we would have to tackle. "There was blood on you: on your jacket, your face, your hands. How'd it get there?"

"When I listened to her chest, I guess. I was flipped out. But I tried CPR. I tried to help her, I swear I did."

"And then security came to the cabana?"

He whispered: "Shit." Then he said, "Yeah. They surely did."

I skimmed the sheriff's report again. "There's no record of any statement from you. What did you say to the police? Or to security?"

Darrien laughed, displaying the humorless smile again. "I'm a black man in Mississippi. I've got nothing to say to the police."

"Well, that's good."

"Miranda v. Arizona."

I stared through the glass at him, surprised that he knew the "right to remain silent" case name.

"So you've heard of the Miranda case."

"I've read it."

I sat back in my chair. "Really."

"Yeah, I wrote a paper on it at Arkansas State. I was a criminology major." He paused before adding, "Before they took the scholarship away."

I pulled the mug shot of Darrien Summers from my file and studied his battered face. Holding the picture up against the pane of security glass, I asked, "Who did this to you?"

His jaw twitched. "Owens, the club manager. At the club, when Owens and his security goons found me with Jewel's body."

Observing my client through the glass, I was glad I'd slept on it, that I'd come back to give it another shot. Because I really did believe him.

He was wearing jail scrubs. Since we were counting down to trial, I needed to address a practical concern. "When you go to court, I want you dressed like you're going to church on Sunday. Who should I contact to get your clothes? You need a suit."

"My daddy lives here in town; he's got my clothes and stuff. But I don't have any kind of suit jacket, nothing like that. The only jacket I own is my white waiter's coat."

I made a note of that. It wasn't necessary to add that I knew where his waiter's jacket could be found. It was in the evidence room of the sheriff's office, covered in blood. State's Exhibit 1.

We talked a while longer; I wanted to know names of people who might testify for the defense. At length, the short jailer appeared to escort Darrien back to his cell. He shackled him and walked him through the door. I wrapped up my interview notes, jotting down some final thoughts. As I stood up, a tap on the glass startled me. I saw the jailer holding the phone receiver on the other side of the glass.

I picked up, confused. "What?"

The jailer's voice drawled into my ear. "I went to high school with Jewel."

I backed away a step, even though the glass separated us. "That right?"

"A lot of people around here set store by the Shaw family. Lot of people wonder why that boy should even get a trial."

I gave him my best tough-girl face. "Are you one of those people? Maybe I should let the sheriff know."

He hung up the phone and walked away with a nasty smirk. When I put the receiver in place, my hand was shaking. I hoped he didn't see it.

# CHAPTER 7

BACK AT MY office, I sat at my desk, picking at a loose strip of plywood on the desktop while I stared at my phone.

I picked the phone up, dialed the Jackson area code. Put it down again.

I'd sworn that I would never again dial Lee Greene's number. But here I sat, preparing to push those numbers once again.

If there was any other option, I'd gladly pursue it. But I had to provide a suit for my client to wear at trial. A man who faced a jury in his inmate garb sent a clear message: I'm guilty. Convict me. Send me up the river.

My ex, Lee Greene Jr., was a clotheshorse—a trait of which he was supremely proud. And he was tall, about the same height as Darrien Summers.

I swallowed my pride and dialed. As I punched the numbers, it occurred to me that Lee might well refuse to talk to me.

But he answered. When I heard the sound of Lee's voice in my ear, my teeth clenched so hard it almost locked my jaw.

He said, "Can it be? Is this really Ruby?"

He was laughing. It rankled. I kept my cool and answered in a polite voice.

"It's me. How you doing, Lee?"

"It's really you. When I saw your number on the screen, I thought I was hallucinating. Because the last time I saw you, Ruby, you bitchslapped me. Threw a diamond at my head. Then you said you'd never speak to me again."

Pressing the phone to my ear, I held my tongue. The conversation wasn't going as well as I'd hoped.

"Do you recall that? Ruby?"

"Yeah."

"You said—this is a quote—'I'll never speak to you again.'"

I waited to see whether he wanted to unload some more. After all, I was calling to beg a favor.

"Ruby? You still there?"

"Right here."

"Well, damn. This is a red-letter day. To what do I owe this pleasure?"

I bit the bullet. "Lee, you know you're the best-dressed man in Mississippi."

*Grease the pig.*

"That's true," he said, his voice dripping self-satisfaction.

"And I'm over here in Williams County, doing a solo practice. I've got a case going to trial really soon. My client is a young man, and I've just got to get him into a suit. I wondered, you know—could I maybe use one of your castoffs? Something you don't wear anymore?"

Now the phone was silent on his end.

I said, "It would be a real kindness on your part, Lee. An act of charity." To lighten the tone, I added, "You'd be racking up points in heaven."

In a suspicious voice, he said, "What kind of clientele are you representing? What man can't put clothes on his back? Oh, my God, don't tell me—is this a criminal case?"

I should have figured he'd react in just this way.

"Yes. A criminal case."

"What's the charge?"

If I thought I could get away with it, I'd have lied through my teeth. But he could easily check my veracity; all he had to do was go online. "Murder. A murder case." Hastily, I added, "He's innocent."

He laughed with genuine mirth. "Oh, they're all innocent, definitely. Every inmate convicted in Mississippi swears he wouldn't hurt a fly, it was someone else who 'done it.' What on earth are you doing with a murder case?"

"I got appointed."

"Well, that's a hoot. So tell me about this client of yours who doesn't have a stitch of clothing."

I hesitated. It wouldn't advance my cause with Lee to reveal Darrien Summers's race. Lee and his family made no secret of their innate sense of superiority to others. The list of people who were beneath their notice was long. As I held the phone, I wondered yet again how I had ever been drawn to him.

"Lee, you don't really want to hear the details. I'd surely appreciate it if you'd do me a solid. It's not so much to ask, right?"

"Um, don't think I can, Ruby. I really don't relish the idea of a criminal trudging into court in chains, sporting my clothes."

I opened my desk drawer and pulled out the Nicorette box. Chewing down on the tablet, I thought: *I tried to be nice. It's time to play dirty.*

"Lee, I'll make you a deal. You help me out, and I won't tell your mama the real reason I broke off the engagement."

I could hear a sharp intake of breath on his end of the phone.

"You know, you always had a mean streak, Ruby. Ruthless. I tried to ignore it, but it was always there, right under the surface."

I didn't suppose that Lee had shared the real story with his mother, the incident that caused our relationship to end. But I certainly hadn't forgotten it. At our engagement party, I'd walked in on him in a bathroom stall with a kneeling woman. So much for the fairy-tale romance.

"You want to blackmail me. Well, you can't play me. I'm not giving you a suit."

"You sure about that?"

He exhaled. "How about a compromise? I've got someone who might be disposed to help you out. My aunt Suzanne practices in Barnes County. Aunt Suze has a soft spot for charity cases."

I frowned into the phone. He was making it complicated. "But I don't even know her."

"Sure you do. You met her one Christmas. Six feet tall, silver hair, two hundred and fifty pounds. Never saw a buffet she didn't like. She'll probably lend you a hand with your clothing crisis."

"Why would your kinfolks want to help me, when you won't do it? How am I supposed to beg a favor from your aunt?"

His voice had regained its confident drawl. "Give her a call, you'll see. Aunt Suzanne is the black sheep of the family. Because she has a taste for trash."

# CHAPTER 8

WITH TWELVE DAYS to go before trial, I should have been dealing with truly pressing matters. Evidence. Witnesses. Research. Trial strategy. Instead, I continued to obsess about getting Darrien into a decent suit for court. So I drove to the next county to meet with Suzanne Greene. Her secretary had said she had some time free before noon.

I recognized Lee's aunt Suzanne the moment I walked into her office and saw her behind her desk. We had shared a cigarette on the side porch of the Greene family homestead when I'd been invited for Christmas during the courtship. Aunt Suzanne had been the only member of Lee's family who didn't act like they should double-check the silver forks to make sure none were missing.

She waved me into her office. "Sit on down, hon, and let me finish up this letter. It'll just be a minute."

I sat, grateful that she hadn't kicked off our meeting by mentioning the broken engagement. But despite Lee's indication that she might help me out, I was nervous.

While Suzanne worked at her computer, I stole a glance around her office. Her desk had piles of papers and files, scattered legal pads bearing handwritten scrawls. Her walls were adorned with certificates: her license to practice in Mississippi, her diploma from the University of Chicago Law School, and her certificate of membership in the ACLU.

I did a double take, squinting to ensure my eyes didn't deceive me. When I ascertained that the certificate did in fact declare Suzanne Greene to be a member of the American Civil Liberties Union, I felt such a rush of relief that my shoulders sagged.

She turned away from the computer screen and faced me. "All righty, then, Ruby. Tell me what's cooking."

I said, "I have a predicament. Just this week, Judge Baylor appointed me to represent Darrien Summers on a capital murder charge in Williams County."

She rubbed the end of her nose. "The Jewel Shaw murder. It's been all the talk around here for weeks."

"They wanted him to plead guilty, but he wouldn't. Mrs. Greene, he swears he didn't do it."

"That's Ms. Greene, hon. I kept my maiden name. Burned my bra, too, back in the 1970s." Her face lit up with a grin. "But it's a more important source of support these days. Now, Ruby, I do recall hearing some scuttlebutt about your client. Wasn't a story going around that Summers beat up the public defender?"

I grimaced, though it didn't surprise me to learn that the story had made the rounds of courthouse talk.

"He didn't hit him. Just swung at him."

Suzanne folded her arms on her desk and took a long look at me. "So the public defender pulled out, and Baylor appointed a little old girl who's fresh out of school and green as grass." She made an impatient noise with her tongue and shook her head.

Pointing a finger at me, she said, "You watch out for Baylor. I went to undergrad with him at Ole Miss. He was a sneaky asshole then, and he hasn't changed a bit."

Here was a new wrinkle. This case was my worst nightmare. "Okay. Thanks, Ms. Greene; I'll be careful. I called you because there's something I need to get for my client. He doesn't have—"

She cut me off. "Tell me about their evidence. Give me the state's case—nutshell version."

I laid it out for her: the text; Jewel Shaw in the cabana with thirteen stab wounds; my client discovered by her side, covered in her blood.

"What was the murder weapon?"

"No weapon was found, but Jewel's phone was in the cabana, containing a variety of photos depicting a sexual relationship between Darrien and the deceased."

"How bad are they?"

"The selfies? Pretty shocking, I'm afraid."

"Let me take a look."

I was glad I'd brought the file along. I fished out the photocopies for her inspection. She lifted the reading glasses that dangled from a chain around her neck and held them like a magnifying glass.

Suzanne held up the picture from the billiard room. "Look at this. Jewel looks like she just won a blue ribbon at the county fair."

It was true. Jewel was grinning from ear to ear.

She waved the picture at me. "Now, you know these pictures are trouble. The prosecutor is going to use them to rile the jury up, try to prejudice folks against your client. But the fact is, it looks like Jewel took those pictures herself, at a number of different times—and always looked like she was having a good time. A real good time. You can use that." She set the photocopy back down on her desk, in the midst of a pile of documents.

I gave her an earnest smile. "Ms. Greene, the reason I'm here..."

She winked at me. "Don't let's stand on ceremony. Call me Suzanne, hon." She reached into the top drawer of her desk and pulled out a pack of Marlboro Golds. "Do you mind? It helps me to think."

"Go right ahead." I popped a nugget of Nicorette and chewed down hard. "Suzanne, when I bring Darrien into court, he needs to look presentable."

She blew a plume of smoke up toward an antique light fixture. "Have you gone through the phone?"

"Beg pardon?"

"The phone—Jewel Shaw's cell phone. Have you looked through it? Contacts, call history, all that?"

"No, ma'am. I didn't know I could do that."

She unearthed a crystal ashtray from its hiding place under a legal pad. Suzanne took another pull on the cigarette, surveying me over the glasses that now rested on her nose. "Hon, have you gone over to the sheriff's department yet? Have you examined the physical evidence?"

"No," I said, as a new wave of panic gripped me. "I didn't think they'd let me touch it."

She tapped an ash into the ashtray. "Oh, baby girl. Get into that evidence room."

"What if they won't let me in?"

She stubbed out the cigarette. "If you're going to be a defense attorney, Ruby, you're going to have to carry a big stick. I'll send you the form: Motion to Compel." She turned to her computer keyboard and said, "Jewel Shaw was kind of a legend in these parts—and not for doing the work of the Lord, if you catch my meaning."

I nodded, wondering again why the name "Jewel Shaw" rang a distant bell.

"That phone should be full of revelations. Why, she likely had a double handful of lovers."

I was in no position to doubt Suzanne, but at this, I had to speak up. "You mean I should slut-shame her?"

Suzanne picked up the Jewel Shaw selfies that were scattered on her desk and stacked them together, then raised her brow.

I ventured, "I think it's bad practice, in general, to demean women. And really disrespectful when a person is dead."

Suzanne smiled at me. "I was a feminist before you were born, Ruby. Second wave, I think they call me. But you have agreed to defend a man who has been charged with murder. To act as his advocate."

She reached across the desk and dropped the selfies in front of me. "Jewel Shaw is dead. You can't hurt her feelings. If you don't do everything in your power to fight on Darrien Summers's behalf, your client may end up dead, too."

I couldn't muster an argument to that.

In a brisk voice, Suzanne said, "Did you say you were looking for a suit?"

I offered a weak smile; it had occurred to me that we might never address the purpose of my visit. "Yes. Suzanne, Darrien doesn't have anything fit to wear to court."

"I've got you covered. My late husband's closet is still full of his suits. I haven't had the heart to throw them out."

A grandfather clock in her office began to toll; it was noon. I put the photocopies back into my briefcase. "You've been such a help, Suzanne. When can I come by and pick up the suit?"

"When will you need it?"

"We are set for trial in twelve days," I said. I closed my bag and took a step toward the door.

"Stop right there."

I froze.

"You are set for trial in less than two weeks, and you haven't even looked at the evidence yet? Girl, how many felony cases have you tried?"

My armpits began to grow damp. "I've never tried one. I don't have any felony experience. None at all."

Suzanne's reading glasses slipped off her nose. "No felony jury trial experience? And you're defending a black man on a murder charge in Williams County, where they have a monument to the Glorious Confederate Dead on the courthouse lawn?"

When I answered, I was ashamed to hear the quaver in my voice. "I don't know what the hell I'm doing. Don't have a damned clue."

"Y'all are getting railroaded." Suzanne rose from her seat and shouted through the door to her secretary. "Marlene! Lunchtime! I'm taking Ruby to the Dixie Buffet!"

# CHAPTER 9

THE WAITRESS AT the Dixie Buffet gave Suzanne a friendly wave as she approached our booth. "All-you-can-eat shrimp special today, Miss Greene."

"Don't I know it," Suzanne said. "I'll take a big glass of sweet tea with that, please."

"Two shrimp buffets?" the waitress asked, glancing at me.

I raised a restraining hand. "No, thank you. Just iced tea for me. Sweet."

As the waitress walked off, Suzanne looked at me with pity. "You're not anorexic, I hope."

That made me laugh. "Suzanne, I'm broke." My wallet held one worn five-dollar bill, and I might need to pump a gallon of gas into the tank to get my car back to Williams County.

She scooted out of the booth. "Let's get over to the buffet line. My treat."

"No, ma'am," I said, lifting my chin. "You've done too much for me already. I can't add to the debt."

Frowning down at me, she paused at the table side, but I was adamant. "You go on. I'm going to drink my tea."

Suzanne returned with a loaded plate. As she peeled the shell off a pink shrimp, she asked how I was liking Rosedale.

"Just fine. No one knows this, but I'm not strictly new to town. My mom and I lived in Rosedale for a while, back when I was in sixth grade."

As I took a sip of tea, my brain finally made the connection. It hit me with such force that I nearly spit a mouthful of liquid across the table.

"Oh. My. Lord. That's it: Jewel Shaw, at Rosedale Middle School. I was in sixth, she was an eighth grader."

"You just this minute figured that out?"

I picked up the damp napkin under my drink and wiped it across my forehead. "She didn't go by 'Jewel' back then. They called her something else—like Julie, maybe. And we moved around a lot. I changed schools so many times, it's kind of a blur. But Julie—Jewel Shaw. Good God."

A thought struck me. "Does this mean I can't be Darrien's lawyer? Because I went to school with the deceased?"

Suzanne dipped a fried nugget of shrimp into a pool of cocktail sauce. "Well, that depends. Were you and Jewel friends? Were y'all close?"

My laugh sounded bitter. "I didn't run in the same circles as Jewel Shaw."

"Because she was older?"

"Because she was the 'It Girl.' I was the new girl, a tough kid from the wrong side of the tracks."

Maybe that was the most compelling reason I'd returned to Rosedale after the broken engagement. I left that town as a girl just one step up from trash; I would return as a professional, with my head held high.

Suzanne shot a reassuring glance over her glasses. "Good. You can act as Darrien Summers's lawyer, unless you believe your recollection of Jewel Shaw diminishes your capacity to represent the defendant to the best of your ability."

Only the day before, I might have seized upon an opportunity to remove myself from the case. But the more I sunk my teeth in, the more determined I was to hang on. "It's not a problem. I don't have fond memories of Julie Shaw."

The waitress paused at our table. "Miss Greene, they just put out a red velvet cake."

"Honey, would you bring me over a piece? We're brainstorming here."

When Suzanne returned her attention to me, I said, "When I get the chance to see Jewel's phone, I'll be looking for other lurid pictures, right?"

"Oh, yes." The cake arrived. She picked up her fork.

"But how does that help my case, exactly? Is it just about smearing the victim?"

Suzanne was chewing. I had to wait for the answer.

"Honey, you need the pictures to broaden the playing field. The prosecution is framing the case as a love affair gone bad. So you'll want to show that there were other affairs, other lovers who might have wanted to plunge the knife." She plunged the fork back into the cake. "Muddy the waters. Blow smoke. Jump up and down about the missing murder weapon. Yell about other lovers."

"How will that help me to prove that my client is innocent?"

She dropped the fork.

"Whoa, darling. That's not your job. What you have to do is raise a reasonable doubt. That's all. If you can create a reasonable doubt in the mind of the jury, they have to find him not guilty. Hell—raise that doubt in the mind of just one juror with a backbone, and you'll hang it up. There's a unanimous jury requirement in criminal cases. All twelve have to vote Guilty to convict."

"Or acquit. I can't get him off unless all twelve agree on Not Guilty."

"So start your treasure hunt. Go looking for that nugget of reasonable doubt, and beat it like a drum. 'If the gloves don't fit, you must acquit.'"

# CHAPTER 10

I HAD MY dukes up—figuratively speaking, anyway—as I waited for Tom Lafayette to appear in Judge Baylor's courtroom.

The copies of my motions lay before me on the counsel table, with handwritten notes jotted in the margins. I'd filed the original with the court that morning, and dropped a copy off at the DA's office.

The door to the courtroom flew open. Tom Lafayette stormed in, gripping sheets of paper in his fist.

Trying to look cool, I tipped my chair back against the railing and rocked back and forth. Lafayette advanced on me, rattling the papers he held. "What's up with this motion for discovery?"

I sat the chair back on all four legs, afraid that it might tip over, which would endanger my appearance of self-possession. "I want to see the evidence."

"You have it. I provided it to you. You have the contents of the state's file."

"I want to inspect it, in the evidence room. I want to see the evidence with my own eyes. I owe it to my client to know exactly what you're presenting at trial."

He huffed. "You can forget about digging around in the evidence room."

I stole a glance at the handwritten notes on my motion. "I'm entitled to inspect the evidence. It's a right guaranteed by Mississippi Uniform Circuit Court Rule 9.04."

He reached into the breast pocket of his gray pinstriped suit jacket and pulled out a pair of glasses. I was glad I'd worn my black graduation dress, the newest article of clothing in my wardrobe.

Lafayette looked up from the motion I'd prepared. "You've cited subsection A of rule 9.04."

"Yep."

He smiled. "I guess you didn't get around to reading subsection B."

I didn't answer, but I was scrambling to remember: What did subsection B say?

He chuckled. "Get ready for a smackdown, Ruby. You're going to lose this round."

"Oh, so you're a fortune teller *and* a district attorney."

As Lafayette walked to his counsel table, he made a parting shot over his shoulder. "Judge Baylor won't be happy with you. Making trouble, stirring the pot."

*Judge Baylor is a sneaky asshole.*

I shifted in my chair and leaned toward the DA. "I've been a troublemaker all my life. You better get used to it."

The door to Judge Baylor's chambers opened and he entered, robed in black. I jumped to my feet. As the judge settled into his chair behind the bench, he said, "Miss Bozarth, I see you've filed two motions in State v. Summers."

"Yes, Your Honor."

He opened the file. "There's a motion for continuance. Mr. Lafayette, what does the prosecution say to that?"

Lafayette leaned against the bar behind his counsel table. "Judge, the state is ready to proceed. Our witnesses are under subpoena, and we've made arrangements for the forensic expert from the state crime lab to appear. It would work a hardship on us to cancel out at this point."

"Miss Bozarth?"

"Your Honor, I need more time to prepare. The trial setting is only eleven days from now."

The DA pushed away from the bar. "Judge, this isn't a complex case."

I turned on him. "What do you mean? It's a capital murder case."

The judge raised a restraining hand. "Y'all settle down. Miss Bozarth, what do you need to accomplish that you can't get done in eleven days?"

I repeated, "Prepare. I need to prepare for trial."

The judge frowned at me like I was a misbehaving child. "Well then, get to work, ma'am. Miss Bozarth, I have access to the docket for Williams County, and you'll forgive me for observing that you don't have a wealth of cases eating up your time."

My blood started to boil. He turned a page. "There's a motion to compel discovery here. Mr. Lafayette, have you provided Miss Bozarth with the prosecution's file?"

The DA was assuring the judge that he had handed it over when I interrupted.

"I want to see it."

The judge said, "What's that?"

"I want to see the evidence in the property room. To inspect it personally."

Lafayette broke in. "Judge, the prosecution objects to this request. The evidence in this case involves sensitive and personal information—matters which may be protected from tampering by subsection B."

I leaned my damp palms on the surface of the counsel table as I faced the judge. "Judge Baylor, you've entrusted me with the defense of a man charged with capital murder. I want to see that evidence, and I want it today."

The judge adjusted his glasses and lifted a pen. "Miss Bozarth, Mr. Lafayette has a wealth of experience in these matters; whereas you are, as they say, new to the game. I'm inclined to trust his judgment."

"I'll appeal."

Shocked silence followed my statement. It was a gamble, a desperate play.

But I sure had their attention.

The judge's voice cut the air in the courtroom. "What do you mean, you'll appeal?"

I scrambled. What was it called, when an attorney in the midst of the trial process appealed the ruling? I sunk my teeth into the legal term I remembered for certain.

"I intend to do an interlocutory appeal." I paused for a moment; when no one jumped in, I knew I'd used the right term. I went on: "We'll just see what the high court says about your refusal to permit me effective representation. And while we wait for their decision, well"—I shrugged philosophically—"I guess that will provide me the extra time I need."

In the silence that followed, I saw Baylor and Lafayette exchange a look. At length, the affronted look on the judge's face disappeared, and was replaced with a genial smile. The judge said, "I think she's outfoxed you, Tom."

The DA jumped in, "Your Honor, on behalf of the State of Mississippi, I repeat my objection—"

But the judge hushed him with a wave of his hand. "Motion for continuance denied. Motion to compel discovery granted." He signed his name with a flourish of the pen, and pointed at Lafayette. "Tom, let the little lady see your evidence."

The judge handed me a copy of the signed motion and departed abruptly. My knees suddenly weak, I dropped into my chair.

# CHAPTER 11

WITH THE SIGNED motion gripped tightly in my hand, I pushed open the door of Shorty's diner. I spied Shorty sitting alone in the back booth, near the kitchen. He was reading a magazine.

"Shorty," I said, waving the document. "I did it."

He looked up with a smile, and I headed down the aisle to join him. Jeb sat again on a stool at the counter. As I passed, he swiveled around.

"Hey, Jailtime! How's the case coming?"

I turned to face him.

"Why are you always parked on that stool? Isn't there some-place you need to be?"

"Better talk sweet to me, Jailtime. I got jury duty in a couple of weeks."

Shorty came to the rescue, slipping behind the counter. "Ruby's right, Jeb; I ought to start charging you rent. Hey, Ruby—what can I get you?"

"Are you really on the jury panel?" In my imagination, I could see Jeb calling me Jailtime Ruby in the jury room.

Shorty said, "Ruby, he's pulling your leg; you can't take anything he says seriously. Let me get you a cup of coffee. Or would you like a cold Coke?"

"Tea, please. I'd love a sweet tea."

While Shorty poured the tea over ice, Jeb thrust his thumb in the direction of the orange booths. "You lucked out this time; I didn't get called. But Troy over there? He's on the list." Jeb called across the diner. "How about it, Troy? Did you manage to talk the judge into letting you out of jury duty?"

The booths were full, but when I scanned the faces of the diners, the man with the birthmark was staring at me. "No. I'm still on the list." His eyes flitted away.

Shorty took me by the elbow and nodded in the direction of the table he'd just vacated. In the past few days, I'd become a regular at Shorty's; I'd walked through that door three times. I'd refused to let Shorty give me dinner on the house the night before, but when he offered to let me order food and drink on credit and pay at the end of the month, I happily agreed to the arrangement. The knowledge that I would receive a government paycheck in the near future made me feel extravagant.

I picked up the magazine he'd been reading and examined the cover. "Oh. My. Lord. The *National Review?* That William F. Buckley rag?"

"It's chock-full of interesting articles." His mouth twitched when he said it.

"Interesting to Newt Gingrich, maybe. Don't you ever read anything fun?"

He smoothed the cover, plucking off a stray crumb. "For an old political science guy, this *is* fun reading."

Swiveling his stool our way, Jeb interjected, "Your daddy said he was throwing money down the well when he sent you off to school."

Shorty rolled his eyes, but his voice remained good-natured. "Jeb, drink your coffee or I'll make it even thinner tomorrow." He pointed at my motion. "Can I see it?"

I handed it to him; looking at it gave me a thrill of pride. "Absolutely. It's public record."

While he read through it, I drained the tea and sent Suzanne a text, telling her about my success in court.

Shorty looked up from the document. "You really scored. So what's next?"

I glanced over my shoulder, to make sure the prospective juror in the orange booth couldn't overhear. The hum of conversation from the other customers provided cover. In a quiet voice, I told Shorty: "I'm going straight to the sheriff's department, to get inside the property room and check out the evidence."

"We ought to celebrate. Why don't you come over to my place tonight? I'll cook for you."

Unzipping my briefcase, I slipped the motion inside. I took a breath and chose my words carefully. "Shorty, that's flattering, it really is. But I got out of a bad relationship in the past year. I'm still kind of gun-shy."

His face was a blank. "Why do you assume I'm asking you out on a date? Maybe it's just a friendly gesture."

I could feel a blush work its way up my neck. Embarrassed, I scooted down the booth, anxious to make my getaway. "I apologize. God, I feel like an idiot. Excuse me for assuming—"

He reached across the table and grasped my forearm. "Hey, I'm giving you a hard time. Yes, Ruby, I was asking you for a date. But it doesn't have to be anything but a friendly evening. It's food. You gotta eat, right?"

In fact, I would need to eat tonight. And Shorty's cooking was much better than mine. But I was also motivated by a case of loneliness. In the months I'd been living and working at the Ben Franklin, I had yet to make a real friend.

We agreed on seven o'clock, and I got his address on a paper napkin.

I was feeling pretty cocky as I walked out. But Jeb knew how to take the wind out of my sails. As I pulled the door open and the bell tinkled overhead, I heard him shout: "Give 'em hell, Jailtime!"

# CHAPTER 12

I WALKED THE short distance to the sheriff's department. A stern-faced woman wearing a tan uniform sat behind the counter in the lobby.

"Hey! I'm Ruby Bozarth, defense counsel in State v. Summers. I need to get access to the state's evidence, back in your property room."

"Excuse me?" Her expression turned downright forbidding. "Mr. Lafayette didn't send any notice about somebody rummaging around in the property room."

I dropped my smile. And I slapped the signed motion onto the counter.

"It's not Lafayette's call. Judge Baylor has ordered the room opened for me. That's his signature, right there."

She made a show of reading the document from beginning to end, then picked up the phone. "Dusty, there's a lawyer here, says you need to open up the evidence room for her." To the voice on the other end of the line, she said, "Because the circuit judge says so. She's got a court order."

Her brow wrinkled. "If you can't get out here, then send somebody." She hung up the phone and turned away from me.

I thought they might make me cool my heels in the lobby, but within minutes, a uniformed deputy arrived. He approached the woman at the desk. "I'm supposed to watch somebody in the property room."

She nodded in my direction. "Her."

I approached the deputy with a determined step and stuck out my hand. "Ruby Bozarth, counsel for defendant Darrien Summers."

The deputy was a young man, so slight that his uniform hung loose on him, like a boy wearing his big brother's clothes. He took my hand and smiled, a blush washing over his freckled face. "I'm Deputy Brockes. Sorry I didn't know you, ma'am. I'm brand-new."

I waved off the apology. "Me, too, Deputy Brockes. Fresh as paint."

He led me down a flight of stairs into the bowels of the building, then unlocked the property room. I followed him inside. While he searched for the Summers evidence, I looked around. Locked behind a mesh cage marked CONTROLLED SUBSTANCES, I saw powdery substances in plastic bags; other bags looked like they held marijuana.

The deputy returned, rolling a dolly that bore two boxes marked STATE V. SUMMERS. He pointed at a scarred wooden table in the corner. "You want to sit over there, ma'am?"

Brockes's voice was respectful, almost shy. I nodded. "Can we get a little more light in here, you think?"

He squinted up at the fluorescent lights flickering overhead. "No, ma'am, I don't think so. Sorry."

"Okay. Hope I don't get eyestrain," I said as I scooted a metal chair beside the table. "Wouldn't want to sue the county."

He looked frightened. I winked at him, so he'd know I was kidding.

Settling into the chair, I opened the first box. Bloodstained clothes were piled inside. The deputy stood over my shoulder. I turned to him. "You know, this is going to take a while."

He coughed, then thrust his hands into his pockets. "I don't think I'm supposed to leave you alone."

"Because I'm gonna steal y'all blind in here?" Deputy Brockes looked alarmed. I laughed, to reassure him. "Joke. It was a joke."

I pulled a notebook and pen from my bag, along with my cell phone; as I unearthed the evidence from the box, I photographed each item and took detailed notes. The deputy maintained his post beside the table for a while, but as I meticulously inspected each item and made my handwritten notations, he yawned.

"I'm going to have a seat here."

"Sure," I said, as I held up Jewel's dress. It was sheathed in plastic, but the slashes in the fabric had been tagged. I counted them: thirteen.

The deputy sat on the concrete floor, his back against the wall. I worked on in silence. When I completed my examination of the first box and lifted the lid from the second, I glanced his way. Sleeping like a baby. His head had fallen forward, and he snored softly.

I set the box lid on the floor and looked inside. At the top of the items in the box, I beheld it: Jewel Shaw's cell phone.

At last, I might find something that could help my client. I wanted to dig into that phone.

The problem was, it was bagged and tagged, sealed in protective plastic. There was no way to check the phone without shedding all that plastic. It had been marked with the initials of the officer who placed it inside, with a sticker sealing the bag.

Bag or no bag, I had to get to that phone. I made a decision: to hell with the state's chain of custody. I glanced over at my companion, who was still snoozing. Without making a sound, I shifted my chair so that my back faced the deputy. Then I reached into my briefcase and slipped on a pair of gloves with touchscreen tips that Suzanne had loaned to me for just this purpose. After another nervous look over my shoulder at Little Boy Blue, I eased up the custody tag without breaking the tape or tearing the plastic. Breathing out in relief, I removed the phone from the bag.

I knew Jewel Shaw's security code; it was listed in a report in the prosecution file. Working quickly, I accessed the phone. With my own cell phone, I took photos of Jewel's call history, recent texts, and some photos. Though I didn't pause to make a close inspection, it appeared that Suzanne's calculations were on target; Jewel had a lot of "couple pics" with different men.

I heard the deputy stir. My heart nearly stopped.

"Ma'am? You still working on those boxes?"

Scooping the phone and the plastic wrapping into my lap, I said, "It won't be too much longer. You're sure a good sport, Deputy Brockes." I began to repackage the phone. My hands were unsteady as I slipped it back into the plastic evidence bag and replaced the chain-of-custody tape. Turning to face the young deputy, I gave him an apologetic smile.

"No problem." With a groan, he pushed away from the wall and rose, coming to stand over me at the table. I dropped the phone into the box and pulled out a stack of files that rested beneath it.

Then I had a chilling thought. Had I remembered to turn the damned thing off?

# CHAPTER 13

SITTING IN A wicker rocking chair on the front porch of Shorty's house, I sipped cold beer from the can, glad I'd overcome my initial hesitation.

"Shorty, that supper was incredible. Catfish just jumped to number one on my list of favorite foods."

"Old family recipe," he said with mock solemnity. "My daddy knew his way around a catfish, I guarantee."

I rocked in the wicker chair. "And your father was the original Shorty?"

"Yep."

"Because he was genuinely short?"

"About five foot six. I got my height from my mama's side." He stretched out his long legs; they nearly reached to the end of the porch.

I asked, "So why'd you get stuck with the nickname?"

He cut his eyes at me. "I'm a junior, named after my daddy. Clarence Palmer Morgan the Second."

I snickered. "Oh, Lord."

"So you get it?"

I nodded in acknowledgment. It would be easier for a boy to be known as Shorty Jr. Living with the name Clarence Jr. would have made life tough on the school playground.

A chilly breeze made the bare branches rattle in the yard. Shorty said, "Is it too cold for you out here?"

"No. I like it. It beats being cooped up in the Ben Franklin." I shifted my chair so I could see him better in the dim light that shone from the window. "So. You got your poli sci degree at Mississippi State. And what were you going to do with that?"

"I wanted to be a journalist. Sound crazy?"

"Why'd you go all the way up to Missouri after you graduated from Miss State?"

"They have a really good J-school, first journalism school in the country. But Daddy had his stroke. I couldn't stay up north while he was suffering in the hospital. Besides, somebody had to run the business. So I came back." He swallowed beer from the can and fell silent. Then he turned to me and laughed, his good humor restored. "Never say you've kicked the dust of Rosedale off your sandals. Sure as you do, you'll find yourself right back here."

Well, he was right about that. When my mother and I left Williams County over a decade ago, I hadn't figured I'd return.

"Come on, your turn. Tell me a story."

"Oh, my life isn't particularly interesting."

"Now, come on. How about that big bad romance you mentioned today? Anybody I know?"

I shrugged, but he persisted. "Come on—let me know the name of the competition. So I'll be able to tell whether I can kick his ass."

I sighed. It wasn't really a secret. In Jackson and Oxford, it was local legend. "His name was Greene. Lee Greene."

"You're kidding." Shorty barked a laugh. "You mean that guy? *The* Lee Greene Junior?"

I shifted in my chair, uncomfortable. "Yeah. Him."

"Well, I'll be damned. I didn't know I was consorting with royalty."

I took a swallow from the beer can. "Well, you ain't. Obviously."

He cocked his head and studied me. After a moment, he said, "It's easy to see what Lee Greene liked about you. What did you see in him?"

The question made me sit back in surprise. No one had ever questioned Lee's appeal. He was the prince in the Cinderella story; I was the girl in rags, lucky to have him show up with a glass slipper.

To avoid answering, I said, "I don't know how it was that I caught his eye. I wasn't his usual type, believe me. Maybe he was weary of sweet southern belles. Tired of plain vanilla, maybe— I dunno."

Shorty picked my hand up from the arm of the rocking chair. Turning it over, he kissed the palm of my hand. "Maybe he was in the mood for peppermint. Or cinnamon. Or chili powder." His tongue touched the life line of my upturned palm, and I shivered.

"Well, I don't think I'm ready for the details of your relationship with Lee Greene Junior. Tell me something else. One of your youthful triumphs," he said.

I set my half-empty beer can on the floor beside my chair. "My adolescent stories are all kind of pitiful."

"No kidding? Well, good. Tell me a sad one."

"Actually, I went to sixth grade right here in Rosedale. And I was not anyone's idea of a beauty queen. That title fell to Julie Shaw."

He blinked. After a moment, he said in a hushed voice, "You mean you knew Jewel Shaw?"

"No. Yes. I mean, I knew who she was. She was older."

He raised his beer can and chugged from it. "Did you like her?"

"No."

Shorty shot me an appraising look. "That was a quick answer. For someone who didn't know her."

I didn't respond. He reached out and took my hand. "What is it? Did you have a run-in with Jewel?"

I stared at him, wondering whether I should shut up and go home. But it might be a relief to confide in someone, and he seemed so trustworthy, looking at me with those gray eyes.

I dove in. "When we lived in Rosedale, my mom worked on the cleaning staff at the Blue Top Motel, and money was tight. Rosedale Public Schools had a PTA clothing bank, and Mom took advantage of it. I wasn't ashamed. I knew the value of a buck, even as a kid.

"One day, my mom came home with a real prize: a beautiful pink sweater the color of cotton candy, in perfect shape, other than a small bleach stain—hardly noticeable. I wore it to middle school the next day, walking tall."

"Uh-oh. I'm afraid I can guess where this story is headed."

"Yep. I passed Jewel and her circle of friends in the hall on the way to my locker. One of Jewel's friends pointed at me. She said, 'Julie? Isn't that your sweater?'"

The memory made my chest tight. I arched my back, trying to stretch the muscles.

Shorty was still holding my hand. He gave it a gentle squeeze.

"Jewel turned and stared—the first time she'd ever looked

my way. Then she laughed. Said, 'It *was* my sweater. Mom gave it away to the poor when she spilled Clorox on it.'"

Telling the story took me back; I remembered standing by that locker like it was yesterday. Jewel and her cronies whispered. One of them laughed. That was all.

But I threw the sweater in a dumpster after school.

Shorty asked, "So is that why you're defending him?"

Startled, I jerked my hand away. How could he think that? "Hell, no. I'm defending him because I believe he's innocent."

He tipped back in his rocker, nodding. "I get that. A defense attorney is obliged to represent a guy if she thinks he's innocent."

I shook my head. "No, that's not the extent of it. Even if the accused isn't innocent, he is entitled to a defense."

"Now you're mixing me up. Where do you stand, Ruby?"

The conversation was making me tense; it was time to head home. I stood up, thanking him for his hospitality.

"You're not leaving already? It's early."

Moving to the porch steps, I said, "I'd better call it a night. Big appointment tomorrow."

"Who you going to see?"

I didn't answer immediately. I was seeing Darrien's father, at his house across town, to talk about defense witnesses.

Shorty stood beside me and reached out to hold my arm in a gentle grip. "Ruby Bozarth. Don't you trust me? After I fed you catfish and told you my life story?"

It made me laugh, and dissolved the tension. When he gave me a quick kiss, it felt right.

# CHAPTER 14

WHEN I DROVE across town the next day to meet with Darrien's father, I wondered whether it would be tough to locate his home. Oscar Summers lived on the outskirts of Rosedale in a neighborhood where mobile homes were scattered between small frame houses.

I needn't have worried. A black man sat on the steps of a well-maintained house with an attached carport. He was a dead ringer for his son. I pulled up to the gravel curb and cut the engine.

He nodded at my approach, and I lifted a hand in greeting. "Mr. Summers?" I called, though I knew it was Darrien's home. "Have I got the right house?" He rose from the steps, extending a hand. Oscar Summers didn't bother to smile; this was not a social call.

"Miss Bozarth, I appreciate you coming out here today."

"Yes, sir," I said. "Can we go inside the house to talk? We'd probably like some privacy." He turned and walked up the steps, holding the screen door open for me.

Once inside, I looked around the living room. The fireplace mantel was crowded with trophies. A riot of ribbons hanging from the wall looked like blue and red streamers for a child's birthday party, but the gold print on each revealed Darrien's youthful accomplishments: first place, second place, All-District, All-State, soccer, track, MVP, Rosedale football.

As I sat on the couch, I said, "Never saw so many honors, Mr. Summers. I never got a single ribbon at school."

"He was the best, always was. A hard worker. Darrien had natural talents, but he sure worked his tail off." It struck me that he was talking about Darrien in the past tense. It sent a chill through me.

"Mr. Summers, I hope to raise a character defense at Darrien's trial. Can you help me with that?"

He nodded, eager. "He was a good worker. His coach at Rosedale High knows that. Why, he started working at the body shop with me when he was a kid, too young to put on the payroll. Roy would pay him out of pocket."

It wasn't what I needed. "Work ethic is a great quality, no question. But in a case like this, where your son is facing a murder charge, we need to talk about other aspects of character. Like, whether he was known to be a peaceful person." His eyes didn't leave my face. It was a good sign; he had no struggle with the image of Darrien as a peaceable man.

"So tell me about Darrien. I've seen his criminal record; aside from the misdemeanor for marijuana possession, it's clean, not even a speeding ticket. But we're talking about reputation, not just arrest record. Did he stay out of fights?"

"Darrien didn't have to fight. Had nothing to prove." He waved his arm at the awards on display. "Just look. Just look at them."

My eyes scanned the room once again. In a corner, his high

school diploma hung behind glass. I walked over to inspect it. Under the diploma, a second certificate proclaimed: Darrien Summers, Principal's Honor List: Top 10%.

Turning back to face Oscar Summers, I tapped the certificate. "Good grades."

"Mighty good grades. Darrien wasn't going to end up tinkering with cars in the body shop. He was studying criminology at Arkansas State. Planned to get himself a degree in it."

Making a notation on my legal pad, I said, "Darrien mentioned that to me."

"I used to think, maybe he'll end up a detective or in the FBI, something like that. He could've done it, too. But he hurt his knee." His face creased with pain. "Then he got stupid. Went to some damn party, got busted. Losing that scholarship over a joint. Come back home with his tail between his legs."

Scanning my notes, I drew a question mark. "So Darrien was a local sports hero. Hard worker. Good student. Why did he end up waiting tables at the country club? When he left from Arkansas State?"

His face shuttered. "I got him back on with me at Roy's shop. It was that knee. He couldn't get under the cars to work; couldn't squat, knee was too messed up. Roy let him go." He looked away.

"Did you know about his relationship with Jewel Shaw?"

His head jerked back to face me. "He didn't chase her; I'd swear to that on the Bible. It was the other way around. He was a worker, not a player."

"Darrien explained that to me. Just wondered whether you knew what was going on."

"Are you saying it's my fault?"

His voice shook when he asked the question. I backpedaled; spreading blame was not my intention. Moving back to safer ground, I asked for names and contact information on the character witnesses.

He left the room and returned with a phone directory, its pages beginning to yellow. Together we made a list of people who would testify that Darrien had a peaceable reputation.

As he thumbed the pages of the phone book, Oscar Summers asked a question. "Will my boy get a fair trial?"

I looked up from my legal pad. Summers stared down at the phone book, turning the pages. With all the confidence I could muster, I said, "I'll do everything I can to assure that he does."

"Who is gonna be on that jury?"

He was still bent over the phone book, so I couldn't read his face. "We don't know yet, Mr. Summers. The jury is selected right before trial."

Then he looked up, his eyes piercing. "Will it be white?"

I let a long breath escape. "Mr. Summers, we won't know the makeup of the jury until trial. But the jury panel comes from registered voters of Williams County and forty percent of the population of the county is black. So it can't be an all-white jury, can it? That's just not possible." In his eyes, I read skepticism.

"We'll see," he said. "Guess we'll see about that."

Our list completed, I packed up to go. He led me to the door but lingered with his hand on the knob.

With his head bowed, he said, "Promise me you won't let them kill my boy."

The statement knocked the stuffing out of me, but I tried to keep my voice calm as I repeated my stock answer: "No lawyer can guarantee an outcome in any case, Mr. Summers, but I'll do my best to see that your son is acquitted."

Looking up, he fixed his eyes on mine. "Not good enough."

I took a backward step. Though nothing about his demeanor

was threatening, the tension that was building made me distance myself.

"Mr. Summers—"

"I want a promise."

"I promise I'll do everything in my power."

"No." He let go of the doorknob and leaned back against the door, as if he wanted to block my exit. "A guarantee. You tell me you'll set my boy free."

My eyes jerked from his face to the doorknob. I wanted out of that house so bad, I considered making a run for the back door.

"Tell me," he said. And his eyes filled.

When the tears rolled down his face, my resolve broke. I would have said anything to escape that moment.

"Yes," I said in a whisper.

"What?"

"Yes, he'll be acquitted. Because he's innocent."

After I spoke the words, I flew down the front steps to the safety of my car, absolutely horrified. How could I have done it? I'd broken the most basic rule of trial practice: Never guarantee victory.

And even worse, I was a liar. Because there was every chance that we would lose.

Oscar Summers's beloved son might be on death row in less than two weeks.

# CHAPTER 15

THAT PROMISE HAUNTED me over the course of the next week and a half. It hovered over me as I met with the character witnesses Darrien's father had provided, and as I sat at my desk crafting cross-examination questions for the state's witnesses.

When I met with Darrien in the interview room at the jail, seeing the fear in his eyes increase with each passing day, I was reminded of the false promise I'd made to his father, a vow I couldn't keep.

On the Sunday night before trial, I sat in my storefront office, scratching notes onto my jury selection presentation with a pen. The ink grew faint and the pen stopped working altogether. I scratched hard on an old envelope to get it flowing again, but it had given up the ghost.

I pulled open my desk drawer to grab a new one, but the box was empty. Ditto for my briefcase. I started to panic, my breath growing shallow as I sorted through piles of papers on my desk, trying to unearth a writing instrument. *Stupid,* a voice whispered in my ear, *stupid, incompetent*. What kind of lawyer doesn't have a damned pen to her name?

I heard a pounding sound and nearly peed my pants. It was past ten o'clock. No one would come calling at this time of night.

Then a face peered through the storefront window and a hand knocked on the glass. "Ruby! Open up, I've got something for you."

When I saw Shorty's face, I breathed out in relief and un-bolted the door. He walked in, carrying a plate covered with aluminum foil.

"Ruby, where were you tonight? Didn't I tell you we have a fried chicken special on Sundays?"

The aroma of freshly fried chicken drew me close. Leaning over the plate in his hands, I closed my eyes and inhaled.

"Lord, Shorty, that smells like heaven."

Two chairs beside the door comprised my "waiting area" for clients. We took a seat. Lifting the foil, I spied the Sunday special in all its glory: fried chicken, mashed potatoes with cream gravy, green beans. Shorty handed me a fork and a knife wrapped in a paper napkin.

As I dug into the potatoes, I said, "You be sure to put this on my tab."

"No way, baby. I was going to throw it away. Do you know what time it is?"

"As a matter of fact, I do. So what are you doing out and about so late?"

"I was at a meeting. Came back to go over the books at the diner, and I saw your light on. Thought I'd check in on you."

"What kind of meeting?"

He looked away and picked up an ancient *People* from a rack of battered magazines I set out for my clients. "Nothing big. Just a local organization."

"Oh, you're going to make me guess." I looked him up and down, pretending I was trying to fit him in a box. "Lions Club? Rotary? Shrine?"

He gave a half shrug, as if he didn't want to talk about it. I laughed, enjoying the brief distraction from my trial preparation.

"Church choir? Young Democrats? Republicans?"

"Nope. You're not such a good guesser."

I gasped in mock horror. "Square dancing? No!"

"Quit deviling me and clean your plate."

I ate up, so glad to have a hot plate of food that I wasn't even self-conscious as Shorty watched me gobble it down. When I paused to wipe gravy from the corner of my mouth, he said, "Can Lee Greene fry chicken that good?"

I had to laugh. "Oh, Shorty, please. Lee never toiled over a frying pan for me, I promise."

My plate was almost clean, except for a chicken leg for tomorrow's breakfast. "Thanks so much for dinner. I'm going to put this in the fridge for later."

Shorty followed me into the back room. As I set my prize in the fridge, he walked around the space with his hands clasped behind his back.

"So this is home?" he said.

Seeing my dwelling through his eyes was awkward. In a teasing voice, I said, "Let me take you on a tour of House Beautiful. This is the state-of-the-art kitchen," indicating my microwave and hot plate with a flourish of my arm.

"The dressing room is on the right." I had a particleboard dresser and a portable rod for hanging clothes.

"And finally, the elegant bedroom." I scooted to my sofa bed, still unmade from the night before.

When he came closer and took my face in his hands, it didn't take me by surprise. It was a blessed relief to escape from Darrien Summers and his fate, to block it out completely. I pulled Shorty onto the unmade bed, ready for a roll in the hay.

After some much-needed distraction, Shorty didn't suggest sleeping over, for which I was grateful; I still had work to do. As he buttoned up his shirt, he shot me a wink.

"Anything else I can do for you tonight, Ruby?"

"Well, you brought me supper and took my mind off my troubles. That should do it."

He was whistling as he shut the door behind him. Suddenly remembering, I followed.

"Hey, Shorty! You got a pen on you?"

# CHAPTER 16

ON MONDAY MORNING, I sat beside Darrien at the counsel table in Judge Baylor's courtroom. I wore my Goodwill suit, the errant button sewn firmly into position. My client was better dressed than I was, in the navy wool suit that Suzanne Greene had provided. It looked sharp, though as we'd predicted when I'd picked it up, it was a tight fit.

I looked around at the prospective jurors assembled in court. The racial makeup was not what I had hoped: roughly three-quarters of the panel was white, only a quarter black.

Judge Baylor's door swung open, and he emerged from his chambers in his robe. The bailiff called: "All rise!"

"Be seated," the judge said, as he settled into his seat behind the bench. He had a sheaf of papers in his hand. "The following panelists are excused from their duty."

Leafing through the sheets of paper, he called out names; as he did, people left the courtroom. With each departure, my anxiety increased.

He was excusing people of color. My black jurors.

After a dozen or more prospective jurors departed, I jumped to my feet.

"Your Honor! May we approach the bench?"

He looked up from the papers. "Now?"

"Yes, Your Honor."

Lafayette joined me at the bench. The judge said, "What is it, Miss Bozarth?"

"Your Honor, I object to the elimination of these jurors. I demand an explanation."

He leaned back, regarding me with surprise. "Demand? You demand?"

I was starting off on the wrong foot with the judge, I knew that, but this wasn't an ice cream social. "The court is affecting the racial diversity of the panel. Of the thirteen people you excused, eleven were black."

Lafayette shrugged, nonplussed. "The judge is just doing his job."

"What?" I said, in a voice too loud for a bench discussion.

Baylor shook the sheets of paper he held. "You're surely aware that Mississippi has a literacy requirement for jury service."

Did I know that?

"And as the circuit judge, it's my responsibility to remove any panelists whose ability to read or write doesn't stand up to my scrutiny. The panelists filled out these questionnaires this morning. This is standard procedure."

Lafayette's mouth was twitching. My radar was buzzing like crazy.

"This is subjective, an abuse of power by the court."

"Your objection is noted," Baylor said. "Sit down."

Once the preliminary panelists named by the judge had been excluded, Judge Baylor gave us a chance to ask the remaining prospective jurors questions. Lafayette went first. He asked whether any members of the panel were friends or acquaintances of the defendant, Darrien Summers. Only one woman raised her hand: a black woman in her twenties. She said she'd gone to school with Darrien. Lafayette approached the bench; I joined him as he whispered to Judge Baylor.

"I request that prospective juror number nine be struck for cause, Your Honor."

The judge looked at me. "Miss Bozarth?"

"I object to her exclusion. She didn't indicate that she would be biased."

The judge picked up a pen and marked through her name on his master list. "I think it can be assumed." He looked at the woman and raised his voice. "Ma'am, you are excused."

I avoided my client's eye as I walked back to the counsel table.

When it was my turn to address the panel, I seized the opportunity to address the elephant in the room.

"Ladies and gentlemen, my client is a black man; the evidence will show he was having an affair with a white woman, and the prosecution has accused him of causing her death. Is there anyone on the panel whose judgment would be affected because my client is black and the murder victim was white?"

I held my breath as I waited for the response. After a pause, hands came up; some were forthright, some hesitant. I made a beeline to the bench and asked Baylor to excuse them all from duty. The judge let them go.

I returned to the wooden podium and said: "Ladies and gentlemen, Jewel Shaw was a native of Williams County. How many of you were friends or acquaintances of the deceased? Or know her family?"

A score of hands were raised. I followed up and asked whether it might affect their ability to serve on the jury; all of them said it would. At my request, they were struck for cause.

I took to the podium again. "I need to know: Is anyone on this panel a member of the Williams County country club? Or have you eaten at the restaurant where my client was employed?"

Many more hands went up, including prospective juror number 18, a dark-haired man whom I recognized. He was the guy with the distinctive port-wine birthmark that I'd seen at Shorty's diner. I worked hard to knock the country club members and patrons from the panel; but while other jurors were relieved to be released from jury service, he seemed resigned to remaining on the panel.

I zeroed in on him. "Sir, you realize that all jurors in this case must be fair and impartial."

His face was impassive. "I do."

"And there are many people today who feel that, because they are members of that club, and have been at that venue, they can't be fair. You have said you've eaten at the club many times."

He parroted my words. "Many times."

"And you're aware, sir—you are under oath."

He gave a slow blink. "I know that."

"But you're telling us that the fact that you've been at the club many times won't affect your impartiality?"

"No. It won't."

"And you will base your verdict on the evidence alone?"

"I will. Yes, ma'am."

He said everything right. But there was something about number 18 that bothered me. He seemed so bloodless about the process; it was unnatural. And he had given me the creeps back when I'd first encountered him at Shorty's diner. I walked to the counsel table, thinking: *Who in his right mind would want to sit on a sequestered jury in a murder case?* I bent down and whispered to Darrien.

"Do you know him?"

He turned his head to take a good look. "Don't think so."

Even so, I drew a circle around number 18's name on my legal pad. When the time came, I would use a peremptory strike to get rid of him. Because he bugged me.

But Lafayette threw me a curve.

"Your Honor, may we approach the bench?"

When I caught up to him at the bench, the DA was rattling off another list of jurors. "Your Honor, I request that the following panelists be struck for cause: numbers 32, 41, 6, 18, and 14."

I thought I'd misunderstood. "Did you say number 18?"

Lafayette checked over his notes. "Yes. He responded to Ms. Bozarth's question about the country club. Despite his testimony, maybe he ought to go, due to his connection to the scene of the crime."

Judge Baylor said, "Your strikes for cause are granted—except for number 18. He stated under oath that he will base his verdict on the evidence. And Mr. Lafayette, if we eliminate everyone in Williams County who's ever had a bite of food at the club, there won't be enough people left in the county to seat a jury of twelve."

The DA conceded, "Reckon you're right about that, Judge."

Back at the counsel table, I was torn. My impulse was to strike number 18 from the panel, but I'd learned in my trial practice class that if a juror is bad for one side, it's good for the other. If Lafayette wanted number 18 gone, then I shouldn't waste one of my strikes on him. Lafayette would get rid of him.

After we made our final peremptory strikes, the judge called the names of the jurors selected to decide the case. I watched them with an eagle eye. The port-wine-marked man did have a spot on the jury—as juror number 3. Some jurors looked miserable when their names were called; some received the news with resignation. But I watched number 3 as he took his seat, and he made no overt reaction. Nothing at all.

I tried to reassure myself that there was nothing really wrong with number 3. We could do worse. But he gave me a bad feeling.

# CHAPTER 17

THOMAS LAFAYETTE'S CHAIR scraped against the tile floor with a screech as he rose to make his opening statement. A woman in the front row of the jury box grimaced and covered one ear.

"Ladies and gentlemen of the jury, I'd like to thank you in advance for your service in court. This will not be an easy task for any of you. The defendant, Darrien Summers," he said, turning toward my client with a glare, "has been charged with the crime of murder in the first degree."

Darrien twisted in his seat, shooting a desperate look at the jury. I reached out and placed a hand on his arm.

Lafayette swung back to face the jury. "This is what the evidence will show."

In his opening statement, the DA began by setting up the facts: the date and location of offense, the Mardi Gras ball at the Williams County country club, where, he said pointedly, Jewel Shaw was a member and the defendant was an employee.

Then he launched into a eulogy on Jewel Shaw's behalf, detailing her background and accomplishments. When he had been talking for ten minutes straight and had only arrived at her sophomore year in college, I stood up.

"Objection."

The judge looked down in surprise. "On what grounds?"

"Your Honor, this extended biography of the deceased is irrelevant. The purpose of opening statement is to tell the jury what the evidence will show..." I paused and added, "the evidence against my client, Mr. Summers."

The judge glanced at Lafayette. "Sir?"

"I'll tie it up, Judge."

"All right, then. Overruled."

He banged his gavel. I sat down.

Lafayette walked up to the jury box. "Funny thing, the defense trying to prevent me from talking to y'all about Jewel Shaw, the beautiful young woman who was brutally murdered that night. Jewel was found dead in a cabana at the country club, with thirteen stab wounds in her. A man was discovered, crouching over her in that cabana with Jewel Shaw's blood on his hands and all over his clothes. Who was that man? Ladies and gentlemen, he's sitting in this courtroom today: it's the defendant."

Then he pointed the finger of accusation at my client. I wanted to glance at Darrien, see how he was holding up, but I didn't dare to look his way. It might look like we had something to hide.

"Ladies and gentlemen, you'll be wondering—because I know what you're thinking—what was a waiter doing with Miss Shaw in her daddy's cabana at the club? The evidence will show that, too. The defendant had been sexually abusing her over and over again."

"That's a lie!"

Darrien was halfway out of his chair as he spoke the words. It took all my strength to grasp his arm with both hands and jerk him down into his seat. Then I jumped up.

"Objection! Your Honor, the prosecution is misstating the evidence. And the DA is making argumentative allegations in opening statement. . . ." I paused, hoping to frame a brilliant follow-up. Nothing came to mind.

"Overruled," Judge Baylor said, his voice stern. "The defense will have the opportunity to speak in defendant's opening." Judge Baylor pointed his gavel at me. "And Miss Bozarth, inform your client that I will not tolerate any further outbursts."

Returning to my seat, I leaned in to Darrien. "Darrien, you can't do that. Don't jump out of your chair, don't say anything. Just talk through me."

His eyes were frantic. "They're lying about me."

"We'll fix it, when they see the pictures. Calm down, act cool. Shouting out like that doesn't help. Think about what you learned in your criminology classes."

After a long pause, he nodded and settled back into his chair. I turned my attention to the jury. As Lafayette continued his description of the evidence—the slashes in the dress, Darrien's bloodstained jacket, the text sent from Jewel to Darrien, and the pictures of their sexual exploits—my spirits sank. The jurors were eyeing the defense table with increasing suspicion. When he described the coroner's report, and said the medical examiner would show the location of all thirteen wounds, the suspicion turned to anger. The jurors only broke eye contact with the DA to glare at Darrien. Or to glare at me.

The oldsters on the panel, half a dozen men and women with gray hair, had already convicted Darrien in their minds. I scanned the faces of the younger jurors, searching for some holdouts upon whom I might focus my advocacy. A woman in her thirties looked distressed but uncertain; she might listen to me. The lone black juror's face was solemn. And then, there was juror number 3, the man with the birthmark.

Maybe I stared at him too long; maybe I sent him a vibe. His eyes cut away from Lafayette and met mine.

He blinked twice, without expression.

Leaning forward in my seat, I tried to make a silent bid for his support.

His mouth twitched and he looked away, refocusing on the prosecutor.

I clenched the arms of my chair. Was he laughing at me?

"Miss Bozarth?"

I looked up. The judge was addressing me. Had I not heard him?

"Yes, Your Honor?"

"The district attorney has finished his opening. Do you wish to give your statement now, or reserve it for later?"

I stood and gazed at the closed and suspicious faces of our jurors. If I spoke now, I might be able to win some of them back. But to do so, I'd have to tip my hand, and reveal my trial strategy to Lafayette.

I swallowed. "Your Honor, we'll reserve it. For later."

The judge checked his watch. "We'll recess. Court will reconvene in twenty minutes." He struck the gavel.

Darrien tugged at my jacket. "Why didn't you say anything for me? Speak up on my behalf?"

I whispered, "We'll have our chance; I'll do it later, at the end of the state's evidence and the start of our case."

I was ready to explain further when a hand reached from behind the counsel table and squeezed my shoulder with an iron grip.

Twisting around in my chair, I saw Oscar Summers, Darrien's father. "Are you trying to hang my boy?"

# CHAPTER 18

AFTER THE BAILIFF cuffed Darrien and escorted him to the holding cell, I made a beeline for the hallway. Oscar Summers followed.

As I dodged behind the Coke machine, he started in on me.

"What are you trying to do in there?"

"Mr. Summers, please keep your voice down."

"I want to make sure you can hear me. Why aren't you fighting for my boy?"

I beckoned for him to stand beside me, so that the soda machine could block our confrontation from curiosity seekers who were roaming the halls. He stepped in close to me, effectively trapping me between the humming red machine and the wall.

"Mr. Summers, you've got to understand how the process works. The state goes first; they have the burden of proof. They put on their case. Then we have our turn. I'll make an opening statement and put on our evidence, call our witnesses."

He moved in closer. I could smell the coffee on his breath.

"By the time you get around to defending Darrien, those twelve people gonna have their minds made up." He pointed a finger at the courtroom. "Did you pick that jury? Eleven white people, only one black one, a woman. Why'd you do that?"

It wouldn't calm him to hear that I shared his apprehensions.

"It's Williams County citizens who have sworn they'll base a verdict on the evidence. We just have to play the hand we're dealt."

A young woman walked up and slipped coins into the Coke machine. Oscar Summers started to speak, but I gave a quick shake of my head. After the woman's can fell from the machine with a clunk and she wandered off, he spoke again, in a soft voice that held a hint of a warning.

"That talk about playing your hand? I don't see that you're risking anything. But my boy's life is at stake. And you promised me." His voice was a hoarse whisper. "You said you'd set my boy free. I'm holding you to that."

When he reminded me of my rash promise, I shut my eyes, a childish reflex. I tried to move away, but my back was literally against the wall.

*Get a grip,* I thought.

I raised my chin. "I was wrong to tell you that, Mr. Summers. I can only promise that I'll do my best. But I shouldn't have made any guarantee. There are no guarantees at trial."

His face contorted. "You can't take it back."

He was getting loud again. I glanced down the hallway; people were turning to stare.

"You can't tell me that, then take it back. My son's life—we're talking about Darrien's life."

I tried to ease around him, sliding my shoulders against the Coke machine, but he blocked me with his arm. "This conversation isn't over."

I heard change jingle in the Coke machine again. A head peered around the side; it was Shorty.

"Everything okay, Ruby?"

I took a deep breath and pasted a smile on my face.

"Hey, there! Shorty, this is Oscar Summers, Darrien's dad. Mr. Summers, have you met Shorty Morgan? He has the diner on the square."

Oscar Summers's arm dropped back to his side. He gave a grudging nod. "I go there sometimes."

Shorty held his hand out. "I appreciate your business, sir. And let me say: you've got a fine lawyer here. Ruby Bozarth is going to kick some ass in that courtroom."

Summers suffered the handshake, but didn't acknowledge the endorsement on my behalf. Shorty pushed a button and picked up a can of Coke from the dispenser. He held it out to me.

"You thirsty, Ruby?"

Gratefully, I popped the top and swigged from the can.

Oscar Summers remained at my side. I said, "Let's talk later, okay? I'll share my strategy with you as soon as I get a chance."

He left us then, and I sagged against the side of the red machine, grateful for its support even though it buzzed like a beehive.

Shorty leaned close and whispered, "Are you going to be all right?"

"I'm a basket case. I want to run and hide."

His fingers rubbed the back of my neck. "You're going to be just fine. The diner will be overflowing when the judge breaks for lunch, so I'll save a seat for you at the counter. I'll put a Reserved sign on your favorite stool."

It was nice to have someone looking out for me. I felt my eyes begin to sting. Covering my weakness with a smirk, I asked whether fried chicken was on the day's menu.

"Oh, hell no. Good thing, too. I know what you'll do for a plate of fried chicken."

I gasped with mock outrage but didn't have a chance to make a snappy comeback. The bailiff shouted down the hall, "Court back in session, Miss Bozarth."

# CHAPTER 19

THAT MORNING, PATRICK Stark, the sheriff of Williams County, sat on the witness stand. He was a squat figure of a man whose tan uniform barely covered his paunch, and his ginger hair was combed over with a pouf.

During direct examination by Lafayette, the state's physical evidence had been introduced. Jewel Shaw's bloody purple dress was admitted into evidence and circulated around the jury box. Some jurors were quick to pass it off. Others handled the plastic shroud reverently. Only juror number 3 seemed unmoved by the exhibit. I couldn't tell whether his lack of reaction boded ill or well for Darrien.

The DA asked Sheriff Stark about the telephones. A brief introduction of Darrien's phone showed his receipt of Jewel's text directing him to the cabana. They spent far more time on Jewel's phone, encased in the plastic bag I'd opened in the evidence room at the sheriff's department. I fidgeted in my seat as the sheriff and the DA handled the plastic-wrapped phone, anxious they might notice my intrusion into the exhibit.

But after the phone was introduced into evidence, Lafayette dropped it on the prosecution's counsel table and left it there. He pushed a flash drive into his laptop and directed the jury's attention to a large screen in the courtroom.

The first image caused Darrien to jerk violently in his chair. Draping an arm around his shoulders, I gave an urgent whisper.

"Pull yourself together."

His eyes met mine, and he nodded, placing his hands on the tabletop, and sat perfectly still.

The picture blown up on display was one of Jewel's selfies; she'd captured a shot of herself astride Darrien.

When Lafayette finished his direct examination of Sheriff Stark, he turned to the judge.

"Your Honor, I offer State's Exhibits One through Thirteen into evidence."

The judge peered down at me. "Miss Bozarth?"

I huddled with Darrien.

"Darrien, he laid the foundation for his exhibits. We can object to them, but the judge will overrule us."

He spoke in a hushed voice. "So we'd end up losing that fight, plus the jury will think we're trying to hide something from them."

His perception impressed me. I whispered, "You'd be great in criminology. You're a natural."

He almost cracked a smile, but as he straightened in his seat, his face regained a grave expression.

I stood. "No objection."

"The exhibits will be received. Miss Bozarth, your witness." And he inclined his head toward the witness stand.

"Sheriff Stark, did you conduct a search of the cabana at the Williams County country club?"

He cleared his throat before answering. "I did. Me and two deputies."

"The physical evidence identified in court today—the dress, the Mardi Gras beads, two telephones, the blood samples— were those all discovered at the scene?"

"They were. I said that already, when I testified for Tom."

"Did you conduct a thorough search, Sheriff?"

His eyes narrowed.

"I always do."

"But on this particular occasion—your search of cabana six—was it thorough? Conducted in a professional manner?"

He leaned forward in his chair. "I know what you're getting at."

I took a step closer to the stand. "Answer the question: yes or no."

Lafayette jumped up. "Your Honor, she's badgering the witness."

I shot him a look and was about to protest, but Judge Baylor intervened. "Answer the lady's question, Pat."

The sheriff shifted back in his chair, watching me with a shuttered face. "Yes. Thorough."

I faced the jury. "Sheriff, where is the murder weapon?"

He sighed. "I don't know."

"Did you look for it?"

"Of course I did. You know, he could've stashed—"

I cut him off in a ringing voice. "Objection, Your Honor: speculation."

The judge said, "Don't speculate, Pat."

"Sheriff, what was the diameter of the cabana? How big of a space are we talking about?"

"I don't recall a measurement, can't rightly say."

"Well, then, let's narrow it down. Bigger than a football field?"

Another sigh from the witness stand. "No."

"Okay, we'll scale back. Big as this courtroom?"

"No."

I walked over to the jury room. It adjoined the courtroom, and the door was located right outside the jury box. I turned the knob and pushed it open. "About the size of the jury room?"

He leaned over his seat and peered into the space. Most of the jurors did the same. Inwardly, I warmed; they were paying attention to me. "Yeah, that might be about right."

I shut the door. As I advanced on the witness stand, I said: "So three law enforcement professionals conducted a thorough search of a space as small as the jury room, and couldn't turn up a weapon."

"We didn't. Didn't find it in there."

I walked to the counsel table and leaned against it. "Sheriff, when my client was apprehended in the cabana, did he have a weapon in his possession?"

"No. Not that I know of, anyway."

I pushed away from the table. "Let's be clear. Did he or didn't he?"

He met my eye with a look that was unmistakably hostile. "He didn't."

I walked to the podium to glance at my notes. The sheriff volunteered: "She was stabbed with a weapon like a knife. He'd have access to knives in the kitchen at the club."

My head jerked up. "Objection!"

"Sustained."

I took a step to the bench. "Ask that the jury be instructed to disregard."

The judge said to the jury, "You will disregard the sheriff's last statement. About the knives in the kitchen."

*Oh, my God,* I thought—*now they've heard it twice.* I moved on.

"Sheriff, you identified an image from Jewel Shaw's phone:

an image which depicts the deceased and my client engaged in what appears to be a sexual act."

His mouth twisted. "Appears to be."

I turned to Lafayette. "Can you display that image again please, Mr. Prosecutor?"

He blinked in surprise and turned to the bench.

"Your Honor?"

The judge shrugged. "It's been admitted."

The photo appeared on the screen. I studied it. "Sheriff, who is on top?"

He gaped at me. "I beg your pardon?"

I walked over to the screen and tapped it. "Who's on top, Sheriff?"

He turned to the judge. "Your Honor, this don't seem right."

Lafayette took the cue from his witness. "Your Honor, I object; the defense is disrespecting the memory of the deceased in the presence of her loved ones. The Shaw family is present in the courtroom, Your Honor."

I didn't need to look out into the courtroom gallery to ascertain whether it was true; I could feel daggers in my back. "Judge, it's their exhibit. It is the state's evidence."

"The defense may continue. But I warn you, I expect discretion and decency in my courtroom."

Turning back to the sheriff, I said, "Is she restrained?"

"What do you mean?"

"Is she tied up? Chained down?"

"Not that I can see."

"All right, then." I paused to study the image again. "Sheriff, would you say she's happy?"

"How would I know?"

"How do you usually detect whether a person is happy?"

"I don't know."

"Well, Sheriff—wouldn't you say that when someone is happy, they're wearing a smile?"

I took my pen and pointed at Jewel Shaw's face. "Tell me honestly, Sheriff—would you say she's happy in this picture? Or sad?"

He was spared the necessity of answering, because the bell in the courthouse began to toll. It was high noon.

Judge Baylor banged the gavel. "Noon recess. Court will reconvene at one o'clock."

I stormed the bench. "Your Honor, I haven't completed my cross-examination of this witness."

But the judge was already rising from his seat. "You'll have the opportunity to continue. After lunch." And he slipped away into his chambers.

Lafayette nearly knocked me down as he raced to confer with the sheriff. And before the courthouse clock struck for the twelfth time, the bailiff was escorting Darrien to the holding cell.

Court was over for the morning.

Just when I was on a roll.

# CHAPTER 20

A CRUSH OF people crowded outside Shorty's diner. When I squeezed through the door, I saw that Shorty had kept his promise: a single stool was unoccupied, and it sported a RE-SERVED sign.

I slipped onto the stool and signaled the waitress, who was juggling water glasses.

"Joyce, I know it's crazy in here, but could you get me a cheeseburger?"

She smiled. "Shorty said to take care of you. I'll get you a sweet tea too, hon, in a to-go cup."

Lord, yes. Sweet tea. When she delivered it, the bell jingled over the front door. I glanced over my shoulder. It was Judge Baylor's bailiff, leading the jury. The twelve jurors followed him in single file.

Shorty pushed through the swinging doors of the kitchen and called to the bailiff. "I've got the back room all set up for you."

As Shorty scooted around the counter, the bailiff said, "Judge says he don't want you sending a waitress in there. I'll take their order and bring it out."

"We'll take good care of you." Shorty shouldered his way into the aisle. To the line of jurors, he said, "Good to see y'all today."

"Shorty, no talking to the jurors. They're sequestered."

I swiveled my stool to face them as they filed past me on their way to Shorty's private dining room. I couldn't speak to them, but I was determined to make eye contact and offer up a smile.

Several jurors cut their eyes away from me or glanced without response. But an older man gave me a nod. That was progress. The younger woman I'd pinned my hopes on smiled at me.

Shorty was an arm's length away from me. As the last of the line filed past, I trained my smile on juror number 3, the port-wine man.

But he wasn't looking at me. He was looking at Shorty.

Shorty didn't speak to the juror. But he extended his hand.

Not so strange, I thought. Juror number 3 was a regular customer.

But as the juror grasped Shorty's outstretched hand and pumped it, he mouthed something to Shorty. Shorty nodded and backed away.

As the jury disappeared into the back room, I called out to Shorty. I wanted to ask what juror number 3 had said to him. But he turned away from me and ducked into the kitchen.

Seemed like Shorty and the juror had more than a casual connection. Maybe it could work to my client's advantage. I opened my briefcase and dug out the jury selection file. I zeroed in on juror number 3: his name was Troy Ellsworth Hampton. Shorty had never mentioned him.

Pulling out my phone, I tried a Google search. It was a shot in the dark, but the name was sufficiently uncommon that I might get a hit. What the search revealed nearly knocked me off my stool.

Because juror number 3 appeared on the Facebook page for the Council of Aryan Citizens of Mississippi. A post showing a picture of the recent installation of new officers bore his image. It was unmistakable. The birthmark made him instantly recognizable.

And scanning a list of individuals present at the installation, I saw a familiar name: Clarence Palmer Morgan Jr.

I dropped the phone into my briefcase. What on earth was Shorty doing in a hate group?

And what the hell was a card-carrying white supremacist doing on my jury?

A wave of anxiety seized me; I had to get out of the diner. The waitress set the plate with my cheeseburger on the counter just as I grabbed my bag and slipped off the stool.

"Ruby! You're not leaving? Hon, that's your order."

I just shook my head and headed for the door. Behind me, she called, "Ruby! You want it to go?"

I pushed through customers who were waiting for a table. Before I reached the exit, I felt a tap on my shoulder.

Turning to see who had touched me, I was confronted by the angry face of a rail-thin middle-aged woman dressed in black, with diamond studs in her ears.

Oh, shit. Jewel Shaw's mother.

"I know you," she said in a breathy whisper.

My head was spinning; I had neither the time nor the inclination to go around the ring with Jewel's mother.

"Beg pardon." Because I was trying to be polite. "I have to go."

She clutched the jacket of my suit. *Dear God,* I thought, *don't let her pull the buttons off.*

"You are trying to disgrace my daughter. I heard you. No decent person would speak ill of the dead like that."

I pulled away and managed to get my hand on the door. But before I made my exit, she had the last word.

"Don't fool yourself—people remember. You're that Bozarth girl. Your mama was a cleaning lady—just like a Negro. You were trash then, and you're still trash."

# CHAPTER 21

THE WORD *TRASH* echoed inside my head as I tore across the street. I was so shaken by the revelations at lunch that I failed to see a car approaching at a fast clip. It swerved to avoid hitting me, and the driver laid on his horn and gave me the one-finger salute.

Mrs. Shaw's furious insult should not have been at the forefront of my thoughts. I had bigger things to think about, matters of profound significance to my client. And to me.

When I reached the front of the county courthouse, I dropped onto a cold stone step and tried to figure out what I should do with the information I'd stumbled upon. My head was buzzing; it prevented me from thinking clearly. My primary focus should be exposing juror number 3 as a liar who was unfit to serve on the jury. But I couldn't stop thinking about Shorty; why would he associate with the Aryan Citizens? Which led to the follow-up: did I have a lick of sense when it came to choosing my romantic partners?

I heard Mrs. Shaw's whispery voice again. *Trash.*

I literally shook myself and pulled my phone out of the brief-case. Suzanne. I should call Suzanne Greene. She'd know what to do.

When she picked up, the sound of her voice helped to calm me down.

I spoke with the phone pressed close to my face. "Suzanne, I've uncovered something about one of my jurors. I think I need a mistrial."

"Mercy, girl. What's going on? Which one?"

"Juror number three: Troy Hampton. He's an officer of a white supremacist group."

Suzanne's voice crackled through the line. "Is he KKK?"

"No, it's another one: Aryan Citizens of Mississippi."

"Different name, idea's the same," Suzanne said in a weary voice.

I hunched over the phone. "Suzanne, I covered the race issue in voir dire, and he didn't respond. He was under oath. I'm go-ing to see Judge Baylor and tell him what I know."

I stood up on the step, brushing off the back of my skirt. But Suzanne's voice in my ear brought me up short.

"No—don't do that. You keep that card up your sleeve for now."

On Suzanne's end of the line, I could hear the clatter of plates in the background; she was probably at the Dixie Buffet. My empty stomach twisted. With a pang, I regretted leaving my cheeseburger behind at Shorty's—and there was no way I'd be darkening the door of his business again.

I spoke softly into the phone, since people were coming up the steps. "Suzanne, why wouldn't I go to the judge?"

Her voice was sharp. "Let this play out. Do more research on juror number three; get your ducks in a row. If you win at trial, you'll never need to use it; Darrien will walk. But if you lose, juror number three has given you a basis for a motion for new trial, and fodder for a successful appeal. You have an ace up your sleeve, but hold on till you need it. If you play it now, best you can hope for is a mistrial, and you'll have to start the trial process over again from scratch."

I walked to the courthouse entrance with slow steps. People were returning from the noon break. The recess was almost over.

"I'll do what you recommend, Suzanne."

"Good." She was chewing. "Get back in there and keep swinging. Anything else I can help you with today?"

I ducked behind a stone pillar so I couldn't be overheard. "One more thing. What do you know about Shorty Morgan? He owns the diner on the square here in Rosedale."

In the moment of silence before she replied, my heartbeat accelerated.

"Shorty? Let me think. Nice young man, I've heard. Fries good chicken."

Her bare bones commendation wasn't enough to reassure me. What had I hoped she might reveal? That Shorty had an identical twin who was a racist and had stolen Shorty's identity?

Baloney. As I ended the call, my suspicions about Shorty consumed me. Seized by paranoia, I pondered: maybe the Aryan Citizens wanted inside information on the Summers case and had tasked Shorty with the job of prying information from me.

My stomach twisted. I'd made it so easy for him. Easy as pie.

And where had I first encountered the mysterious juror number 3? In an orange booth at Shorty's diner.

Closing my eyes, I indulged in another fit of self-loathing. I had fallen into bed with a manipulator, a man I barely knew. Bet he thought it was a hoot.

The tower clock struck one.

# CHAPTER 22

BACK IN JUDGE Baylor's courtroom, we resumed our positions. Sheriff Stark sat on the witness stand; I faced him, leaning on the lectern near the jury box; and the DA was poised at his counsel table. Darrien sat at the defense table alone, with his father keeping watch behind him.

Judge Baylor said to the sheriff, "Pat, let me remind you: you're still under oath."

"Yes, sir, Judge."

"Miss Bozarth, you may continue."

I needed to make some headway. "Sheriff Stark, I believe you've testified that you examined Jewel Shaw's telephone."

"I did."

"And you looked through her photo history, the pictures on her cell phone. Correct?"

"Yes."

I smiled, encouraging. "Sheriff, you have testified regarding photos of Jewel Shaw and my client. But there were other pictures on Ms. Shaw's phone, isn't that true?"

His eyes cut away from me. "She had a lot of pictures."

"That's true. And isn't it also true, Sheriff, that a number of those shots depict Ms. Shaw in the company of men other than Darrien Summers?"

"They might have. I don't know."

I walked close to the witness stand. He was clamming up, afraid to give an answer that would hurt the state. "Oh, come on, Sheriff. Did you or did you not see pictures of Jewel Shaw with a variety of male companions on her cell phone?"

"I can't remember every picture on her phone."

He didn't want to play ball with me. With a nod at the jury box, I walked to the DA's counsel table and picked up State's Exhibit 5, the phone that belonged to Jewel Shaw.

Lafayette demanded in a whisper, "What are you doing?"

I didn't answer, just ripped the plastic cocoon off Jewel Shaw's phone.

Lafayette jumped to his feet. "Your Honor, the defense is tampering with the state's exhibit!"

I held it up so that the judge—and the jury—could see it. "Your Honor, I'm not harming the exhibit in any way."

Lafayette moved toward the bench with a full head of steam. "I want to know what Miss Bozarth intends to do with the state's exhibit."

*Gonna make the sheriff eat his words.*

"Use it to cross-examine this witness, Judge."

In the days prior to trial, I had studied Jewel's phone history; I knew the pictures on that phone. I had determined in advance precisely which ones I intended for the jury to see. Jewel Shaw hanging off a blond surfer type. Jewel Shaw in the nude, riding piggyback on a suntanned Hispanic man. Jewel Shaw lifting her shirt on Bourbon Street, with the caption "Begging for beads!"

At Lafayette's insistence we approached the bench, and after a whispered consultation, Judge Baylor said I could proceed. With a cocky air, I walked the short distance to the podium. My excitement mounted; I was going to make headway with the phone information and initiate a tangible contribution to Darrien's defense. I'd start taking charge—just as soon as I turned on Jewel's phone and revealed its contents.

Holding the phone in my hand, I tried to turn it on.

The phone was dead.

As I stared at the dark screen, a voice in my head whispered: *Karma.* Or the ghost of Jewel Shaw.

# CHAPTER 23

THAT DAY, COURT ran so long that the sun was setting when the state called its last witness. A shaft of light shining through the windows on the west side of the courtroom illuminated the faces of the jurors as they sat in the box. They looked strained, weary.

So was I.

Lafayette approached his final witness. "State your name, sir."

"Stanley Forsythe."

"And what is your occupation?"

"I'm a photographer. I have a studio here in Rosedale."

"What kind of photography do you do, sir?"

"Weddings, graduation portraits, family portraits. My clients can have traditional sittings in my studio, but I also go out on location, take photos in natural settings."

Lafayette grinned at him. "Like my daughter's graduation picture? You went to the high school stadium as a background for her in her cheerleading uniform, ain't that right?"

From my seat, I said: "Objection. Irrelevant."

The judge adjusted his glasses. "Sustained."

The DA glanced at me with a careless shrug of his shoulders. He'd made his point. He was a local baron, firmly woven into the tapestry of the community. I was the outsider.

Turning back to his witness, Lafayette said, "Sir, in February of this year, did you have occasion to be present at the Mardi Gras ball at the Williams County country club?"

"I did."

"For what purpose were you there?"

"The club hired me to take photographs of the event. It's an annual tradition."

"Posed photos?"

"No. Candids. For the club newsletter."

As he testified, I was doing a slow burn. I'd seen the photographer's name on the state's witness list, and tried to contact him half a dozen times, even going to his studio the Saturday before trial began. He wouldn't talk to me.

The DA set up two easels near the witness stand, then picked up a large mounted exhibit from his counsel table.

Lafayette placed the exhibit on one of the easels. "Mr. Forsythe, I show you what's been marked for identification as State's Exhibit Thirty-three. Can you identify it for the jury, sir?"

Looking at the exhibit as Forsythe responded, I clutched the pen in my hand so hard that I cracked the plastic casing. The exhibit was a blown-up photograph of Jewel Shaw, taken at the ball. It was a full-length shot in a glorious riot of color: her purple dress, her shining golden hair, her laughing face behind the glittery green Mardi Gras mask. The image seemed to vibrate with life and vitality.

I cut my eyes at the jury, to measure the impact the photo had on them. They looked like mourners at the funeral service. My lone black juror was fumbling with a packet of Kleenex tissues. She wiped her eyes.

*Lord help us.*

Lafayette said, "Mr. Forsythe, what time was this photograph taken?"

"Ten fifteen p.m. My equipment records the times of each photograph."

In a voice of deep solemnity, he asked, "Is State's Exhibit Thirty-three a fair and accurate representation of Jewel Shaw at 10:15 on the night of her death?"

"It is."

The DA turned to the bench. "Your Honor, the state offers State's Exhibit Thirty-three into evidence."

"Miss Bozarth?"

I didn't huddle in conference with Darrien. I wanted the moment to pass as quickly as possible. "No objection."

Lafayette walked back to the prosecution table and hefted a second exhibit, identical in size.

He placed the exhibit on the second easel. It was an image that had been admitted into evidence earlier: State's Exhibit 10. Jewel Shaw lay dead in her bloodstained dress in cabana 6, her arm dangling off the chaise. Her sightless eyes were open. Blood matted the golden hair and the green and gold beads at her neck.

Lafayette bowed his head, like a man preparing to launch into prayer.

"No further questions."

# CHAPTER 24

"YOUR HONOR, THE state rests."

Lafayette's voice rang with self-satisfaction.

Judge Baylor said, "It's been a long day. Ladies and gentlemen, we'll recess until tomorrow morning."

When he stood to leave the bench, I rose, and remained standing as the sequestered jury passed by my counsel table. Keeping my posture rigidly erect, I tried to make eye contact with the jurors, but they all avoided my gaze—with one exception: juror number 3. He smiled, showing his teeth. I narrowed my eyes, thinking: *I know all about you, Mr. Aryan Citizen.*

As the courtroom emptied out, Darrien slumped down in his chair. "Ruby, it looks bad."

I dropped into my chair beside him and spoke in a whisper. "It's not over. We get our chance tomorrow."

He wiped his face with a hand that trembled. "I've been watching that jury. They hate me."

"We'll turn it around. We have ten witnesses coming in to-morrow morning who will testify about your character."

His hand left his face and he looked at me. "Will it help?"

"You bet it will. The jury has only heard one side. And there's something else."

I was so deep in conversation that I didn't see Lafayette ap-proach. "Ruby."

My head jerked up. He was standing a foot away. "What do you want?"

He pulled a face. "Don't bite my head off. I have a disclosure to make. A witness I may call."

I wanted to tear out my hair. "You just rested."

"I'll call him as a rebuttal witness. After the defense rests."

The bailiff was shackling Darrien, preparing to take him back to jail. "Ruby?" he said as the cuffs clicked shut.

To Darrien, I whispered, "I'll be in to see you tomorrow morning, before court. I found out something that can help our case, something major. But we need to talk privately."

He nodded an acknowledgment, but as he walked away, I sensed fear radiating from him.

Lafayette rested a hip on my table. He held out a sheet of pa-per. It read: "State's rebuttal witness: Phillip Nelson, Assistant Public Defender."

I looked up. "That doesn't make any sense."

The DA was smug. "Makes perfect sense."

"Phillip Nelson was the public defender who represented Darrien before I was appointed. He can't testify against his for-mer client. That's not ethical."

With mock patience, Lafayette said, "I'm anticipating a char-acter defense. I contacted a couple of those names on your witness list. They told me you'll be calling them to swear to Mr. Summers's peaceable reputation."

"So?"

"You think I'll be sitting on my hands, doing nothing to combat it? Girl, you've got a lot to learn. 'Mr. So-and-so, would it affect your opinion if you knew that Darrien Summers attacked his attorney in a court of law?' I'll get to ask that question in cross-ex."

A flush crawled up my neck. I should have anticipated that.

"And then, when you're done, I'll need to call the victim of the assault. To show the jury that, once again, I'm telling them the whole truth and nothing but the truth."

"I'll object. It's not proper," I said, with more confidence than I felt.

He slipped off the counsel table, knocking my pen to the floor as he did so. I bent down to pick it up; Lord knows I didn't have a wealth of writing implements.

"Make all the noise you want. It builds such trust with the jury when you try to conceal the facts."

He actually chuckled as he walked over to his own table and packed up his exhibits. I should have known he would attack my character defense. My inexperience had caused me to fail my client yet again.

I wanted to lay my head on the counsel table and howl. I shook with the effort to retain control.

An arm slipped around my shoulder. I smelled a whiff of tobacco.

With a start, I twisted around in my chair. Suzanne Greene was leaning over the wooden bar that separated the public gallery from the lawyers and judge.

Behind her reading glasses, her eyes twinkled. "Pack up your stuff and meet me at my office in forty-five minutes. I've got something for you."

I searched her face. She looked like a bearer of good news,

but my spirits were down too low to try to guess what it might be.

"What is it?"

She patted my shoulder.

"You'll see."

"Is it a cyanide tablet? Because I'd like to swallow one right about now."

Her hand, still on my shoulder, gave me a firm shake. "I don't like that talk. Don't you dare give up. The cavalry has arrived."

# CHAPTER 25

AFTER I PARKED my car behind Suzanne's office building, I pulled out my phone to see whether any new catastrophe had occurred. There was a text from Shorty.

*Hey darling! Should I drop by tonite with covered dish?* It was followed by a winky face emoji.

Staring at the phone, I considered angry replies or accusations.

Instead, I deleted the message. As I walked to Suzanne's office, I berated myself once again. When it came to men, I didn't have a lick of sense.

The door was unlocked. I walked into the lobby and called out: "Suzanne?" Then I saw a sight that made me trip over my own feet.

Lee Greene Jr. My ex-fiancé. Standing in front of an antique mirrored hat rack in the lobby, admiring his reflection.

"Lee," I blurted.

He was straightening a striped bow tie at his neck. Glancing my way, his face broke into a smile. A sardonic smile.

"Well, I'll be damned. If it's not my old heartthrob, Ruby Bozarth."

I clutched the briefcase he'd given me behind my back, hoping to hide it from view. "I'm here to see Suzanne. She's helping me."

"That's what I hear. Sounds like you're chasing my aunt all over the state, begging for her favors."

I flushed. Had Suzanne characterized me in that fashion?

Lee gave himself a final once-over in the mirror, and said, "I shouldn't be surprised. You always were hungry for the Greene family legacy."

I took a step in his direction. "The hell you say. Seems like I told you to take your legacy and shove it up your snobby—"

He cut me off with a laugh. "There's that junkyard dog I used to adore. You never change, Ruby. Awful glad I found out in time."

A sheaf of papers sat on the empty receptionist's desk. He picked them up, and called out to the back of the office. "Aunt Suze, I'm heading out. Thanks for letting me use your printer."

Suzanne's voice echoed down the hallway. "Glad to help. Is Ruby out there?"

"She is, ma'am." Lee tucked the papers into a leather portfolio. "I'm off to Vicksburg. It's been a pleasure."

"Ruby! Back here! In the library!"

Entering the book-lined room, I was taken aback to see the man sitting beside Suzanne at the conference table.

It was Stanley Forsythe, the Rosedale photographer. And he didn't look happy.

Dropping my briefcase to the floor, I said, "Well, this is a surprise."

Suzanne was puffing on a Marlboro Gold. "Y'all haven't been properly introduced. Stanley, this is Ruby Bozarth. She's a friend of mine. My protégé, you might say."

I slid into a chair at Suzanne's right. "Mr. Forsythe and I met over the phone last week. I wanted to get together with him, but he was too busy."

"Well, he's got some free time now. All righty, Stan—let's see those Mardi Gras pictures."

Stanley Forsythe had a laptop computer in front of him. His hand made a damp print on the black surface. "I don't know about this, Suzanne. The DA said that my images are state's evidence."

I was wild to see the pictures he had withheld from me. I popped a piece of Nicorette and said, "Mr. Forsythe, if it's regarded as state's evidence, then I'm legally entitled to inspect it. Judge Baylor signed an order saying so."

He wiped his sweaty hands on the legs of his pants. "Maybe I should ask Lafayette first."

Suzanne flicked an ash. "Open the damn computer and pull up those shots. You're acting like a kid stealing candy at the Piggly Wiggly."

"I don't know, Suzanne. It doesn't feel right."

She peered at him over her reading glasses. "Since when did you start doubting my legal judgment? You know, Stanley, you wouldn't be in business today if I hadn't won your divorce case three years back."

That did the trick. He opened the laptop and pulled up the file containing the photographs he'd shot at the Mardi Gras ball. I left my chair and walked closer to look over his shoulder.

We surveyed the images on the screen one by one. Jewel Shaw appeared in many of the shots. The camera captured her at dinner with her parents, laughing with young people in party clothes, dancing to the band.

The time that the photos were taken appeared on the screen, as he had explained in his testimony. We studied pictures of Jewel taken later in the evening.

"Look there," Suzanne said, tapping the screen. "Something's wrong."

I'd seen it, too. Jewel appeared in two pictures taken after eleven that night. Her party girl smile had disappeared. In the final image she looked angry, and her feathered mask didn't hide the indignant scowl on her face.

"Jewel's not having fun," I said.

I leaned in to examine the final shot of Jewel. Her angry face was not the only one captured: other masked people were snapped, including a dark-haired man. He appeared to be trying to lean out of the shot. I pointed at his figure on the screen.

"This guy doesn't like having his picture taken."

His masked face was turned away from the camera, but a red mark showed up outside the black mask's coverage.

My heart rattled in my chest. "Mr. Forsythe, can you enlarge the image on the screen?"

He tapped at the computer. Jewel's scowl was life-size on the screen, and I could see that the red mark on the black-haired man was a birthmark. A port-wine stain birthmark.

# CHAPTER 26

IT WAS A gamble.

Back in court the next morning, I heard the courthouse clock strike nine. Judge Baylor was seated at his bench. I stood beside my counsel table with my back to the jury. I couldn't face them, not yet. What if I couldn't keep a poker face?

Looking down at Darrien, I raised my brow. We had spent the past hour in the holding cell, conferring in whispers.

He glanced at the jury box behind me, then met my eye. He nodded twice, a bare movement of his head.

Time to roll the dice. In reality, I was a stranger to games of chance. But Suzanne, a regular patron of the casinos in Tunica, Mississippi, had given me the counsel of a seasoned player: go all in.

My dallying apparently made the judge impatient. "Miss Bozarth, is the defense ready to proceed or not?"

"Yes, Your Honor." I cut a glance at Lafayette. He held a notebook; on its cover, in bold black ink, he'd written: *Character*

*Evidence Cross-Examination.* Apparently, the DA had seen our witnesses lined up in the hall outside the courtroom.

I had been nauseated all morning and had even tried to vomit before I left my office. But when I saw the DA's pad, a tiny thrill of pleasure shot through me. Lafayette was in for a surprise.

When the judge invited me to make my opening statement, I hesitated. I had no intention of revealing our evidence before it unfolded. So I marched to the jury box and launched into an oratory on the legal presumption of innocence.

Lafayette jumped up. "Objection, Your Honor; this is argument."

"Sustained. Miss Bozarth, confine your statements to the evidence."

Unruffled, I nodded at the jury and walked back to the counsel table. "Your Honor, the defense calls Stanley Forsythe to the witness stand."

The photographer walked into the courtroom. He paused before the bench. The judge said, "Mr. Forsythe, you're still under oath. Be seated."

On my laptop, I pulled up the Mardi Gras photo depicting Jewel Shaw's angry expression, taken around 11:00 p.m., and displayed it on the courtroom screen. I asked the witness to identify Defendant's Exhibit 1.

Stanley Forsythe said, "It's a candid photograph, taken at the Mardi Gras ball at the Williams County country club."

"Can you tell the court the time at which this picture was taken?"

"Just after eleven. At 11:03 p.m."

"Mr. Forsythe, is Defendant's Exhibit One a fair and accurate representation of the individuals you photographed at the Mardi Gras ball on that night?"

"It is."

"Mr. Forsythe, has Defendant's Exhibit One been changed or altered in any way?"

"No, ma'am."

"I turned to the judge. "Your Honor, the defense offers Defendant's Exhibit One into evidence."

The judge glanced at the DA. "Mr. Lafayette?"

"No objection."

I nodded politely at the photographer. "The defense has no further questions of this witness."

"Mr. Lafayette, you may cross-examine."

"No questions." He looked sulky. He'd pushed his "character witnesses" pad to the side and was doodling on a fresh legal pad. The top sheet had a line of question marks.

The sight made me want to grin. But I wore a stoic expression as I said, "The defense calls Sheriff Patrick Stark to the witness stand." While the bailiff called his name in the hallway, I was amazed to notice that my nausea had disappeared.

As the sheriff took his seat, the DA caught my eye and gave me a "What the hell?" look. I ignored it.

Stepping over to the prosecution table, I picked up one of the state's exhibits lined up on its surface: Jewel Shaw's cell phone. Without asking leave, I walked up to the witness stand and handed it to the sheriff.

"Sheriff Stark, I've handed you State's Exhibit Five. This is the cell phone that belonged to the deceased, Jewel Shaw—isn't that right?"

His face was closed. "Yeah."

"Sheriff Stark, please tell the court: what is the security passcode for Miss Shaw's phone?"

"Don't know. Can't remember it off the top off my head."

Yeah, baby. I was ready for that. I'd dealt with the sheriff's selective memory before.

"Mr. Stark, would it be helpful to refresh your recollection with the sheriff's report you prepared in this case?"

I handed him the report. Grudgingly, he recited the passcode. I walked over to my briefcase, pulled out a portable phone charger, slipped the phone from its plastic wrapping and plugged it in.

It took a minute to charge. Leaning against the counsel table, I waited, smiling. For the first time that day, I turned my face to the jury box.

Some jurors looked impatient, others confused. And one of them looked tense. Nervous.

Juror number 3 was starting to sweat. Beads of moisture were visible on his upper lip.

Once Jewel's phone was powered up, I handed it to the sheriff.

"Sir, I'm showing you the phone history on State's Exhibit Five, the cell phone of Jewel Shaw. Please read off the number of the last call received by the deceased."

He did.

"Was the call received on the date of her death?"

"It was."

"What time was it received?"

He glanced down. "Eleven sixteen p.m."

I said, "Is there an identifying contact name?"

"Nope." His eyes met mine with a challenge. "No name."

Time for the grand gesture. I extended a hand; he placed the phone in my palm. With a fingertip, I hit the number on the screen. And I waited.

We'd done the homework. But any number of things might prevent the outcome I was praying for.

As the silence dragged on, my nausea returned so sharply, I nearly gagged.

Then I heard it: a buzz. The humming sound of an incoming

call on a muted cell phone. My head jerked to the right: the sound was coming from the jury box.

The jurors looked around in confusion. When the humming ceased, I held up the phone and hit the number again.

When the second round of humming began, I strode to the jury box and leaned on the railing. Juror number 3 sat in the middle of the front row. I focused on him. His fellow jurors were staring at him as well; it had become clear that he was the source of the noise.

Holding Jewel's phone so that the screen was visible to the jury, I cocked my brow and gazed down at juror number 3.

"You gonna answer that?"

# CHAPTER 27

JUROR NUMBER 3 met my eye with an unblinking gaze, but a droplet of perspiration trickled in a wet path from his temple to his cheek.

When the humming ended for the second time, I walked to my computer, tapped a key, and enlarged the photo on display on the computer screen. With a quick adjustment, I centered it on the face of the masked man leaning away from the camera.

"Sheriff Stark," I said, walking to the screen and pointing at the image. "Can you identify the individual depicted in the Defendant's Exhibit One?"

The sheriff leaned forward in his chair, studying the enlarged image with a perplexed expression. As he squinted at the screen, juror number 3 stood up in the jury box.

I heard a gasp; it may have come from my own chest as I watched to see what he would do next.

To the woman on his right, the juror excused himself in a courtly fashion as he stepped over her feet. He nimbly passed the other jurors in the front row, making his way past their knees without stumbling. At the end of the jury enclosure, he stepped down onto the floor of the courtroom and walked the short distance to the adjoining jury room. Without a backward look, he opened the door and walked inside, pulling the door shut.

I swung around to face Judge Baylor. He was staring slack-jawed at the jury room door. "Your Honor?"

When the judge didn't respond, I ran to the jury room and tried to twist the knob. It wouldn't turn. Putting my shoulder to the door, I tried again.

"Judge. He's locked himself inside," I said.

The courtroom had been buzzing with speculative murmurs since the juror made his exit. When I made my announcement, the volume intensified to a roar. The hubbub must have awakened the judge's senses; he banged his gavel twice.

"Order. Order!" Judge Baylor waved his bailiff over. "Get that door open and get him out of there."

The bailiff, an aged courtroom veteran, wrestled with the knob. He tried to shake it, pull it to and fro.

Judge Baylor said, "Use the key, for God's sake."

A sheepish look crossed the bailiff's face. He pulled a ring of keys from his pocket and turned the lock. He twisted the knob; I saw it turn. The door remained closed.

The bailiff turned to the judge and spoke in an apologetic voice.

"Can't get inside, Judge. Something is blocking the door, I reckon."

From the corner of my eye, I saw Darrien rise from his seat at the counsel table.

"Your Honor, I can get it open," he said.

He could, without a doubt. But Judge Baylor shook his head.

"No, thank you, Mr. Summers. Be seated, sir." He leaned toward the sheriff, who still sat on the witness stand with his hands dangling between his knees.

"Pat, get up and get into that jury room."

The sheriff rose eagerly; he strode to the door and lifted his booted foot. With three stout kicks, he opened the door, shoving the heavy conference table that had blocked it from the inside.

Once the door cracked open, I scooted next to Sheriff Stark and peered into the room.

The table still blocked the door from opening all the way, and a dozen chairs were pushed from their orderly placement. But it was plain to see that aside from the table and chairs, the room was empty.

The only movement in the jury room came from the lone window. It was wide open. A curtain fluttered in the wind.

# CHAPTER 28

I DIDN'T ENTER the jury room. I just stood in the doorway and stared at the open window, trying to get my head around it.

A hand grasped my shoulder and gave me a shove. I stumbled and grasped the door frame for balance as Lafayette charged into the empty jury room. He looked around, but aside from the table and chairs sitting askew, there was nothing to be seen.

He swung around, turning to me with a frantic look.

"What the hell is going on?"

The calmness of my voice amazed me. "We just lost one of our jurors."

"I know that; I've got eyeballs in my head. What I want to know is," and he advanced on me with an accusatory finger, "what in God's name are you up to?"

I left the doorway and walked up to the screen, where the party photo was still on display. I pointed at the masked man, running my finger down the red line of the birthmark that the mask didn't cover.

"Didn't you see that?"

He took a step forward for a closer look. "Doesn't mean anything."

"Are you insane? At the least—the very least—it means we've been trying the case to a man who was at the scene of the Mardi Gras party and didn't bother to let us know. But Tom, that's not all."

I grabbed the cell phone from the counsel table and showed him the phone history. "Tom, I dialed this number—the last call received on the night of Jewel Shaw's death."

He stared at the phone. A look of dread came into his eyes. "And it rang. In the jury box."

"Yep. Sure did."

He rubbed his forehead. I said, "Have you figured it out? You're prosecuting the wrong guy, Lafayette."

"Ruby!"

Darrien was calling to me from the defense table; his father was behind him with a hand on his shoulder and a baffled expression. I hurried over to them.

Oscar Summers spoke first. "What the hell is going on here?"

I didn't bother to whisper; the cat was way out of the bag. "One of the jurors went AWOL: juror number three."

Darrien grasped my arm. "What happens now? Are they gonna let me go?"

I bent down so that I could speak into his ear. "Too soon to say. But Darrien, I think things are finally going your way."

His father interrupted. "That white man with the red mark on his face—did he run out because he's the one who did it?"

Lafayette was at the bench, waving his arms. The judge called to me, but I could barely hear him; the sound of sirens outside muted the voices in the courtroom.

I gave Darrien's shoulder a squeeze. "Be right back." I hustled up to join Lafayette at the bench.

The witness stand was empty. Judge Baylor said, "Miss Bozarth, I dispatched the sheriff to run down that juror."

"Good. Excellent. Hope he remembers to advise him of his rights before he questions him."

Lafayette ignored me. "Your Honor, what do we do now?"

"Danged if I know. I've served this county for nineteen years, practiced law here for decades. But I've never seen anything like this." He craned his neck, checking out the remaining eleven jurors. I turned to look, too. Most were huddled in groups of two and three, whispering. The lone black woman sat with her arms crossed. She smiled at me.

The judge called to the bailiff. "Leon, take the remaining jurors into the jury room until further notice."

The bailiff stuck his head into the jury room. "Kind of a mess in there, Judge."

"Straighten it up, then." A pulse was pounding in the judge's temple. He stood abruptly and addressed Lafayette and me. "Meet me in chambers."

Another wail of sirens soared through the open window.

Lafayette turned on his heel and walked to the prosecution table. I followed close behind him.

"Sure hope they catch that dude," I said.

No response. With his back to me, Lafayette bent to pick up his briefcase.

I said, "Hey, Tom. If the sheriff apprehends him, you know what I think you ought to do? If I were you, I'd have the sheriff impound that guy's vehicle and do an inventory search of it."

He jerked around to face me. The hair at the crown of his head was tousled. "Don't tell me how to do my job."

Raising my hands, I backed away. Back at the defense table, I took a moment to advise Darrien that I was heading off to meet with the judge in chambers, and I'd let him know what happened. Behind Darrien's shoulder, Oscar Summers actually winked at me.

With my adrenaline pumping, I turned to focus on the prosecution table. From my vantage point, I could see Lafayette pull out his cell phone. Though the courtroom was noisy, I was pretty sure I heard him say: "Tell the sheriff to impound the car when they catch him."

I bowed my head so nobody could see my satisfied grin.

# CHAPTER 29

WHEN LAFAYETTE AND I joined the judge in chambers, he was shaking tablets into his hand from a bottle of Advil. He dry-swallowed them, and then shouted at his clerk through the open door. "Grace! Where's my Coke?"

She hurried in with a can and a cup of ice, then disappeared, pulling the door shut behind her.

Ignoring the cup, Judge Baylor gulped from the can. As he set the can on his desk, he let out a soft belch.

"Beg pardon," the judge said, placing his hand on his abdomen. "All right, Tom, Ruby."

I noted with a start that for once he had addressed me by my first name. "How do you want to proceed?" he asked.

I opened my mouth to answer, but Lafayette jumped in. "I hate to do it, Judge, but I'm going to have to ask for a mistrial."

"No, no, no," I said, leaning forward on the seat of the wing-back chair. "Not good enough. The defense requests a judgment of acquittal."

The DA gnawed on a thumbnail. "No way. You can't be serious."

"Oh, I'm totally serious." I crossed my legs, swinging my left foot and displaying a shoe with a heel that was worn down to the metal stud. "I'm serious as a heart attack."

"We have an alternate," Judge Baylor said.

Lafayette shot us a look of disbelief. "Is that what you want? Just proceed with the trial like nothing happened?"

"Oh, something definitely happened," I said. Both men focused on me. "I have other witnesses I can call. Got ten character witnesses out in the hall. And while they're testifying about what a fine young man Darrien Summers is, I'll betcha the jury will be thinking about juror number three. Wondering where he is."

The DA shifted his eyes away from mine, so I tapped him on the arm.

"Don't you think that they'll be wondering why that juror ran off after I showed the picture of him at the Mardi Gras ball? And called him on Jewel Shaw's phone?"

Judge Baylor sighed. "Sweet Jesus." He stood abruptly, jerking the zipper of his black robe. He yanked the robe off and threw it over his chair, then loosened his tie.

He turned to the DA. "Tom, what do you know about this guy? What's his name?"

"Troy Hampton," I said.

"I don't know him," Lafayette said.

"Didn't you try to get rid of him? Strike him for cause?"

Lafayette pulled at his thumbnail. "I don't know him personally; I've seen him around. Didn't particularly want him on the jury. Not comfortable with his politics."

I tried to keep my voice steady. "Politics? What kind of politics?"

Lafayette shifted in his seat. "Not politics, exactly. Associations."

"And what might those be?"

"Some ultra-conservative views, I guess. Stuff I'm not personally comfortable with."

I snapped. "Thomas Lafayette—were you aware of any hate group activity on his part? Sounds like you were. And yet you remained silent about it during voir dire, when he testified under oath that my client's race wouldn't have any bearing on his verdict."

Lafayette and Judge Baylor exchanged a look. When the DA spoke, he chose his words carefully.

"I didn't have any hard evidence of the guy's activities. In my position, I hear a lot of things. But it's vital that I exercise discretion."

"Baloney," I said. "Judge Baylor, I want to make a request for judgment of acquittal, and I want it on the record."

"Fine." He shook the Advil bottle again.

"And I need to make a record regarding the DA's prior knowledge of juror number three's 'political associations.'"

"I object to that," Lafayette said. "I don't like that."

"I don't care whether you like it."

A timid knock sounded on the inner door. Grace opened the door just wide enough to poke her head through.

"Judge Baylor?"

"*What?*"

His voice was so loud that her head jerked back and hit the door frame. She spoke in a whisper. "The sheriff is coming. He needs to see you."

"Good. Send him in." In a more civilized tone, he added, "Thank you, Grace."

We sat in silence for long minutes as we waited for Sheriff Stark to arrive. The heel of my shoe had developed a wobble. When I reached down to investigate, it fell off onto the floor.

*Shit.*

While I struggled to stick the heel back on, the sheriff walked in. When I saw him, the heel slipped from my fingers, unheeded by anyone, including me.

Stark was sweating, though the day was cool. Damp spots showed on the front and back of his tan shirt, and his armpits were soaked.

"We got the car."

"Good. Where is he?" the judge said.

"No, not him. The car. It was deserted, sitting on a side road on the east end of town."

The judge sighed, a soft exhale. "Well, I'll issue a warrant. Contempt of court, leaving the trial when he'd sworn to serve. One of your deputies can try to run him down."

He stood and picked up the black robe. "Let's get back to court. Miss Bozarth, you can make your request on the record, but with all due respect, ma'am, I'm inclined to follow the DA's recommendation. I believe I'll declare a mistrial."

The disappointment might have knocked me over, had I not been seated. I ducked my head, picking up my fallen heel. By some miracle, I successfully jammed it into place.

Sheriff Stark cleared his throat. "Judge, I impounded that car and did an inventory search of the vehicle. Like Tom told me."

I glanced at Lafayette. He wouldn't look at me.

"What did you find. Drugs? A million dollars? A dead body?" The judge pulled a face as he zipped up his robe.

"No, sir, Your Honor. Didn't expect to find nothing. But in the trunk, I looked under the tire well. Danged if I didn't see something strange."

"What?"

He held a small trash bag. I'd been so busy with my shoe, I hadn't noticed it. Reaching inside, the sheriff pulled out a clear plastic evidence bag.

"I think it's one of those Mardi Gras masks."

I leaned forward to get a better look. It was smashed in places, the worse for wear. But it was a green Mardi Gras mask, with the remnant of a blood-stained feather.

Just like the mask Jewel Shaw had worn at the Mardi Gras ball.

# CHAPTER 30

IT WAS COLD outside the county jail. I pulled my suit jacket tightly around me as I lingered by the back door.

When I'd initially arrived at the jailhouse exit, I stood alone; but a crowd shortly began to gather. TV news vans pulled up to the curb. A local reporter for the Rosedale weekly paper hurried across the street, waving his arm.

I twisted my head his way, unable to discern whether the newsman was waving at me. A body slammed into me from the back, lifting me off the sidewalk and swinging me off the ground.

I let out a shriek. But when he set me on my feet, I was relieved to see that the unexpected embrace came from Oscar Summers. He was beaming. Traces of tears tracked down his cheeks. "You did it. You kept your promise."

Oh, Lord—that promise. I'd never be so foolhardy again. But this time, I'd lucked out. I returned his hug, gasping as he nearly squeezed the wind out of me.

In the doorway of the exit, Darrien appeared. TV cameras zoomed in, and photographers pushed toward him. He searched the faces in the crowd, then Oscar shouldered through the media crush and clutched his son to his chest.

A reporter jostled me. "Can you give me your reaction to the judge's decision?"

I hadn't prepared anything clever to say. "I'm delighted," I said, smiling, as Darrien moved through the crowd of press and extended his hand. I grasped it; he put an arm around me and we grinned like crazy at each other.

The reporter persisted. "Is that all?"

My head was muddled by the crazy day, but I pulled it together sufficiently to add: "My client's innocence has been established. Judge Baylor entered a judgment of acquittal. Darrien Summers has been cleared. Today, justice has been served in Mississippi."

They shouted more questions, begging Darrien for a statement, but he turned to his father and said, "I just want to go home, Dad."

Oscar Summers gave a decided nod. To me, he said, "Miss Bozarth, some friends and family are coming by the house. We'd be proud to have you join us."

I took his hand. "I'll drop by later on, Mr. Summers. Y'all are so kind to include me. But a friend wants to meet me for supper first."

Minutes later, I was maneuvering my battered car up the private drive of the Williams County country club. I entered the club and walked up a flight of stairs into the dining room.

The club manager, Bert Owens, was holding a whispered conversation with two men. When I walked into the room, he strode toward me.

"Ma'am, this club is for members only."

My face flushed, but I met his eye without blinking. "I'm a guest. Meeting a friend for dinner."

Suzanne Greene was seated at a back table, near the doors to the patio. She lifted a hand in greeting. "Ruby!"

With a grim face, Owens led me across the room to Suzanne's table. It was the peak of the dinner hour, and many patrons' heads turned to stare as I passed. I lifted my chin and made my victory lap with a swagger, thinking: *Hey, Rosedale—knock this chip off my shoulder.*

As I set a napkin in my lap, Suzanne reached over to give my arm a squeeze. "You did it, darling. You're the talk of Mississippi."

Glancing around, I said, "I'm the topic of conversation in this room, anyway."

"Baby, you made the evening news—all over the state. You're on the screen in Jackson!" She gave a happy sigh and took a hearty swallow from a cocktail glass. "I always believed in you. Feel like you're my own."

A white-haired waiter came up. I knew him: it was Anthony Phelps, one of my character witnesses. After we exchanged a friendly greeting, Suzanne ordered a round of mojitos. After several sips, I launched into a description of the furor created by the discovery of Jewel's mask.

"At first, Lafayette put up a fight. He said he wouldn't withdraw the charges until the mask went through testing at the state lab, to ascertain that it was actually Jewel's."

"And that would take time. Do you mean to tell me that Lafayette wanted to make that innocent young man languish in jail while they waited for test results?"

"Uh-huh. And here's the thing: both the DA and the judge wanted the final decision to be on the other one's head. Baylor wanted Lafayette to withdraw the charge against Darrien, but Lafayette wanted it to be the judge's call."

"So the friends and family of Jewel Shaw..."

"Wouldn't be unhappy with them. So I asked that they do some internet research on that juror—Troy Hampton—just to see how that might impact their decision. Oh, Lord, Suzanne—you can't imagine all the stuff we uncovered."

"Like what?"

"I'd just scratched the surface before. We found social media sites where he'd posted crazy rants about how Mississippi should criminalize black-and-white relations. And since the government won't do it, he said vigilantes need to take it into their own hands. With the death penalty."

Suzanne drained her drink. "Just when you think things have changed in Mississippi, you encounter a nut job like that juror."

"Not only is he a murderer—he wanted Darrien to pay the price. When I think of what Darrien has suffered..." I'd already asked Suzanne for enough favors to last a lifetime, but I had one more request. "Suzanne, he should be back in school. I don't have any contacts, but I wondered whether you might know how to pull a string."

"Enough said. I'll get on it. I know some people in higher ed."

Our waiter came back to the table and announced the dinner special: fried catfish. I followed Suzanne's lead and ordered it. As he walked away, Suzanne said, "So your professional life is golden; you're walking on sunshine. How's your love life?"

If it hadn't been for the cocktail, I'd have dodged the question. But it loosened my tongue. "Suzanne, begging your pardon—I have the shittiest taste in men. If it wasn't so pitiful, it would be downright funny."

Anthony appeared and set down three plates of catfish. He bent to whisper in my ear, but he spoke so softly, I couldn't catch what he was saying.

"Anthony, can you speak up, please?"

He glanced over his shoulder. "Mr. Owens says we're not supposed to say anything. But you need to know, Ruby. He's here."

"Who?"

"Him. You know. He's in the men's locker room."

He said more, his mouth close to my ear, but I couldn't hear it. The sound of sirens rang through the room.

# CHAPTER 31

I RAISED MY voice to a near shout. "Anthony! Are the police here?"

"Yes, ma'am, I reckon so. Mr. Owens has him cornered in the locker room."

"Who is cornered?" I asked, but on some level, I knew the answer.

Anthony tapped his cheek. "The man with the red face."

Suzanne leaned over in her chair. "What is going on, Anthony?"

"The cleaning staff found that man messing around in the locker room. He'd climbed up on top of the lockers."

"What on earth?" Suzanne demanded.

The country club members were leaving their chairs, racing to the patio. The sirens stopped, so Anthony lowered his voice. "He was in the men's locker room. He's got no call to be in there. Only golf members are allowed."

"What was he doing?"

"Standing up on top of the lockers. Lifting up the ceiling tiles, feeling around under them."

"The ceiling tiles?"

"Yes, ma'am. And when the cleaning lady said he wasn't supposed to be up on those lockers, he jumped right down. But he was holding a knife. She seen it plain as day."

I reeled as the implications hit home. "He pulled a knife? From under the ceiling tiles?"

"Big old straight-edge knife. She told me it was dirty. You reckon it had dried blood on it, maybe?"

"Yeah. I bet it did."

Anthony said, "Cleaning lady about had a heart attack. Ran out in the hall, screaming for Mr. Owens. Security pinned the dude down before he could leave."

I jumped from my seat and joined the others who were rubbernecking at the patio doors. I got there in time to see the sheriff swing open the back door of his patrol car, place his hand on the dark head, and shove the handcuffed man inside. Through the car window, I saw his profile: it was juror number 3.

I walked back to the table. Suzanne said, "Did you see him?"

I nodded. She said, "Anthony filled me in. He hid the weapon in the locker room. Sounds like it's been concealed in there since the night Jewel died."

So, I thought. All the pieces of the murder puzzle were in place. And with Troy Hampton in custody, it was really over. As I sat in my seat, I could feel my pulse racing. I made a silent vow: I would never again get involved in a homicide defense. It could eat me alive.

Suzanne was staring at me. "Anthony, would you bring Ruby a fresh drink? Looks like she needs it."

"Yes, Miss Greene."

I looked down at the plate of catfish but had no appetite for it. Then I was struck by the presence of the third plate. Puzzled, I asked Suzanne whether someone was joining us.

She craned her neck, checking out the dining room entrance. "I think he just walked in." She stood and grabbed her purse. "I'm going to have a smoke on the patio. Be right back."

I watched her walk through the patio doors, then turned to the entrance and was appalled to see Shorty Morgan heading straight for our table, dressed in a sports coat and gray slacks.

He sat down, cool as a cucumber. "Hey, stranger."

I'd have liked to knock him out of the chair, but I was in a formal setting. Instead, I jumped out of my seat and reached for my briefcase.

Shorty rose and seized my elbow. "Why have you been giving me the cold shoulder? Ruby, we need to talk."

I jerked my arm from his grasp. "You're a damned hypocrite."

He had the good grace to look abashed. "How did you find me out?"

"On the internet, you idiot." I grabbed the lapel of his jacket and pulled him closer, so I wouldn't have to raise my voice. "You were playing me. You're a racist. What was your angle? Were you reporting my trial strategy to your buddies in the Aryan hate club?"

He leaned in close and whispered in my ear. "Sit. Down."

I sat. But not because he told me to. I wanted to hear his flimsy explanation.

Still speaking in a low voice, Shorty said, "I'm a political scientist, not a racist. And I was doing research, undercover."

That set me back. I studied his face. "What kind of research?"

"I'm writing an article for an academic journal. I do have ambitions higher than frying a chicken. Did you know that?"

He picked up his fork, took a bite of catfish, and dipped it in the tartar sauce. As he chewed, he screwed up his face in disgust. "That tartar sauce wasn't made in-house. What kind of joint are they running here?"

Settling into my chair, I watched him as he took another bite. He seemed sincere—and not just about the tartar sauce. My instincts said I should believe him, but, admittedly, my gut instincts were only right about half the time.

He set his fork down, reached out, and placed his hand over mine. I liked his hands.

# CHAPTER 32

I HAD A million questions about Shorty's Aryan brotherhood research, but just then Suzanne came flying in from the patio, her lit cigarette between her teeth.

She jerked the Marlboro from her mouth and extinguished it in the tartar sauce. "Good God almighty, kids. We have to go. Now." She glanced at Shorty's place setting; only the plate of fish and a water glass sat before him. "Thank goodness, Shorty, you haven't been drinking. You can drive."

As she pulled her purse onto her shoulder, I rose from my seat. I would follow anywhere Suzanne led. Shorty was slower to react. "Miss Greene, may I ask where we're headed?"

"Vicksburg." She waved at the waiter. "Anthony! Put it on my account. We're out of here."

"What's in Vicksburg?" I asked.

She gripped my arm and whispered. "My brother just called. His boy Lee is in jail. He's in terrible trouble—some charge of a partner dying during a sex act."

I backed away. The mention of my ex-fiancé set off alarms in my head. And I had sworn off a career in murder defense only moments before.

"Suzanne, I'm awful sorry—for you and your family. But if Lee is in trouble, I don't see what in the world it has to do with me."

She grasped my hand, pulling me forcibly from the table. "Ruby, he needs legal help. Now."

I resisted, leaning back in a game of tug-of-war. "Suzanne, Lee won't want me there, I assure you."

She stopped in her tracks, turning to face me with a steely gaze over her spectacles. "Sugar. He asked for you by name."

As Suzanne strode from the dining room, I followed behind, moving on autopilot. Shorty caught up to me and took my hand again. I was grateful for the warm clasp of his fingers.

So much for that vow.

It looked like I was headed to Vicksburg on a new murder case.

# CHAPTER 33

I SMOOTHED A wrinkle in my skirt as I sat beside Suzanne at the counsel table in the Warren County courtroom in Vicksburg, Mississippi. We were waiting for the Vicksburg police to escort Lee Greene over from the county jail for his arraignment.

The wrinkle was stubborn. No matter how I tugged at it, the crease remained in the black fabric. Suzanne pinched me lightly on the arm.

"Quit fidgeting," she whispered.

My hands stilled. Lee Greene always looked like a million bucks. When we were dating, he'd eye what I was wearing and shake his head. *Walmart? Or Old Navy clearance rack?*

The door to the courtroom opened, and a man in an orange jumpsuit entered, escorted by two plainclothes police officers. The prisoner in orange shuffled with an uncertain gait, his hands cuffed in front of him.

I blinked. It took a moment before my brain made the connection. The stumbling figure in orange was my old fiancé, Lee Greene Jr.

As he neared the counsel table, Suzanne stood and placed an arm around his shoulders. "Sit in the middle, hon. Between Ruby and me."

Lee nodded, collapsing into the chair. I stared at his profile before looking away in embarrassment. His hair, always perfectly groomed and parted on one side, was a greasy tousle. His hands, spread before him in the handcuffs, were dirty. And he smelled to high heaven: stale booze and body odor.

Suzanne was talking in a low tone. "We're going to get you out of here, Lee. We're taking you home. Your family is here for you, sugar."

It was true. I stole a glance over my shoulder at Lee's parents, who were sitting in the courtroom gallery. Lee Sr.'s face was frozen with shock. His wife was sobbing, her head bent low.

The judge entered, and we rose. Suzanne and I had to help Lee to stand, each of us gripping him under an arm. When the judge began to read the charge against him, Lee turned to Suzanne and whispered.

"I didn't do it."

"Shush, honey. Just be quiet now."

The judge's voice droned on, reading the legal language: Lee had committed the crime of capital murder by causing the death of Monae Prince during an unnatural sex act. Lee swayed on his feet. I grabbed his arm with both of mine to steady him. He looked down at me with unfocused eyes.

"Ruby, I don't know what they're talking about."

Suzanne's voice rang out. "Defendant pleads not guilty. We request that a reasonable bond amount be set."

The judge gave Lee a wary look, then turned to the DA's table. "What does the prosecution recommend?"

The assistant district attorney stood. I recognized him; he was a guy who'd been two years ahead of me at Ole Miss. Not the brightest dude in law school. Suzanne could tackle him with one hand tied behind her. He said, "We request that the defendant be held without bail."

Behind me, I heard a voice cry out: "No!" Then Lee's mother wailed aloud.

Suzanne proceeded as if she hadn't heard the interruption. "My client has no criminal history—as the DA is perfectly aware. He is not at risk of absconding, and he poses no danger to the community."

"We contest both of those points," the ADA said.

But the judge waved a hand and the ADA fell silent. "I'm setting the bond at one million dollars."

I gasped. Who could make a million-dollar bond? Lee would be in lockup until trial, and that could take several months, maybe even longer.

When the judge moved on to the next docket item, the ADA sidled over to our table. He didn't acknowledge me and addressed Suzanne.

"Looks like your client will be a guest of the Warren County jail for a while," he said with a snotty smile on his face.

Suzanne didn't return the smile. "Lee will be out today," she said, opening her purse and stuffing her pen inside with an angry thrust.

I followed suit, pulling my Coach briefcase onto the table and placing the file folder inside.

The ADA said, "That's brave talk. You got a million bucks in your purse, Miss Greene? Or maybe your colleague stuffed the money in her briefcase."

I clutched the briefcase to my chest in reflex. No danger that he'd find a stash of cash on me. I had less than twenty dollars in my possession.

Suzanne pulled up to her full height and eyed the lawyer.

She cut a formidable figure: six feet of affronted southern dowager. In a tone of voice I'd never heard her use before, she said, "Young man, don't underestimate us. And don't insult me."

*A property bond*, I thought. The ancestral Greene estate, outside of Jackson. It was worth well over a million. I glanced down at Lee in his orange suit and thought: *Good God, I hope he doesn't run off. If Lee jumps bail, his parents will be homeless.*

He caught me staring. "Ruby, you have to help me."

I sat again, and placed a hand on his arm. "Your aunt Suzanne and I are going to do everything we can."

He bent his head close to mine. I had to steel myself not to back away from the smell.

"Ruby, I wouldn't hurt a fly. You know me."

The ADA had moved on, so we weren't in danger of being overheard. I said, "We'll get to the bottom of this, Lee. Tell me: What happened with this woman—Monae Prince?"

He gave me a glassy stare. The white of his right eye was so bloodshot, it was hot pink. "I can't tell you."

I patted his arm. "Of course you can, Lee. I've entered my appearance as your counsel. You can tell me anything. It's privileged. What do you remember?"

He let out a sound that was a cross between a giggle and a groan. "That's just it. I can't tell you because I don't remember. Anything."

His gaze drifted sideways, and he said again: "I don't remember anything. Anything at all."

# CHAPTER 34

THE FOLLOWING MONDAY I sprinted across the courthouse lawn in Rosedale, racing to the Ben Franklin. The Greenes were due at my office any minute, and I didn't want them to cool their heels in front of a locked door.

Once inside, I did a quick pickup, stuffing loose papers into a desk drawer and wiping dust from my desk with a wad of Kleenex. My office was a humble spot to hold a meeting, but they were driving to Rosedale to accommodate my court schedule. I'd had a first appearance on a new child custody case that morning, and I'd asked the Greenes to meet at my office rather than Suzanne's in the next county.

I checked the time, relieved to see that the Greenes were running late. It occurred to me that it would be wise to run a brush through my hair. The heated exchange earlier in court had probably made me look frowzy.

When I walked into the bathroom behind the office area, I froze. It was a disaster. I'd rushed out at 8:50 that morning, leaving my makeup strewn across all surfaces. I snatched up my cosmetics bag, spilling loose powder in the process. Cursing, I picked up the can of Comet cleanser and shook it over the sink, then dumped some green powder into the toilet bowl for good measure. Working fast, I cleaned the sink, and was scrubbing at the rust-stained bowl with a toilet brush when a voice caused me to look up.

"Ruby?"

They were standing in the bathroom door. All of them: Suzanne, Lee, and Mr. and Mrs. Greene. I dropped the brush into the toilet bowl as if it had burned me. Mr. Greene looked away, embarrassed. His wife stared at the toilet like she'd never seen one before.

Suzanne said, "Honey, we just wanted to make sure you were here. We'll wait out front."

I nodded. As they turned away, I spoke. "I'll just wash my hands." I tried to look poised when I joined them a moment later. Suzanne was seated at my desk. The Greenes sat in the folding chairs I'd lined up in anticipation of the meeting. I slid into the chair beside Lee. Looking up, our eyes met.

He was himself again: his hair was precisely parted, and a perfectly folded pocket square peeked out of his jacket. I gave him a reassuring smile, which he did not return.

His eyes shifted to the damp spots on the sleeves of my blouse where the toilet water had splashed me.

Suzanne rummaged in her purse. "Ruby, honey, can you get me an ashtray?"

I paused, taken aback. I didn't own an ashtray, not anymore. Racing into the back room, I found a dirty coffee mug that could serve. It took a minute to wash it out. When I returned to the office, Suzanne was smoking a Marlboro. Lee had a box of cigarettes in his hand: Nat Shermans. He opened it, extending the box to me. "Want one?"

When I shook my head, he lit one for himself. I placed the mug where both Suzanne and Lee could reach it.

Suzanne adjusted her reading glasses and shuffled through pages in an open file folder on the desk. "Ruby, did you look over the results of the blood test we did on Lee?"

"I did." The printed copy of the test results was in the top drawer of my desk, but I felt awkward moving Suzanne out of the way to retrieve it. "The blood alcohol was lower than I expected."

She puffed on the cigarette, looking at Lee over her spectacles. "He was locked up for well over twenty-four hours before we were able to get a sample drawn. I'm surprised they found anything at all."

I turned to him. "Lee, did they take a blood sample while you were in custody?"

He barely gave me a glance. "I don't know."

There it was again: his lack of recall. I heard Mr. Greene speak in an undertone. "No one in our family line has ever been a drunk."

Lee turned on him. "I am not a drunk, sir."

"Well, you're saying you don't remember anything that happened that night. Clearly, you were drunk. Blind drunk. Or were you high on drugs?"

Though Lee's head was turned away from me, I saw a cord of tension rising in his neck. "I don't do drugs of any kind."

"Well, you must have been doing something of some kind. Consorting with a streetwalker at the Magnolia Inn in Vicksburg, where anyone could have seen you."

Suzanne broke in, to my relief; the father-and-son battle was not advancing our cause.

"Brother Lee, you need to focus. Our problem isn't that Lee employed a streetwalker. It's that she was found dead in bed with him. That's the problem we're dealing with here. I have a task for you. Since my nephew can't fill in the blanks and the blood test is inconclusive, I'd advise you to hire a detective."

Mrs. Greene's voice piped in, a high soprano. "The police will surely look into this and find out that Lee didn't do anything bad."

"Sugar," Mr. Greene said, "the police in Vicksburg are not on Lee's side."

"How can that be?"

Suzanne ignored her. To her brother, she said, "Lee, get the best private investigator in the South. I can give you some leads."

Mr. Greene nodded and squeezed his eyes shut.

Mrs. Greene leaned sideways in her seat and caught my eye. Making a vague gesture with her manicured hand, she said, "Ruby, do you really live here? In this old dime store?"

My spine stiffened. "Yes, ma'am, I do."

Lee interjected, "Ruby's lived in worse places." He lifted the cigarette to his lips and took a pull, then exhaled a plume of smoke.

Lee's father's complexion was turning a dangerous scarlet shade. "Good God almighty, what does it matter where the girl lives? My family is in crisis, our good reputation in tatters." He slammed his fist on the top of my desk, and I jerked in surprise. "Suzanne, what do you intend to do about this? How will you clear my boy's name?"

Suzanne slapped a file onto Mr. Greene's clenched fingers, and he hastily removed his hand from the desktop. When she spoke, her voice was stern.

"I'm going to do it one step at a time. This isn't a magic act; it's the legal profession. We'll put one foot in front of the other." She dropped her cigarette into my coffee mug. It was still burning. A white snake of smoke wafted out. "Now do I have your attention? Can we get back to a reasonable discussion?"

No one spoke. Suzanne barreled on.

"Lee, have you been in touch with your firm in Jackson? Are they standing by you?"

"The law firm has suspended me. Indefinitely." The hand holding his cigarette trembled.

"That won't do. We'll have to come up with something to occupy you. When we go to trial, we don't want the DA to paint you as idle."

I spoke up. "Maybe Lee could do pro bono work. Take cases for free."

He snorted as Suzanne shook her head. "I think Legal Aid would be hesitant to take him on, considering the charge he's facing."

Lee's mother clapped her hands like a child. "I know just the thing. Lee can spend his time at Big Brothers Big Sisters. We donate every year."

Her husband grasped her hands and gently pushed them into her lap. "Honey, they won't entrust a child to his care."

The cigarette in Lee's hand shook until he dropped it into the cup, but his expression was stony. "Daddy's right, Mama. No one is seeking out my company. The only creature who's glad to see me right now is old Georgie."

I remembered Georgie well: he was Lee's aged golden retriever, his longtime pet. During our courtship, I sometimes wondered whether Lee preferred Georgie's company to mine.

But it gave me an idea. "Lee loves animals. Maybe he can work gratis at an animal shelter."

Suzanne snapped her fingers. "Bingo! I'll call the Humane Society in Barnes County."

His father muttered, "My only son, working at the dog

pound." When Suzanne pinned him with a look, he cleared his throat and said, "Have you seen the medical reports?"

"The blood test is negative for drug use and only shows residual alcohol. But his system could have flushed the drugs out before we got him to a lab. So it doesn't explain the memory loss." She shook another cigarette out of the pack. "Lee, what was the name of the man you met with in Vicksburg that night? The one you had dinner with?"

"Cary Reynolds. An old frat brother. He wanted legal advice."

Suzanne made a note with her free hand, while the other brandished a fresh Marlboro. "We'll talk to this Reynolds fellow, see if he can fill in some of the blanks."

Mrs. Greene spoke again. "If Lee doesn't remember doing anything wrong, how can they put him in jail?"

Lee's head dropped, and he heaved a sigh. He knew the answer, even if his mother didn't.

Suzanne said, "Honey, if you think that's a defense to murder, you're wrong."

Mrs. Greene gasped and covered her mouth with a handkerchief. Mr. Greene squeezed his wife's hand and asked, "This trumped-up charge about a streetwalker overdosing on drugs—how serious can they be? What kind of penalty are we looking at, Suzanne?"

"Brother Lee, they've charged it as capital murder."

"But—a dead prostitute, for God's sake. What's the maximum penalty?"

I lowered my eyes so I wouldn't have to see the faces of Lee's parents when Suzanne answered.

"Death."

# CHAPTER 35

THE OFFICE SMELLED smoky after the Greenes departed. I opened the windows over my sofa bed, hoping the fresh air would clear the lobby.

The effect was not immediate. I popped a nugget of nicotine gum and headed back to the courthouse, thinking I'd give the office a little time to air out.

I cruised past security and was surprised to see Thomas Lafayette sitting on a wooden bench in the courthouse lobby, reading a newspaper. I walked over to say hello, since I had time to kill.

"Hey, Lafayette. Is this the new annex for the DA's office?"

He looked up from the paper and made a face. "My clerk came down with a stomach bug. Didn't make it to the bathroom. They're cleaning the carpet." He turned a page of the paper. "I wouldn't go in there for a while if I was you."

"Enough said." I sat beside him on the bench and pulled out my phone to check my email.

The DA nudged me with his elbow. "You made the paper again."

I hadn't seen it. I wanted to play it cool, but I was curious. "Which one?"

"Vicksburg. It's got a picture."

"Of me?" I leaned over to look, ignoring Lafayette's mocking snort.

"No, it's not your picture; it's your client. Lee Greene Junior, the prince of Mississippi."

He held the open page wide for me to see. "It's a before-and-after shot."

The images on the page made me wince. Next to a black-and-white professional head shot of Lee, the paper had run a color shot of him in handcuffs in his orange jail scrubs, escorted into court by two Vicksburg policemen.

"Lord help us. I hope Lee doesn't see that. It will drive him crazy."

"He's bound to see it. That picture has run in papers all over the state."

I made a face, pretending disinterest. "I wouldn't know."

He folded the paper and looked at me with a wrinkled brow. "You mean you're not following the media coverage on this?"

I shrugged. "Not really. I'm super busy."

He stood so abruptly, I looked up in surprise. Tucking the paper under his arm, he started to walk away. Then he paused, turned around, and came back to the bench where I sat.

Lafayette tossed the folded newspaper in my lap. "You should be cataloguing it."

"What?" I tried to hand the paper back to him, but he wouldn't accept it. "Why?"

With a hiss of disgust, he shook his head. "Why I have to counsel a defense attorney on strategy, I swear I do not know." He took a step closer and whispered. "Venue."

"Venue," I repeated.

"Don't be stupid," he said. "Is that where you want the case to be tried? In Vicksburg, where they've followed the case in the press every day?"

Finally, I got it. The DA was right. We needed a change of venue to get the case transferred out of Vicksburg and into another county, where we could get a jury panel that hadn't been exposed to so much pretrial publicity. I opened my briefcase and stuffed the newspaper inside.

I needed to initiate an internet search for all the news stories on Lee and the Vicksburg murder case. So that we could get the trial out of Vicksburg.

Lafayette was walking toward the staircase. I jumped off the bench and caught up with him.

"Suzanne Greene probably has already thought of that. The change of venue."

He ignored me and started to climb the stairs. I took them two at a time so that I could block his path.

Standing in front of him on the stairway, I said, "But I appreciate the advice. What I'm curious about, Lafayette, is why you'd lend me a hand. Why are you helping me out?"

I searched his face as we stood, waiting for an answer. Finally, he spoke.

"Do you know who y'all will be going up against in this case?"

I paused, confused. "At the arraignment, the DA's office sent a guy I remember from law school. So maybe he's handling it."

Lafayette snorted again at my reply, and dropped his voice. "Isaac Keet. Keet will prosecute this case for the DA's office in Vicksburg. Keet is going to eat you alive."

A chill ran through me, even though I'd never met the man. Keeping my voice nonchalant, I said, "He won't be able to intimidate Suzanne Greene. She's the toughest litigator in the state."

Speaking in a whisper, he said, "It's personal for Keet. He despises people like Lee Greene."

"What do you mean, people like Lee?" But I had a sneaking suspicion.

"You know. The old family name, old money, privileged southern white man. He'll try to cut him down to size."

He swung past me and continued up the stairs. To his back, I asked: "Yeah? How can you be so sure?"

"Because he's done it to me."

# CHAPTER 36

IN THE PAST, Thomas Lafayette hadn't always shot straight with me. But he was right about one thing.

Isaac Keet, the Vicksburg DA, was good. Terribly good.

When we appeared in the Warren County courtroom before Judge Ashley on defendant's motion for change of venue, Keet commanded the courtroom from the outset. He walked into court with erect military bearing, marched up to our counsel table, and tossed Suzanne's motion next to her coffee cup.

"Ms. Greene, you injure me. Do you really believe your client can't get a fair trial in Warren County?"

Suzanne gave him a measured glance over her glasses. "I'm dead certain he can't, Mr. Keet. And I'll prove it to the satisfaction of the court."

She placed a hand on my shoulder. "Mr. Keet, this is my co-counsel, Ruby Bozarth. I don't think y'all have met."

I stuck out my hand and he shook it briefly. Though I started to say I was pleased to meet him, he cut me off before I could finish uttering the pleasantry.

To Suzanne, he said, "Will your client be in court today?"

"He's sitting two rows back, with his mama and daddy. Mr. Greene will come to the table when the hearing begins."

Isaac Keet looked over our heads to the row occupied by the Greene family. With the ghost of a smile, he said, "Well, I'll be. Sure wouldn't have recognized him from his mug shot."

As he turned away, I heard Lee's mother speak in her warbling soprano. "Who was that black man? The one talking to Suzanne?"

A whispered hiss sounded in response, then I heard her speak again, her voice spiking in shock. "He's the district attorney?"

Mrs. Greene's voice carried like an opera singer's. I fervently wished that her family would shut her up or leave her at home.

Mrs. Greene was interrupted by the judge's appearance. Judge Ashley was a veteran of the bench. I'd done a little homework to get some background on him: he was over sixty and had served as judge for nearly twenty years. His thin hair was combed straight back over his scalp and looked as if he might have touched it up with Clairol for Men.

Suzanne took the lead in the hearing, introducing copies of articles from the *Vicksburg Post* and playing recordings of news stories regarding the murder case that had run on the local television channels. Isaac Keet tried to object, claiming she had improperly laid the foundation for one of the videos, but Suzanne won that fight. The judge admitted the evidence.

While she and Keet addressed the court, their voices projected at such a booming volume that I was tempted to cover my ears. The courtroom was large, but it didn't require this degree of amplification.

But the judge appeared not to notice that they were shouting.

Judge Ashley said, "Does the defense wish to put on further evidence in support of the motion?"

Suzanne smiled. "The defense calls Carol Sheppard to the witness stand."

An older woman dressed like a Chico's ad was sworn in. Once on the witness stand, she turned to Suzanne with a smile.

Suzanne asked whether she had heard of the case of State v. Lee Greene.

"Yes, I have."

"What have you heard?"

"There was a murder at a hotel in Vicksburg. The Magnolia Inn. It's a sordid case. Lee Greene was charged with the murder of a young woman."

"Where did you hear this information?"

"It's been all over the news. I take the *Vicksburg Post,* and I watch WBTV3 every evening. And I hear stories."

Suzanne nodded in agreement, her face grim. "Ms. Sheppard, based on the media coverage in this case, do you think that Lee Greene can get a fair trial in Warren County?"

"No. No, I don't."

Suzanne raised her chin. Though she stood just a few yards from Judge Ashley, her voice boomed.

"No further questions, Your Honor."

The judge nodded at Keet. "Your witness."

He launched out of the chair and advanced toward the witness. "Ma'am, are you acquainted with the defendant?"

"No."

"His family?"

"Yes. His aunt Suzanne. The attorney."

Keet's face broke into a grin. "Ah—Ms. Greene, counsel for the defense. How long have y'all been acquainted?"

"Oh, years and years. We met at Ole Miss."

Keet turned to pin Suzanne with an accusatory look before turning back to the witness. "Begging your pardon, ma'am—then your friendship has been of a long duration?"

"Yes. It has."

"And y'all are close friends?"

"We are." Ms. Sheppard beamed at Suzanne from her seat on the witness stand. I wanted to squirm; I knew where Keet was headed. I sneaked a glance at Suzanne, but if she was worried, it wasn't apparent. She tapped her legal pad with an ink pen, wearing a serene expression.

"As long as you've been friends—close friends, I believe you said—I bet you'd do about anything to help Ms. Greene and her family. Isn't that true?"

Though I'd never handled a change of venue hearing, I knew that Keet had found the crack in the plaster. I ducked my head, awaiting disaster.

But Mrs. Sheppard stiffened and turned a sharp eye at Keet. "I beg your pardon?"

Keet's voice was like clover honey. "I said: Isn't it true that you'd like to help Ms. Greene?"

Mrs. Sheppard's brow furrowed. "I don't know how to answer that question."

I was impressed; the woman was smart. She looked like a retired schoolteacher, the kind who could subdue a classroom full of unruly adolescents.

Keet doubled down. "Ms. Sheppard, let me remind you that you are under oath."

Her face flushed, and she drew herself up with dignity. "Sir, are you questioning my integrity?"

Keet stepped closer to the witness. "I'm asking you to answer the question."

"All right, I will. Despite my fondness for Suzanne Greene, no sir, I would not commit perjury on her behalf."

Suzanne smiled like the Cheshire cat. And I relaxed. Yes, Keet was good at his job, but he wouldn't outfox Suzanne Greene.

Keet persisted. "Then you've concluded that Lee Greene is guilty of murder."

Beside me, I heard Lee's quick intake of breath. I placed a hand on his arm in a show of solidarity.

"I did not say that."

Keet stepped away, scratching the back of his head, playing the confused interrogator. "But you said that you'd watched a lot of news coverage, and then opined that the media made it impossible for him to get a fair trial. So you must be convinced that Lee's guilty."

"I am convinced that he can't get a fair trial in Vicksburg because there has been so much information disseminated in the press."

"Well, where do you think he can get a fair trial? Seattle, Washington? Bangor, Maine? You do understand the case must be tried in Mississippi."

The witness paused to shoot a schoolteacher frown at the DA. There was a moment of pregnant silence, which was broken when I spoke.

"Rosedale," I said.

At first, I wasn't aware that I'd uttered it loudly enough to be overheard. But when Keet turned a frowning face toward me, it was clear that my voice had carried.

The judge cupped a hand around his ear. "What's that?"

I shot a glance at Suzanne, afraid that she'd give me the evil eye for speaking out of turn. But she shot me a wink and scrawled on the page in front of her:

*Speak up. Deaf as a post.*

I rose, warming to the task.

"Your Honor, the defense has provided abundant evidence that the media attention has tainted the venue of Warren County. My client is entitled to a jury panel that hasn't heard so much detail about the case. I recommend that it be tried in Rosedale."

Suzanne was writing again: *LOUDER*.

I raised my voice, projecting from my diaphragm. "We agree with Mr. Keet on one point: the case must be tried by a Mississippi jury. And we've established that Vicksburg is untenable. We should change the venue to a small town in Mississippi, in a rural county. My practice is in Rosedale, in Williams County. It will accommodate the convenience of defense, and Mr. Keet will have his Mississippi jury panel."

"Objection," Keet said, but the judge held up a restraining hand.

"Isaac, the defense has made their case for the motion, and I'm going to grant it. Mrs. Sheppard," and he gave the witness a courtly nod, "you may step down."

As Mrs. Sheppard made her way past the counsel table, Judge Ashley proclaimed from the bench: "Defendant's motion for change of venue is granted. The case will be transferred from Warren County to Williams County. Ms. Greene, I will travel to Rosedale to preside over the trial, and Mr. Keet will represent the state."

Suzanne stood to reply, and Lee turned on me, his face twisted in apoplexy. With burning eyes, he said: "Rosedale?"

# CHAPTER 37

"SO, YOUR OLD beau doesn't like the idea of trying his case in Rosedale?"

Shorty was stirring an industrial-size pot of grits with a long-handled spoon. I watched him from my seat at the counter, where I mopped up egg yolk with a slice of buttered toast. I'd come to the diner early, while the SORRY! WE'RE CLOSED! sign still hung on the front door.

"Oh, Shorty. Lee was fit to be tied. He said—and this is a quote—'Why don't you keep your goddamned mouth shut?'"

Shorty's eyes narrowed, and he gave the grits such a vicious stir that the white cereal jumped out of the pot and sizzled on the hot burner.

"How did you respond to that?"

"I didn't have to respond. Suzanne jumped in, said the Rosedale idea was a stroke of genius. That it was a better setting than Barnes County, where her office sits, because she's so well-known there. We'd have lost the whole jury panel. She's gotten everyone in Barnes County a divorce or a will, or handled their personal injury car crash. But with Rosedale as our home base, we can operate out of my office on the square and still have the hometown advantage."

Shortly scooped a ladle of grits into a bowl and added a pat of butter. "These are done."

I picked up the salt and pepper shakers. As I seasoned the grits, I said, "And then Suzanne and I had a private chat. That's the big news I came over to tell you."

Shorty put a lid on the pot and then joined me, leaning against the opposite side of the counter. "I'm all ears."

"She wants to go into partnership with me."

His face broke into a smile. "That's huge."

"Oh, Lord, Shorty—you can't imagine how tickled I am. We'll keep both offices: Suzanne's in Barnes County, mine at the Ben Franklin. Greene and Bozarth, Attorneys at Law."

"She's lucky to have you."

"I'm the lucky one. She's putting me on salary, plus I'll keep a percentage of my fees. Suzanne says she's getting too old for solo practice. She can cut down her hours now, because I can make appearances on her behalf."

"What's she paying you?"

I paused, reluctant to answer. My mama was always skittish talking about money. She was strict in her code of conduct, even if she was a cleaning lady.

I dipped a spoon into the buttery grits and popped it into my mouth. I regretted the move immediately.

"Too hot," I groaned with my mouth full.

"Girl, you know better than to eat grits before they've had a chance to cool down. I'd call you Goldilocks, except your hair is such a pretty chestnut brown."

I pushed the bowl away and took a long swig of ice water.

Shorty reached for my hand and gave it a squeeze. "I didn't mean to be nosy."

I waved off the statement. "I'm too closemouthed; can't help it. But this much I'll say: it's enough for me to move out of the back of the Ben Franklin. I'm going apartment hunting today. Ain't that cool? Suzanne has already cut me a check. I feel rich as a Lannister." We'd been watching *Game of Thrones*.

Leaning across the counter, he kissed me and said, "You're a Stark."

I laughed. "Pretty sure I'd be a peasant, pushing a plow in the fields." Another happy thought struck me. "Shorty—I can get cable TV. Finally."

I tried to pull my hand back, but he held on. "Ruby, I've got an idea. Let's go to Little Rock. When you have a day or two free?"

That was a quick change of topic. "What's in Little Rock? Other than the big city lights?"

"My mama. She moved there when I took over the diner, to be near her sister. And I want you to meet her."

The suggestion caused my heart rate to accelerate. The last time I'd been presented to a boyfriend's mother, it had been a disaster. Mrs. Greene had taken one look at me and decided I didn't come up to snuff. Not much had changed.

I didn't have to reply, because someone was pounding on the glass door. Shorty looked past me, squinting at the entrance. "It's Jeb. Right on time for breakfast."

Picking up my briefcase, I said, "I'll check my calendar. But Shorty, Suzanne is going to be keeping me real busy." And I planned on remaining far too busy to meet anybody's mama.

He turned away, pulling a set of keys from his pocket. As he unlocked the front door, he said, "You let me know."

"I'll do that," I said.

Then I fled.

# PART TWO

# SIX MONTHS LATER

# CHAPTER 38

AS THE MONTHS rolled by, I was busy. My own clientele had picked up; not only was I getting walk-ins at the Ben Franklin, but Judge Baylor had actually begun sending guardianships and juvenile appointments my way. And, true to her word, Suzanne kept me on the run. Our partnership, proudly announced in black paint on the storefront glass of the old Ben Franklin, was so successful that some days passed without my finding time to spare a thought about State v. Lee Greene Jr.

This was not one of those days.

We sat around the conference table at Suzanne's office in Barnes County, thirty minutes up the highway from Rosedale. No one spoke. I stared at the landline phone sitting on the conference table, waiting for it to ring.

Mr. Greene shifted in his seat. "Suzanne," he said, but she waved a hand to silence him.

"Hush. We'll talk afterwards."

On cue, the phone rang, and Suzanne pushed a button to answer. "This is Suzanne Greene. We're on speaker."

"Miss Greene, this is Judge Ashley's clerk in Vicksburg. I'm going to go ahead and connect y'all."

We waited. After a tense moment, we heard a man's voice. "Hello? Hello?"

I pressed my lips together; it wasn't a fitting moment for laughter. But the judge acted like he'd been born before Alexander Graham Bell invented the telephone.

"Judge, Suzanne Greene here."

A third voice chimed in. "Isaac Keet, Judge Ashley. I'm on the road. Tell your clerk thanks for patching me in."

Keet's voice was totally chill; I envied him. But then, he wasn't confronting the possibility of a family member or an ex-lover going to prison for life. Or worse.

The judge spoke again. "Glad to get y'all on the phone. I have a new development, something I want to throw out there."

I met Suzanne's eyes across the conference table. She looked wary.

"What's up, Judge Ashley?" Her casual tone contrasted with her guarded expression.

"I have a personal injury jury trial set on my calendar, a month away. It was a big old pileup on Interstate 20. I gave it a whole week of my docket."

There was a pause, then Isaac Keet's voice broke in. "Didn't I hear they settled that up?"

"Yes, sir. All the parties have come to terms. Didn't even have to do it on the courthouse steps." The judge cleared his throat. "I bet you can guess what I'm about to propose."

Suzanne leaned across the table, focusing on Lee and his parents. Silently, she shook her head.

The DA's voice came through the speaker, smooth as silk. "The state can be ready for trial, Your Honor. I give you my word on that."

Judge Ashley said, "I appreciate that, Isaac. But it will be the defendant's call. This is a faster track than we'd generally see in a murder case in Vicksburg. If Miss Greene opposes it, I'll find another case to fill that space."

When no one spoke, he added, "Or I guess I could go fishing. Take some time off."

Suzanne took a deep breath and said, "Judge, while we appreciate the opportunity, I'm afraid the defense will have to decline."

In the conference room, Lee stood up. "I want it."

Suzanne gaped at him. Before she could open her mouth, Lee spoke again. "Next month. Let's do it."

The speaker crackled with Judge Ashley's voice. "What's that? Who's talking? Isaac, was that you?"

"Not me," the DA said.

Suzanne pointed a threatening finger at Lee, and he dropped back into his chair. "Your Honor, sorry for the confusion. I'll need to communicate your proposition to my client. May I get back with y'all on this?"

"Yes, ma'am, Miss Greene. You let me know."

"I will. And I'll be quick about it."

As soon as the judge said good-bye, Suzanne cut off the call with a vicious thrust of her forefinger. Then she turned on Lee.

"Are you crazy?"

Lee didn't respond. He just set his jaw and met her glare.

She said, "I know you haven't dirtied your hands with criminal defense, so you may not know a basic fact. In criminal cases, delay is good for the defense. Bad for the prosecution."

She was right. But I kept my mouth shut. Suzanne didn't need me to make her case.

"As time goes by, witnesses' memories fade. They leave town. Evidence can be lost. The community forgets. Our potential jurors' feelings of outrage will dissipate. This is what we want."

"I don't care," Lee said, his voice sulky as a child's.

"You better care. And another thing, young man: we don't have a defense. Have you thought about that? Do you care?"

Mr. Greene spoke up. "I've paid a fortune to that private detective out of New Orleans. What happened to my money?"

They turned to my end of the table. Four sets of blue eyes focused on me. I had been the contact with the PI.

I spoke, trying to sound assured, as if the eyes of the Greene family didn't rattle me. "I'm meeting with him this week. He says he's uncovered something about the victim. He has a lead."

"Is that all?" Mr. Greene shook his head in disgust.

Lee looked away from me and focused on the tabletop. "I want this behind me. Do you know what I'm going through? I can't show my face in Jackson. My only distraction is the dog pound in Barnes County. The rest of the time, I'm back in my old bedroom at Daddy and Mama's, staring at the fucking wall."

Mr. Greene slapped his hand on the conference table. "You mind your language. Your mama is present."

Suzanne stood and walked out of the conference room. I sat in silence, staring at the law books lining the shelves on the wall, until Lee spoke.

"Ruby, what do you think?"

The question surprised me so much, I did a double take. Lee was looking right at me, his eyes imploring. I chose my words with care.

"Lee, you know Suzanne is right about the benefit of letting time pass. But I'm also sympathetic to your situation. You're going through hell."

Mr. Greene coughed and I realized my gaffe: more bad language assaulting Mrs. Greene's ears. I soldiered on.

"Until we get the report from the private investigator, we're in no position to decide. Let's hold off."

Suzanne barreled through the door with an appointment calendar in hand. "The week the judge has offered—I have multiple conflicts."

Her brother looked at her in indignation. "You'll have to cancel them."

She dropped the book on the table with a bang. "Your son is not my only client. I have a law practice. I have people counting on me."

Mr. Greene roared, "Your family is counting on you."

I rose. It was time. "Whoa," I shouted.

They swiveled in their seats, astonishment on all faces. The family resemblance was remarkable.

In a softer tone, I said, "Let me hear out the investigator, what he's learned. Whether he's found us a witness. Then we'll see where we are."

Everyone sat down. Suzanne lit a Marlboro. Lee pulled out his blue box of Nat Shermans. He opened the box and offered me one.

My hand reached for it. But I thought better of it. I shook out a Nicorette instead and thought: *Darrien and Oscar Summers were a walk in the park. The Greenes will be the death of me.*

# CHAPTER 39

SITTING IN THE parking lot outside a bar in a sketchy Vicksburg neighborhood, I was nervous. I was about to meet the man who could be the basis of our defense in the murder case.

Not the private investigator—I'd talked with him earlier in the week. He had set up this meeting.

He'd told me to wait for my witness outside a dive called the Twilight Inn. I was looking for a black man in his thirties, with a goatee, driving a late-model Volvo. He was a detective named Guion who worked vice in Vicksburg.

If ever I'd longed for a nicotine buzz, this was the night. But I'd sworn off Nicorette, decided to kick it altogether when I nearly accepted that cigarette from Lee Greene. I unwrapped a stick of Juicy Fruit gum and chewed on it. It made a poor substitute.

A Volvo pulled into the lot. The driver met the description the PI had provided. I tossed the gum wrapper onto the floorboard of the passenger side and grabbed my briefcase.

The bar was dimly lit, but even so, it was clear that I was the only customer wearing a business suit. I drew a couple of curious stares, which I ignored. My target sat in a booth at the rear. I joined him.

A waitress walked up. "What can I get y'all?"

The man said, "Bud. Draft."

I smiled, trying to act natural. "Same."

When she walked away, I said, "I really appreciate you coming out here to meet me, Detective Guion."

He shook his head with a humorless laugh. "I gotta be crazy. This is the kind of exposure I absolutely do not need."

The waitress walked up with two mugs of beer, and we fell silent. I reached into my purse for money, but Guion said, "We'll run a tab."

Once she walked away, I said, "I'm sorry for your loss. Monae, I mean. Miss Prince."

He gave me an incredulous look. "Monae was my snitch."

"Yes. So sorry."

"My snitch. Not my little sister."

I shifted in my seat. This was new territory for me. I didn't know the dynamics of undercover police relationships. "I'm sorry. I mean, sorry that I misunderstood."

I needed to get a grip, quit making so many apologies. Reaching into my briefcase, I said, "So how long have you been working undercover for the Vicksburg police department?"

He reached across the table and seized my arm. "Don't."

"What?"

"Don't pull anything out of that bag. Not a phone, not a file, not a pencil. If you do, I'm walking out of here."

He released my arm, and I sat back against the booth. "I can't record this?"

"Nope."

"Then I'll need to take notes. For my recollection."

He looked me up and down. "You're pretty young. I bet you have a good memory. You're gonna have to rely on that."

I leaned in toward him. In a harsh whisper, I said, "You know I can depose you. Then we'll have an excellent record."

"That's not the deal. I've been working my tail off to nail a crime ring in Vicksburg, and I'm not going to let you blow it wide open. Not yet."

He took a swallow of beer and studied the mug, wiping the condensation on the glass with his finger.

Still whispering, I said, "You're a detective. You have an obligation to respect court proceedings."

Before he spoke, he looked away, as if he were scoping out the room. "I'll talk to you tonight. I'll testify at the dude's trial. I know you can make me appear by subpoena. But I don't want to publicly reveal any details of the investigation before I have to. Not ready to do that."

I zipped my briefcase shut. He had the whip hand. I needed his information. And I needed to keep him cooperative.

"Okay. Deal. So Monae died of a drug overdose when she was in bed with my client. And my client has been accused of causing Monae's death. We need to know—did she have a drug history, to your knowledge?"

"Hell, yeah. That's why she was in prostitution. Got the drug habit, turned to the sex trade to support it."

My knee started jiggling under the table. This was what we needed. "So she was a drug addict and a prostitute?"

"Yeah."

"But the police report says she was seventeen. How did she get so deeply involved in the lifestyle at seventeen?"

When the detective laughed, I was taken aback. I hadn't intended to amuse him. He said, "Right, the investigative team at the hotel, they found an ID on her, said she was seventeen. Shit. That girl hadn't been seventeen for a long time."

I cocked my head. "Huh?"

He reached into his jacket and pulled out a folded sheet of paper, then pushed it across the table. I picked it up before it could get wet from the rings of moisture left by the beer mugs.

Studying the sheet, I said, "I don't get it. She was twenty-three?"

"Yeah."

I looked up. "But you didn't share this with the murder investigation?"

"I ain't sharing shit. From what Monae told me, someone I know could be on the payroll. Fuck them. I don't know who to trust."

I gave him a sunny smile. "I guess you have confidence in me. You're giving me valuable information."

He spoke in a voice that was deadly serious. "I'm keeping a lid on you, baby."

This cop was as prickly as a porcupine. I tried a sarcastic tone. "You don't trust anyone you work with in Vicksburg?"

"I didn't say that." He looked up, as if he were thinking. "I trust some of the undercover cops. Beau George—I trust him."

"Didn't you trust Monae?"

Again, the look—like he was talking to a kindergartner who wasn't particularly bright.

"Monae was a snitch," he said, as if that explained everything.

"How did you meet her?"

"I busted her. For drug possession. Opioids. Then I turned her. Offered immunity if she'd give me information. Tell me about the other players."

"What other players?"

He didn't answer. Just stared at me over the mug while he took another swallow. He wiped beer from his mustache and said, "You'll find out when I make the bust. Might be someone you know."

I tried another tactic. "So Monae was twenty-three, a prostitute by profession, and a known drug abuser. How long had she been engaged in a criminal lifestyle?"

"For a while. She fell into it not long after she left Ole Miss."

Now it was my turn to stare. "Ole Miss?"

"Yeah, she had a scholarship, freshman year. I never said she was stupid." He paused, thinking. "Actually, I guess she was. Pretty stupid to get involved with drugs and the sex trade."

"So who was her pimp?"

He reached across the table and pushed my untouched mug closer to me. "Drink your beer. We're done."

I clutched the beer mug. "But I want more information."

"We're done talking for tonight." He began to slide out of the booth.

"No, please. Don't run off yet."

Pausing, he gave me a hooded look. In a cynical voice, he said, "If you want, I'll let you pick up the tab. You can put it on your client's bill. Pretty sure he can afford it."

"When can I see you again?"

"I'll let you know."

Frustrated, I jerked some cash out of my bag and let him depart. When he was out the door, I slipped out to the safety of my car.

Ten minutes later, I sat in my car a block from the bar, parked under a streetlight. By the light overhead, I wrote on my legal pad like a madwoman, recording every detail of the conversation that I could remember. My confidence in my young brain's recall didn't match the faith of my new witness.

My new star witness. That vice detective was going to save the day.

Scanning the notes, I saw the words I'd recorded to describe Monae: snitch, criminal, prostitute, opioids, liar. A chill ran down my spine.

In less than a year, I'd defended two cases in which a woman had been murdered in connection with a sex act. Both times, I had to go on the attack against a dead victim.

I never intended to devote my legal career to this brand of representation. Sitting in the car, I promised myself: when I wrapped up this murder trial, I'd seek out some happy cases. It took me a minute to conjure up an example of a happy case, but I thought of one. Adoptions. I'd do an adoption for free, just for the pleasure of it.

My cell phone hummed; I'd had it on mute in the bar. I glanced at it, irritated by the interruption. But when I saw Suzanne Greene's name, I picked up.

"Hey, Suzanne."

"Well? Did he show?"

Her voice crackled through the phone. I was tempted to hold it away from my ear.

"He sure did. Just left him a while ago."

"And?"

"It's good. Really good. I don't know how your New Orleans private eye uncovered him, but it's worth whatever the Greenes paid. This Vicksburg cop is a gold mine."

"Well, New Orleans. They know how to find the seamy side." She paused, then asked, "Did he tell you everything? Everything we were led to expect from the PI's report?"

"Pretty much. He was holding back, I'm certain. But he spilled the beans on Monae. We can counter the prosecution's case."

I thought she'd be happy, but Suzanne said nothing at all. Finally, I said, "Suzanne? Did you hear me? The vice cop will make a great witness for Lee. I guarantee it. I've got a nickname for him: we can call him Detective 'Reasonable Doubt' Guion."

She sighed. "Well, hell."

Surprised, I sat, waiting for her to elaborate.

"There'll be no holding them back now. Lee wants that early trial setting, and my brother is backing him up. Looks like we're going to trial."

Before she rang off, I heard her mutter: "Son of a bitch."

# CHAPTER 40

I CUSSED OUT loud as I steered my car to the Barnes County Humane Society. It was the Saturday before trial, and I'd been phoning Lee all afternoon, but he hadn't seen fit to answer my calls.

Pulling into the gravel drive, I recognized the shiny black BMW parked beside the tumbledown shelter and breathed out in relief. Clutching a sheaf of printed notes, I slammed my car door behind me and hurried down an uneven path to the facility. When I saw a man emerge from a rough shed adjoining the main building, I paused.

He was dressed in jeans and a T-shirt, and carried a large bag.

"I'll be damned," I whispered. It was my client.

"Lee," I called, waving my papers. I doubled my pace and met him by the shed.

Lee let the bag slip to the ground and stood up. His hair was tousled. He shook it back and swiped at grime clinging to his shoulder.

"Hey," I said. When he didn't respond, I pointed at the bag resting at his feet. "Looks heavy. What are you toting?"

"It's dog food," he said stiffly.

"That makes sense. It's a big old bag." I bent my head and shuffled through the papers in my hand. "You wanted to look through the jury selection questions in advance of voir dire. I emailed them to you. When you didn't get back to me, I got nervous. I called you a million times, but couldn't reach you. Your mom said you were out here."

He squinted in disbelief. "You called my mother? Really?"

"Is that a problem? I was anxious to reach you." I twisted around, looking for a place to sit, but there were no chairs or benches. "Do you have a minute to run over these with me? See if they look okay?"

He extended his hand. "Just give it to me. I'll look over the questions tonight and get back with you."

"Okay." I placed the pages in his outstretched hand, alarmed to note a mark on his arm—of a recent bite. I almost reached out to touch the spot on his forearm, but dropped my hand. "Lord, Lee. Is your arm okay? It looks like a dog attacked you."

He stuffed the pages into his pocket. "It's nothing serious. My sleeve will cover it at trial."

"What kind of beasts are you handling in there? Is it safe?"

He rubbed the partially healed wound with his hand. "It wasn't her fault. She was in bad shape when they brought her in, and she got spooked. Someone had been cruel to her." He shook his head.

"You take care of yourself. Jury selection is Monday, first day of evidence is Tuesday. We need you in one piece. And Lee: don't be late. We'll meet at my office before court begins, eight o'clock sharp."

He bent down and picked up the bag of dog food, settling it

on his shoulder with a grunt. "You want to come inside? Meet the dogs?"

I took a step back. "Not today, thanks. Gotta go."

He turned and walked to the side door of the shelter. To his back, I called, "Call me if you want to talk about the voir dire questions. Or if you have any last-minute thoughts."

He didn't reply. When he reached for the screen door, it burst open. A huge beast of indiscriminate breed bounded out, barking, and lunged toward Lee. I gasped and stumbled away, poised to run.

The big dog jumped up on Lee, its massive paws on my client's chest. But I heard Lee laugh. He dropped the bag of dog food to the ground and rubbed the dog's head with both hands, speaking to it in a voice I couldn't hear.

I recalled, for the first time in many months, some of the traits I used to admire in Lee Greene Jr.

# CHAPTER 41

I'D TOLD HIM he couldn't be late.

And I'd told him emphatically, right after we finished picking the jury on Monday. "My office, eight a.m. Lee: Do. Not. Be. Late."

On Tuesday, the first day of evidence in the State v. Greene jury trial, Lee needed to appear right on time. Preferably in a dark navy suit and blue power tie.

My watch was moving closer to 8:15 when his car pulled up in front of my office.

The door opened, and Lee walked in. I checked out his attire: gray suit, blue shirt, pink silk bow tie wrapped up in a jaunty pink knot. My frazzled nerves got a shock at the sight of his neckwear.

"Dammit, Lee, you're late. And what are you doing in that tie?"

He looked affronted. His hand flew to his neck in a protective gesture.

"It's a tie. What's your problem, Ruby?"

He'd picked the wrong day to play a power game.

"That tie makes you look like a spoiled frat boy. That is not the impression you want to make in front of this jury, believe me."

I could have elaborated, but we had an audience. Lee's mother and father seemed to use up all of the oxygen in the room. Someone was wearing a musky perfume that made my eyes water.

Mr. and Mrs. Greene were giving me flinty stares. Even while I held their son's fate in my hands, I was still getting the cold shoulder from the Greenes.

But beneath Lee Sr.'s frown, I spied a beautiful necktie: red and blue striped, and bandbox fresh. I groaned with relief. Pointing at the tie on the elder Greene, I said: "The tie. Mr. Greene, that's what Lee needs to wear in court today. I want y'all to swap."

As Lee jerked out the knot of the pink silk bow tie, he said, "So it's come to this. Taking fashion dictates from Ruby."

That stung. I was wearing a brand-new suit I'd bought for trial.

Since joining forces with Suzanne, I didn't have to wear exclusively thrift store clothes, and I no longer camped out in the back room of the Ben Franklin. I'd moved into a cozy one-bedroom apartment, not far from the town square in Rosedale. But Lee always knew how to make me feel small.

Lee stood in front of my framed diploma from Ole Miss law school. In the reflection from the glass, he expertly tied a double Windsor knot and tightened it at the neck.

Lee's father said, "Where's my sister? Why isn't Suzanne here yet?"

I had been wondering the same thing. Though Suzanne had initially taken the lead as counsel for the defendant, that role was now mine by default. In the past four weeks, every time we'd met with the Greenes, our legal discussions had ended in a bloodbath, with Suzanne and her brother nearly coming to blows.

As a result, Suzanne had stepped back from the case, leaving me as first chair. She'd concluded that it wasn't wise for a near relation to head up the defense. Also, she didn't cotton to anyone questioning her legal advice. And, as she had warned them, she had scheduling conflicts this week.

Mr. Greene spoke in a demanding tone. "I thought she was supposed to provide oversight at the trial."

"She is."

"The only reason I agreed to pay the bill for your representation was because I was assured Suzanne would be at your elbow, watching out for Lee. How the dickens will she run this trial if she won't take the trouble to show? This is my son, for God's sake—her own nephew."

I tried to keep my voice pleasant. "We've been through this, Mr. Greene. Suzanne says that representing a family member in a criminal trial is like a doctor performing surgery on kinfolks. It's a bad practice. But she'll be here, to help out. Suzanne's probably run into some traffic on the highway. She would never fail to show." *Oh, my God, Suzanne, please, please show,* I thought.

In a tight voice, Mr. Greene addressed Lee. "I warned you about this from the outset. I knew we should hire a firm in Jackson, but you insisted that this girl was up to the task."

"Daddy, I know Ruby. She'll be fine. She's a junkyard dog."

I found the description oddly appealing.

Lee asked: "Ruby, have you met with Cary Reynolds? About what his testimony is going to be?"

Lee's mother turned away from the elder Greene; she had been fumbling to tie the pink silk with shaking hands. In a high-pitched voice, she said, "The Reynolds boy? Was he the one you had dinner with that night?"

"Yes, Mama."

"Was he your fraternity brother? I don't know him." Her eyes were glassy, slightly unfocused.

"Of course you do, Mama. You've just forgotten. I was his pledge father in Sigma Nu."

To Lee, I said, "We've talked on the phone, more than once. But I'm running him down tonight, in Vicksburg, if I have to. I won't let Cary Reynolds get on the witness stand until we've met and talked in person. I'll nail down everything, every detail he remembers about the night. He's the last person who saw her alive, other than you."

Lee nodded, silent. His shoulders slumped.

It was true; it was imperative that we nail down the facts about the night of the murder through Cary Reynolds. We had to be entirely clear about what Reynolds, Lee's old frat brother, recalled.

Because Lee Greene Jr.—the former pride of Jackson, Mississippi's social elite, the crown prince of southern gentility—still couldn't remember a thing about the incident.

Not a damn thing.

# CHAPTER 42

I KEPT A close eye on the clock.

Lee and his parents were walking across the street to the county courthouse, but I needed a quiet moment before I joined them in court.

I punched in Cary Reynolds's number on my cell phone and waited. It went to voice mail after four rings. I dropped the phone into my bag, ignoring the invitation to leave a message. I'd try again later, when the court took a recess.

I locked up the office and pocketed the key. I knew I should head straight to court, but the blinking neon bulbs of Shorty's diner, just around the corner on the town square, beckoned to me. Shorty could provide me with a powerful boost, and I needed one this morning.

I made my way to the diner at a trot. The brass bell hanging over the door jingled at my entry. I felt my tight shoulders relax at the powerful smell of coffee brewing and bacon grease.

And the sight of the proprietor.

Shorty looked up from the grill and beamed at me. "Ruby, darlin'! You got time for a bite of breakfast?"

Making my way to the counter, I shook my head. "I just have time for a sip of coffee."

Shorty turned around and grasped the coffeepot by the handle. "Do you want me to pour a cup to go?"

"No—thanks, hon. Just give me a cup and I'll chug it down right here."

After he poured it, he leaned across the counter and gave me a quick kiss. "Don't burn your mouth," he said with a wink.

I took a swallow of the brew. It was just right: hot but not scalding.

He squeezed my hand and rested his elbows on the counter. "Will you come by the house tonight? I can have a plate of fried chicken waiting for you."

Shorty's fried chicken was a temptation. But I had another date.

"I have to drive to Vicksburg tonight. I'm determined to run down a witness."

"Shoot. I'm hungry for a little piece of your valuable time." He flashed a quick smile. "I've got something important to tell you. Well, to ask you, I guess."

"Is it about your research? Did you get a nibble on your article?"

"It's not that. It's better."

The clock was ticking. I took a final sip of coffee and grabbed my briefcase. "Later. Wish me luck."

As I left the diner and strode to the courthouse, a thought hit me. What important matter did he want to ask me about? Was it the apartment? My apartment had a six-month lease, which Shorty knew was coming up for renewal. Did he want me to move in? I wasn't ready. Didn't want to go there.

The last time I'd rushed into a serious relationship, it had been a disaster. And now that I was representing Lee Greene, I was confronted with the reminder of my folly on a daily basis.

# CHAPTER 43

AT THE COURTHOUSE entrance, there was a line to get through security, but I bypassed it. The courthouse buzzed with activity; murder trials were an uncommon occurrence in our little town. Once inside, I dodged through the crowded hallway to reach the courtroom.

I'd just turned the doorknob when my phone started to buzz. It took a protracted moment to unearth it, but when I looked at the screen I was glad I'd taken the trouble.

"Cary? Mr. Reynolds?"

"Who's this?"

"Mr. Reynolds, it's Ruby Bozarth—Lee Greene's lawyer. We've talked before, about the murder trial. How you doing?"

He cleared his throat. "Fine, good. But I'm worried about my brother. How's my boy Lee getting along?"

It was reassuring to hear him refer to Lee as "his brother." "Lee's pretty tense right now, I'd say. The evidence starts this morning. I'll have to be in court in a minute."

"That right? Damn."

A moment's silence hung on the line; I broke it.

"Mr. Reynolds—can I call you Cary? I need to see you, to talk again before you take the stand. How about tonight? Court will adjourn at five o'clock. I could be in Vicksburg at six, six thirty at the latest."

"Yeah, sure. My business stays open till eight o'clock most nights. You want to meet me here? At my lot? Cary's Used Cars and Trux in Vicksburg."

"Perfect."

"Good, then. Look forward to meeting you in person. Sure want to do anything I can to help my old frat brother."

I peeked into the courtroom to check the time. The clock on the far wall said I had a few minutes to spare. "I'll be asking you to tell me everything you remember about that night, when Lee was in Vicksburg for depositions and y'all got together for drinks and dinner."

"Yes, ma'am. Two old buddies, just like old times."

I stuck my head into the courtroom again. Lee shot me an impatient glare, but the DA's counsel table was empty. I ducked back into the hallway.

"So Cary, do I have this right: after dinner, you joined Lee in his hotel room?"

The voice on the other end of the line was urgent, plaintive. "Just popped in to give him a present. Something special for Lee. The Scotch."

I chose my next words with care. "And a woman joined y'all."

He groaned into the phone. "Just another little surprise. I don't mean no disrespect, but she walked in looking good enough to eat. Lacy shorts, fishnet hose, skin like brown sugar."

In the glass panel of the courtroom door, I saw my face twist into a grimace. He was talking about a dead woman. I forced myself to relax my features. "And then the three of you drank the Scotch in the hotel room."

His voice was hesitant. "Well, I poured a round. But when that little girl sat on Lee's lap, I made myself scarce."

"Okay."

"I said—Lee, buddy, I'm gonna scoot on out of here and give y'all some privacy."

I needed more detail. Cary Reynolds's testimony was my only light into the events of that night. The next morning, Lee and the hooker were found in the room, and the girl was dead.

# CHAPTER 44

STILL HOLDING THE phone to my ear, I glanced to my right. Two uniformed deputies lingered nearby. I knew one of them: a young guy, Deputy Brockes. I ran into him at the courthouse on a regular basis. Brockes was a sweet kid.

He stood beside a gray-haired deputy I didn't know too well. Though I encountered most of the sheriff's department personnel in my line of work, the older guy—Potts was his name— was a newcomer to Rosedale, and we had yet to come face-to-face in court. But as I stood in the courthouse hallway, it seemed that Potts was staring me down, right at that moment.

It made me uncomfortable. Was he listening in to my side of the phone conversation? I turned my back to the deputy and lowered my voice.

"Cary, when I come up to see you tonight, we'll need to nail down specifics."

He paused. "Specifics?"

"Yeah. Like, about how much Lee had to drink that night.

How much did he imbibe at dinner? And the bottle of Scotch was empty when the police searched the room—was it full when you brought it in? The hooker—when she arrived, did she appear to be under the influence of drugs or alcohol?"

Cary sighed into the phone. He didn't answer right away. The uniformed deputies, Brockes and Potts, had edged closer. They were seriously intruding on my circle of private space.

Brockes said, "Hey, Miss Bozarth."

I pointed at the phone in my hand. "On a call," I said.

He went on as if I hadn't spoken. "I'll be in the courtroom with you this week. The Vicksburg judge asked for extra security, since it's a murder trial. Old Potts here is going to have to ride patrol without me." Brockes was puffed up with importance, and his face shone with pride.

On the phone, Cary Reynolds said, "Are you talking to somebody?"

"Sorry." I turned my back to the deputies. "What were we talking about? The hooker. Tell me more specifics."

In a voice of concern, he said, "I want my testimony to be helpful, I surely do. But I don't know if I can recall every minute of that night. It was a while back, you know? I do know about the Scotch. It was a new bottle. Is it okay if I testify to that?"

My reflection revealed that I was frowning again. If I didn't stop it, I'd be a wrinkled-up crone at the age of twenty-seven. Cary needed to help me establish the plausibility of the defense. The hooker who came into Lee's room that night died of an overdose of drugs and alcohol while she and Lee were in bed, and the DA intended to pin that death on Lee Greene. I needed to plant a reasonable doubt and convince the jury that the OD could have been a result of the woman's own actions.

But I also played by the rules. "Cary, you have to tell the

truth. You'll be under oath." The court reporter walked up to her seat near the witness stand, signaling that court would convene soon. I said again: "So we'll meet tonight at your lot, and you'll come to Rosedale to testify in the case—right?"

"Sure, I'll be there. I owe him."

# CHAPTER 45

AS I SAT beside my client at the counsel table, I checked the time over my shoulder. The big courtroom wall clock read 9:08.

But the prosecution table was empty, the bailiff's desk was unoccupied, and the judge's seat at the bench was vacant. I pulled out my phone to ascertain whether the courthouse clock was running fast, but no. Nine past nine in the morning.

Lee Greene jabbed me with his elbow. "Where is everybody?"

"Dunno."

I smelled it again: the cologne. It was my client. Seemed like the scent hovered around him in a cloud.

Lee's parents were seated behind us, in the front row of the gallery. His father leaned over the railing that separated the spectators from the court. In a whisper, he said, "Doesn't court start on time in your county?"

I peered into the hallway, where no court personnel could be seen. "Well, it usually does."

Mr. Greene leaned in closer; I could feel his breath in my ear. "And where is my sister? Why isn't Suzanne here?"

I'd been wondering the same thing. I sent up a silent entreaty: *Suzanne, come and rescue me.*

In the meantime, it fell to me to solve the mystery of the missing courtroom personnel. I left the counsel table and approached the court reporter, a gaunt woman with a helmet of hair dyed midnight black.

"Roseanne, have you seen the DA this morning? Isaac Keet— the guy from Vicksburg?"

She nodded as she inserted a roll of paper into her reporting device. "He's been hanging around since eight o'clock. I saw him talking to the judge."

I didn't like the sound of that. The DA had no business conferring with Judge Ashley outside my presence. It was called ex parte communication, otherwise known as "woodshedding" the judge. It was not an ethical practice.

I felt like odd man out with Judge Ashley, anyway, since both he and Keet were from Vicksburg; they clearly enjoyed a private camaraderie. Thank goodness Ashley had agreed to let me try the case in my own backyard, in the Rosedale courthouse. It was a lucky break. I needed the hometown advantage.

The court reporter was staring at me over the top of her eyeglasses. I hoped it wasn't because I was wearing yet another scary expression. I said, "Thanks for the info, Roseanne. Guess I'll go crash that party." I opened the door that led to the judge's chambers.

I bumped into the Vicksburg DA—literally. Isaac Keet took a step back into the narrow passageway. "There you are," he said. "I've been looking all over for you."

Snappish, I said: "I'm not hard to find, Isaac. My office is across the damned street."

Yes, my nose was out of joint, but I also was attempting to cover for the fact that Isaac Keet intimidated the shit out of me.

I squared my shoulders and said, "So if you're trying to justify your private communications with Judge Ashley on the basis that I'm out of pocket, let me set you straight: it won't fly."

He flashed a rare smile, startling in its intensity. "I get it. You're showing me what a tough cookie you are. Showing me who's boss."

I glanced away, uncomfortable with his sharp eye. It took all the nerve I possessed to match Isaac Keet blow for blow in court. He had every advantage over me: age, maturity, experience. He was old enough to be my daddy (by Mississippi standards, anyway). He'd served overseas in the navy for eight years. And in the past fifteen years, he had risen in the ranks of the Vicksburg DA's office.

In our conferences with the Greene family, I'd expressed my concern about being outmatched by Keet. Lee Sr. had seconded the emotion. Suzanne waved my concern away; she claimed that juries like a fresh, young warrior.

And my client's mother had also brushed off my concerns—on a different basis. *No one will take that prosecutor seriously, for goodness' sake. I don't think I need to explain why.*

She didn't. Her meaning was crystal clear: Mrs. Greene thought he would be disregarded because he was black. Every time that woman opened her mouth, I thanked the gods that I was not a member of the Greene family. I had dodged that silver bullet.

Facing Isaac Keet in the passageway, I said, "So what were you and the judge chatting about this morning? Do y'all run late like this in Vicksburg? We like to start on time here in Rosedale. Of course, we're just a small town—"

He cut me off. "You're right; I was talking with the judge.

I had to share some news—shocking news—about a law en-forcement associate. That's why we're running late." He glanced up and stared at the overhead light in silence for a moment. When I opened my mouth, he spoke again before I had the chance.

"Before the start of evidence, I'll give you another shot. Does your client want to plead guilty?"

I pulled a face of disbelief. "Are we back to this? How many times have I told you? This case is overcharged. Capital murder, for the accidental death of a sex worker with a drug history?"

Keet ran his hand over his close-cropped hair, which was starting to gray. "Yes, seems like you mentioned that."

"I think it's terrible, absolutely offensive, the way district at-torneys abuse the capital murder charge. You file these death penalty cases to scare the defendant into a plea bargain. You use the charge as a club to beat them over the head. How do you sleep at night?"

The smile flashed again. "Like a baby."

His taunt made me even more irate. "Has it occurred to you that the state can't show a motive in this case?"

He shrugged. I went on, my voice rising.

"No motive. Why on earth would Lee Greene want to kill this woman? The Rosedale jury is going to see right through your paper-thin case. I haven't kept it a secret from you: I have a wit-ness who will testify that the deceased prostitute was involved in drugs as well as the sex trade."

He leaned back against the wall. In a voice that was not unkind, Keet said, "My last plea offer was a reduced charge: vol-untary manslaughter. If Greene will plead to manslaughter, I'll recommend five years. That's the best I can do."

I shook my head. "No way. My client didn't kill her."

Keet said, "Aren't you going to communicate the offer to

your client? In Vicksburg, the defense attorneys usually let their clients decide." There was an edge in his voice. "But as you say—this isn't Vicksburg."

I frowned. He always made me feel like a kid. "I'll tell him. But I know what he'll say."

"Good. Tell him pretty quick, Ruby. The offer is good today only."

Keet held a folded sheet of paper; he opened it and stared at the sheet. It was upside down, from my angle, but I recognized it at a glance. It was the defense witness list, a disclosure that I had provided to Keet prior to trial.

In a quiet voice, he said, "Before we start with opening statements, I feel duty-bound to share some crucial information with you."

I let out an impatient huff. I was sick of the delays; it was time to get moving.

"What?"

Keet examined my witness list for another moment. Running his finger under a name, he said in a grave voice, "One of your witnesses won't be testifying."

"Why not?" I asked.

"Because he's dead."

# CHAPTER 46

HE WAS DEAD. Gone, just like that. Keet told me he'd been shot to death in his vehicle, the late-model Volvo I'd seen outside the sketchy bar. He was at the side of the road, just outside of Rosedale. Probably appearing in response to the pink subpoena that he had been served to testify for the defense.

I sat in court, trying to get my head around it. When Isaac Keet stood to present his opening statement, my hand slipped into my briefcase to rummage inside it. My right hand moved of its own volition like Thing, the disembodied hand that would send my mama into gales of laughter when we watched reruns of *The Addams Family.*

The hand was hunting for a box of Nicorette gum in my bag, because I needed a shot of nicotine. I needed it bad. But there was nothing hidden in the recesses of my bag, since I'd nobly decided to swear off the gum.

My client was giving me a quizzical look, which brought me back to the business at hand. I ceased digging in the briefcase and sat up straight in my chair, with my eyes glued to the DA's back. To occupy my hands, I grasped a felt-tipped pen and uncapped it.

Isaac Keet said, "Ladies and gentlemen of the jury, this is what the evidence will show."

Beside me at the counsel table, Lee held a pen as well: a Montblanc fountain pen. He scrawled on a legal pad without looking down, then pushed the pad in front of me. It read: *Vice cop dead? What will you do?*

Lee was echoing my thoughts. The same refrain had pounded in my head since Keet dropped the bomb on me outside the judge's chambers. I was so shell-shocked by the news of my star witness's demise, my mind was frozen in question mark mode.

How would I launch a defense without my star witness? Detective Guion was an encyclopedia of information about the life and times of Monae Prince.

That vice cop was my smoking gun. But he was dead. And dead men tell no tales.

Forcing my attention to the DA, I tried to focus. He was describing the state's charge against my client, and when he spoke Lee's name, he wheeled around and pointed a finger at him.

Lee was prepared. It's an old prosecutor's trick, confronting the accused with the finger of guilt. Lee raised his chin and stared calmly at Keet.

Keet turned back to the jury. "The victim of the crime was Miss Monae Prince. Ladies and gentlemen, in the course of this trial, there are some difficult facts you'll have to hear about Miss Prince."

I cut my eyes at Lee. He scrawled on the pad again: *Suck the poison???*

It sounded like Keet was gearing up to suck the snakebite in opening statement. I had wondered how he would handle the issue of Monae Prince's occupation. When preparing my own notes for opening statement, I'd tried to predict whether the district attorney would be forthcoming in front of the jury or whether he would play coy.

Keet grasped the sides of the podium that faced the jury box. I could see the tendons in the back of his hands.

"Miss Prince had been lured to the hotel room in Vicksburg—the hotel room of the defendant, Lee Greene—for a reason that will appall y'all, ladies and gentlemen. She was there because Lee Greene solicited her services for the purpose of prostitution."

"Objection," I said, starting to rise. I had evidence to the contrary; the hooker was Cary Reynolds's idea, not Lee's. But Judge Ashley dismissed me with a wave of his hand. "Overruled. The defense will have its turn shortly, Ms. Bozarth."

I sat.

Isaac Keet's voice rolled out like spun silk as he continued his statement to the jury. "Yes, ladies and gentlemen, Monae was in the company of the defendant that night as a call girl. A prostitute for hire. But, ladies and gentlemen, Miss Prince wasn't only a call girl. No, indeed."

I leaned forward, curious to hear what was coming. So did several of the jurors.

"She was a young girl. Monae Prince was an adolescent, a girl of tender years. If life was always fair, Monae would have been living with a family who loved and cared for her. But life can be hard. She was a girl living in dire poverty, without protection or support of family. And she was only seventeen years old. Seventeen, ladies and gentlemen."

I kept my poker face intact when he beat the point home about Monae's tender age because I knew better. At the time of her death, Monae Prince was old enough to vote and buy booze in Mississippi. The Vicksburg vice detective had said so.

The dead Vicksburg cop.

My mind started into overdrive again. How would I establish the evidence that the Vicksburg detective would have provided about the deceased's background? I needed to tie her to the drug underworld. I'd been confident that we could prove that Ms. Prince was an enthusiastic consumer of illegal drugs. But with the vice detective dead and gone, who would contest the state's position that Monae Prince was a helpless girl at Lee's mercy?

Isaac Keet was wrapping up. He paced in front of the jury box, and said, "I see that some of y'all have been glancing over at the defendant, taking a look. And I suspect I know what's going through some of your minds this morning."

He stopped pacing. He stepped right up to the jury box and grasped the railing. "I know that some of you may find this unthinkable. You see the defendant sitting there in that fine new suit, holding a fancy writing pen. His pen costs more than my shoes, you know that?"

"Objection." I shot up from my seat. "Mr. Keet's comments are irrelevant and outside the scope of the evidence."

"Sustained," the judge said.

As I took my seat, I could hear Lee beside me, breathing rapidly. His blood pressure must have spiked.

Isaac Keet waved off my objection like a buzzing horsefly. "As I was saying: you're asking yourselves a pertinent question. Why would a prosperous, educated man from a good family callously cause the death of a poor teenage girl? Well, I have the answer. Ladies and gentlemen, some people in our society suffer from a disease of entitlement. There's a word for it: 'affluenza.' Lee Greene had a bad case of affluenza—and young Monae Prince died as a result."

As Keet turned away from the jury box and walked beside the counsel table, his eyes were twinkling. He had the nerve to wink.

Oh, I knew what he was communicating. He'd stolen a march on me. I had scoffed at him less than an hour earlier, mocking the state's inability to produce a motive for the killing.

Affluenza.

Well, so much for my motive argument. I took my felt-tipped pen and struck a paragraph from my own opening statement.

# CHAPTER 47

MY TURN.

The judge's voice split the air in the crowded courtroom: "Ms. Bozarth, the defense may now address the jury with opening statement or reserve it for the beginning of defendant's case."

He made my ears ring. I'd learned that Judge Ashley was nearly deaf in one ear. But stubbornness made him resist the use of his hearing aid on most occasions. As a result, he tended to speak at a high volume.

I rose. "If it please the court."

He leaned back in his high-backed leather chair. "You may proceed."

Clutching the manila folder that held the printed pages of my opening statement, I walked to the podium, casting a sharp eye on the jury of seven women and five men. I hoped my outward expression was serene, because my brain was frantic. And the pages of my presentation to the jury, which had been pristine an hour prior, were marked with so many slashes of red ink, it looked like someone had hemorrhaged on it.

When I had crafted the opening statement on Sunday night, I'd planned to attack the state's case without revealing what the details of the defense would be. That's what Suzanne had advised.

*It's a tactical plan,* she had said, blowing a cloud of Marlboro smoke in my office at the Ben Franklin. *Don't reveal your cards.*

I'd followed Suzanne's advice to the letter, because Suzanne had thirty years of courtroom experience. Plus, she did a lot of gambling at the Mississippi riverfront casinos.

I shot a glance at the courtroom gallery, looking in vain for my partner. With a flash of panic, I wondered again: where the hell was Suzanne Greene?

Spreading the ink-slaughtered pages out on the podium, I smiled at the twelve people in the jury box.

"Ladies and gentlemen, I'd like to thank you in advance for your service in the trial. My client and I know that jury service involves a sacrifice, and Lee Greene and I appreciate y'all doing your civic duty."

A woman in the front row nodded. That was good; it was a start, anyway. I saw her eyes slide to my right, sneaking a look past my shoulder. She was probably checking Lee out.

It didn't necessarily hurt to have a good-looking client wearing a well-cut suit. If we were lucky, a couple of women on the jury would develop a crush on Lee during the trial. That could be his "get out of jail free" card.

I spoke in a sober tone as I talked to the jury about the deceased, Monae Prince. Instead of serving up bombshells, I skimmed the surface of her seamy background. After all, with the detective lying in the county morgue, I wasn't yet certain how much of Monae Prince's seedy life would get into evidence.

I was treading lightly, soft-pedaling the prostitution angle. So it startled me when I heard the DA slam his chair into the railing behind the counsel table.

I jumped and turned with a jerk. Isaac Keet was on his feet, his wooden chair tipped backward at a dangerous angle.

"Objection!" he shouted. Even the deaf judge winced at the noise.

"What?" I snapped.

Keet stepped away from the counsel table. "Your Honor, I will not stand silently by while she maligns that poor dead child."

I shook my head in amazement. "What are you talking about? All I said was that she engaged in prostitution. You already said so yourself. You told the jury she was a hooker in your opening statement."

"Hooker?" His nostrils flared. "Your Honor, did you hear the terminology Ms. Bozarth is using? It is offensive."

Judge Ashley scratched at his receding hairline. "Mr. Keet," he began, but the DA cut him off.

Advancing in my direction, Keet said, "I told this jury that the defendant—your client, who is so appreciative of the jury's service on his behalf—lured the murder victim into an act of prostitution."

Keet was an arm's length away from me—and from the jury. My face burned; I could feel the blood flushing my cheeks. I turned to the judge. "Judge Ashley, the defense requests that you tell Mr. Keet to sit down."

The judge tugged at his deaf ear. "Let's all settle down. Tensions are running high. Mr. Keet, your objection is overruled."

I watched as Keet strode back to his counsel table. As he straightened his chair, he fixed my client with a look of pure disgust. Lee cringed slightly in his seat, as if he'd been threatened.

Sweet Jesus.

Turning back to the jury, I took a breath and said, "The evidence will show that my client did not solicit the deceased. He did not lure her to his hotel room in Vicksburg. She appeared without his prior knowledge. The defense will provide uncontroverted testimony that Monae Prince had been contacted by another individual, without my client's knowledge or consent."

I paused in confusion for a moment. Hadn't I intended to avoid revealing the defense evidence? Isaac Keet's theatrics were getting me flustered.

It was time to transition, to build up a contrasting image for the jury's benefit: Lee Greene, Mr. Wonderful.

"Y'all may not have heard much about my client, Lee Greene. He's from over in Jackson, where he practices corporate law with one of the leading firms in our state capital. Lee grew up just outside Jackson, on a piece of land that's been in the Greene family for nearly two hundred years. He got his undergraduate degree and his law degree from Ole Miss. Graduated with high honors."

I paced to the left, to make sure I was engaging all of the jurors. "But in addition to a distinguished legal career, Lee Greene is also committed to public service. He's a lifelong member of the Calvary Presbyterian Church, he's a member and officer of his Rotary group, and he's also a leading supporter of and fund-raiser for the charitable organization in Mississippi that is building homes and schools in poverty-stricken areas of Nicaragua. A school currently under construction there will bear his family name. And he devotes countless hours of volunteer work to the Humane Society of Barnes County, caring for abandoned animals."

I paused, turning to look at Lee, hoping the jurors would follow my lead. He was wearing a saintly, benevolent expression. Glancing back at the jury box, I saw yet another woman look at him with approval.

I continued, my voice firm. "Clearly, as you will see, Lee Greene is not a man who would commit the lurid crime with which he is charged."

"Objection."

This time, Isaac Keet didn't shout, didn't shove his chair. When I turned my head, he was leaning against the railing with his arms crossed.

"Your Honor," he said, in a voice that was deadly calm, "I'm going to have to ask that Ruby Bozarth be censured."

I was so shocked that I sputtered, and it took a few seconds before I could respond clearly. "What on earth are you talking about? Your Honor, I object to the DA's continual interruptions. There is no basis for this, none at all."

Keet went on, as if I hadn't spoken. "Ruby Bozarth is an officer of the court—and yet she knows that what she is telling the jury is untrue."

I clenched my fists and stuffed them into my pockets. "What are you even talking about?"

"Her supposed presentation of the defendant as a clean-cut paragon who'd never do anything wrong? Never hurt a living soul? Ms. Bozarth, please! Your Honor, it's well known that defense attorney Ruby Bozarth refused to marry defendant Lee Greene because of his sexual proclivities."

I gasped. I opened my mouth to speak, then snapped it shut. Exactly how should I respond to Keet's scandalous statement?

Because, after all—it was the truth.

Judge Ashley cupped his hand around his ear. "What's that you say?"

# CHAPTER 48

"YOUR HONOR, MAY we approach the bench?" I struggled to regain my composure in addressing the judge.

Judge Ashley invited us up with a wave. As I walked the short distance to the bench, my ears hummed like a beehive. If I didn't settle down, I might end up as deaf as the judge.

Keet was waiting for me. He had the nerve to smile as I approached. "What's the matter, Ms. Bozarth? You're red as a beet."

The bees in my ears hummed with an angry buzz. "Your Honor, the defense requests a mistrial."

Judge Ashley's brow furrowed. "Beg pardon? Did someone say mistrial?"

Isaac Keet laughed out loud. "Now who's got the thin skin?"

The judge inclined his good ear in my direction. "Ms. Bozarth, did you say you want a mistrial?"

"Your Honor, the district attorney's untoward comments—which are irrelevant and immaterial—are highly prejudicial to my client."

Keet smiled again. "But are they true?"

I could feel the blood in my face; I suspected that I was, as Keet claimed, red as a beet. And as for his objectionable comment: how could I deny it? I had, in fact, broken off my engagement with Lee Greene due to his sexual proclivities.

In a furious whisper, I said to Keet: "How dare you inject my personal life into this case, in the presence of the jury?"

Keet bent his head and spoke softly into my ear. "When you've been around a while, you'll learn a thing or two about trial practice. For example: all's fair in love and war, as the saying goes."

Judge Ashley leaned toward us. "Can y'all speak up?"

Keet raised his voice. "Your Honor, the defense has informed me in the past that the state's case is baseless and flawed because we cannot, in Ms. Bozarth's opinion, show a motive for the crime. The State of Mississippi has a duty to let the jury know the defendant's mind-set. His elitist, misogynistic temperament is at issue in this case. Maybe Ms. Bozarth can't recognize it because she shares his elitist background."

He looked over for my reaction. But he'd revealed he didn't know his opponent as well as he thought. Because I'd learned how to fight off bullies at an early age.

I lifted my chin and addressed the judge. "I request the court instruct the DA and the jury that this prosecution is about facts, hard evidence, and not gossip and innuendo." I shot Keet a glare. "You, sir, should be disciplined."

He grinned. "I'm frightened."

While we wrangled at the bench, the elderly bailiff and young Deputy Brockes sat at the bailiff's desk at the far end of the bench. The old bailiff nudged Brockes, and they spoke in whispers. Deputy Brockes hid a smile with his hand.

I wanted to snap. Apparently, we were providing entertainment for the courthouse staff.

Looking back at the judge, I spoke firmly. "Judge, I need a ruling on my request for mistrial."

The judge made a face. "Are you sure you want to do that, Ms. Bozarth? We've got the doggone jury already seated. Me and Isaac, we've come in from Vicksburg for this special setting. Do you really want it reset? To start the process all over again? It might be another year, maybe longer, before I can fit it into my calendar."

At the mention of the jury, I glanced over to gauge their reaction to the drama that was taking place. Three of the jurors looked bored. A couple were exchanging looks of impatience.

And one woman on the jury was casting sympathetic, longing eyes at Lee Greene.

Maybe a mistrial wasn't such a good idea.

The main door to the courtroom creaked open and closed with a bang. Many heads turned to see the county sheriff, Patrick Stark, walk into court, accompanied by Potts, the nosy deputy whom I'd encountered in the hallway. Deputy Potts lingered by the door, but Sheriff Stark marched to the bench, his boots treading heavily on the tiled floor.

"I need to talk to you, Your Honor."

The judge looked astounded by the interruption. "What?"

The sheriff walked up to the empty witness stand and sat on the wooden seat. "Judge, I've got to take my deputy out of here."

"What's that? Who?"

Sheriff Stark edged closer and set his elbow on the bench. "My deputy."

"Who's your deputy?"

"Young fellow assisting your bailiff over there: Deputy Brockes. I got to take him away."

Judge Ashley rubbed his head. "This is a murder trial, Sheriff. I need security. Why do you need your man right now?"

At the bailiff's desk, Brockes must have overheard the exchange. He rose to his feet, a look of confusion clouding his face.

The sheriff dropped his voice to a gruff whisper. "I need him for the investigation into the shooting of that Vicksburg detective."

That grabbed my attention. I moved down the bench, to be closer to the sheriff. I wanted to hear exactly what he said. The Vicksburg detective's fate was intimately tied to the fate of Lee Greene, and the outcome of my case.

I needn't have bothered to elbow my way closer. The judge waved his black-robed arm at the sheriff. "Speak up, sir. What is it?"

In a booming baritone, Sheriff Stark said: "We have the weapon that killed the Vicksburg detective. It's registered to that boy there." He cocked his head and nodded in Deputy Brockes's direction.

"And it's got his prints."

# CHAPTER 49

I SWUNG AROUND and checked out Deputy Brockes. It appeared that Brockes had also overheard the sheriff's pronouncement. His face had blanched, and his jaw opened and shut, and then opened again.

"I-I—n-n-never," he said, sputtering.

Sheriff Stark left the witness stand, and with a jerk of his head, he signaled to Deputy Potts in the back of the courtroom. Both lawmen advanced on young Brockes. Brockes backed away, shaking his head.

Sheriff Stark said, "You need to come along, son."

"Why? Wha-What for?"

The sheriff lowered his voice, but he was only a few feet away from me. I could hear him clearly.

"Looks like you're a suspect in the investigation of the Vicksburg man's death. I expect we can clear it all up. I'm sure we can. But we need to have a talk, Deputy."

He grasped Brockes by the elbow, but the young man jerked his arm away.

"Wasn't me. I don't know nothing about that Vicksburg man, nothing except we seen him in his car that night. Ain't that right, Potts?"

Deputy Potts had reached his partner's side. His face was grave as he looked to the sheriff for direction.

The pitch of Brockes's voice rose to a whine, childlike in its intensity. "We pulled him over, is all. It was Potts that said to do it. 'Pull that Volvo over,' he told me. 'It didn't signal right.' He was fine when we let him go. Fine as frog hair."

He turned to his partner. "Ain't that right, Potts?"

Potts didn't respond. The sheriff reached for Brockes a second time; again, Brockes snatched his arm away.

The sheriff said to Deputy Potts: "Cuff him."

With a stony face, Potts pulled the handcuffs from his belt. It took both men to hold Brockes as they clicked the restraints shut. I had to look away; it seemed disrespectful to witness the scene. I turned my focus to Judge Ashley. He and Isaac Keet were exchanging a look.

"Getting kind of rowdy in here, Judge," Keet said.

For once, I was in agreement with the DA. The spectators in the gallery were buzzing with talk; more important, the jurors were craning their necks to see the drama unfold.

Judge Ashley banged his gavel. "Court will be in recess for fifteen minutes." To the bailiff, he said, "You'll probably need to accompany the jurors to the restroom facilities."

The bailiff spread his hands in a helpless gesture. "I can't watch over the ladies' room and the men's room at the same time. I've only got one set of eyes—"

The judge cut him off. "My court clerk will assist. Carla!" he said, pointing to a woman who lingered near the judge's chambers exit. "Assist with the ladies. Please."

And Judge Ashley disappeared.

# CHAPTER 50

I HEADED FOR the defense counsel table and walked into the cloud of scent. My nose began to drip. As I dug a wad of Kleenex from my briefcase, I said, "Lee, you can't wear that cologne. It's driving me nuts."

"It's my new signature scent." He looked down at my briefcase. "Is that the bag I got you for graduation? You still carry it, after all this time. That is really touching."

I shoved the briefcase under the table. "Don't flatter yourself. I don't carry it for sentimental reasons."

"Maybe you carry it because it's nicer than anything you can afford," he whispered.

I rolled my eyes. That stuck-up son of a bitch. Even if it was true.

Lee drummed his fingers on the wooden tabletop, watching as Deputy Brockes was escorted out of the room, still protesting. After the officers departed, he laughed and said to me in a confiding tone, "Jesus Christ—that Barney Fife deputy doesn't know when to keep his mouth shut. Glad I'm not representing him."

"What are you talking about?"

"That little deputy they just dragged out of here. What an idiot. I wouldn't want to represent a dumbshit like him, that's all I'm saying."

I stared at him for a long moment. It seemed to me that maybe Lee didn't have a grasp on reality. We were sitting in a Mississippi courtroom where he was on trial for a murder charge. And if I couldn't figure out an angle to get the dirt on the victim into evidence, the only legal work Lee would do in the future might be as a jailhouse lawyer in a Mississippi state prison.

I needed to make Lee concentrate on his own situation. "Since I'm seeing Cary Reynolds tonight, I want to be fresh. Give me the background on y'all's friendship."

Lee waved it off. "We're brothers, Ruby. It's all good."

"So you stayed tight after college."

"Well, no. It doesn't work like that."

"Did you talk regularly?"

"No. Lord, I don't think we'd talked in years. But he followed me on Facebook. I posted a picture of dinner at that barbeque place in Vicksburg, and he messaged me."

"And?"

"And he said he wanted to see me, next time I was in town. He wanted some business advice. I was going to Vicksburg anyway, on depositions. So we made an appointment to have dinner while I was in town."

I was about to ask a follow-up question when I caught sight of the DA exiting through a side door. In his absence, I needed to have some straight talk with my client. "Lee, the DA brought up his plea bargain offer again this morning."

"I don't want to talk about it."

He stood up abruptly and turned away, but I grabbed his coat sleeve. "Lee, it's my duty to tell you what he offered."

He wrenched his sleeve from my hand. "You're wrinkling my jacket."

I stood beside him and spoke into his ear. "Keet will accept a plea of guilty to voluntary manslaughter. If you plead, he'll recommend five years."

Lee's head dropped and he let out a groan. I went on: "Lee, with your clean record, and the victim's seamy background, you might have a shot at probation." When he didn't speak, I said, "I'm not saying you should take the offer. But you should think about it. Talk it over with your parents. And your aunt Suzanne."

He shut his eyes and laughed softly. "Aunt Suzanne."

When he lifted his chin and looked at me, his typical demeanor was back in place. "I have an answer for you, Ruby. The suggestion that I claim any responsibility for that woman's death is appalling to me. I've told you: I have no recollection of doing anything criminal."

I nodded. "Yeah. No recollection. And I've told you, Lee: your lack of recall doesn't help your case. Because you know as well as I do that voluntary intoxication is not a defense for this crime."

His eyes flashed. In a dangerous voice, he said, "Thanks, counselor—so glad to see you're on my side. Here's a thought, Ruby: maybe the girl at the hotel drugged me. You know it's not my custom to experience blackouts."

I pondered the possibility. It would help our case, but it just didn't make sense. Why would the girl drug him, then give herself an overdose?

# CHAPTER 51

I PUSHED MY files into a neat pile on the counsel table while I watched Judge Ashley fiddle with his ear. He turned to look at Isaac Keet, and I saw a pink plastic device in the judge's ear canal.

I breathed a sigh of relief: thank goodness. Maybe we wouldn't have to shout our secret conferences at the bench.

Addressing the jury, Judge Ashley instructed that they were to disregard the events that had occurred prior to the recess. He then asked me if I wished to continue my opening statement, which I declined. Finally, to the DA, Judge Ashley said, "Call your first witness."

Keet stood. "The State of Mississippi calls Juana Gomez."

The bailiff, now stationed at the courtroom entrance, opened the door and called out the name. A young woman entered, wearing a high-necked black nylon dress. Once she was inside, the bailiff murmured instructions to her and she approached the bench.

"Raise your right hand," Judge Ashley said, and she complied.

"Do you swear that the testimony you're about to give is the whole truth?"

"I do," she answered, with a decided nod.

"You may be seated."

She took her seat on the witness stand, pulling the hem of her dress down to her kneecaps.

Isaac Keet said in a solemn tone, "Please state your name."

In a heavily accented contralto voice that carried to the back of the room, she said, "Juana Maria Gomez."

"And what is your occupation, Ms. Gomez?"

"I work in housekeeping at the Magnolia Inn." She paused and added, "Magnolia Inn, in Vicksburg."

Keet nodded with approval. "And by Vicksburg, you're referring to Vicksburg, Mississippi?"

I could've objected to leading the witness, but there was nothing to be gained by it, so I kept my seat.

"Yes, sir. Mississippi."

"How long have you been employed in that capacity?"

She blinked; there was a moment's pause. "How long have I worked there? Two years, almost."

Keet strolled to the jury box and leaned on the wooden railing. "Ms. Gomez, let me direct your attention to March of this year. Specifically, March twenty-third. Were you working on that date?"

"Yes, I was working."

"What shift, if you recall?"

"Early shift. Seven to three."

He reached out with his right hand and grasped the oak railing. "Let me direct your attention to 11:15 a.m. on March twenty-third. Could you tell us what happened at that time?"

She shifted in her chair and faced the jury, taking care to

cover her knees. He'd trained her like a professional witness. I was impressed in spite of myself.

"Checkout is eleven."

"Objection." I rose to a half-stand. "Not responsive."

The judge gave me a glance. "Sustained."

Keet shot me a scornful look. It was a small matter. I knew he would redirect her. I just wanted to remind the jury that I was on the playing field.

"Ms. Gomez, what precisely did you do at 11:15 a.m. on that date?"

She looked at the defense table with trepidation, then said, "I knocked on the door. The door of room 113."

"And why did you do that?"

"Because I needed to get in, to clean. He should be gone. Because," and she looked my way again, triumphant, "checkout is eleven."

"What happened when you knocked on that door?"

"No answer. So I used my key and I opened it."

"Then what?"

She exhaled audibly. "I peeked in. Only opened the door partway. I said, 'Housekeeping,' like they tell us to."

"Was there any response?"

"No. No one said nothing."

"Then what happened?"

She turned to face the jury again. "I stepped inside and you can't believe what I seen."

"Objection," I said, but the judge waved me down.

"Just tell the jury what you saw, ma'am," Judge Ashley said.

She dropped her voice to a husky whisper. "I saw there was a black girl's arms tied to the headboard of the bed, with duct tape. And a white man was on top of her."

"What did you observe about the man in room 113?"

"He was naked with no sheet or blanket or nothing."

"Ms. Gomez, what, if anything, were the people in bed doing?"

"Well, they don't move, so at first I thought they were asleep. But the man's face was so white, maybe they are not breathing. Maybe they're dead. But I must have made a noise because he opened his eyes, he lifted his head. I thought he looked like a ghost. He scared me so much I couldn't even move, not at first."

"What happened next?"

"I looked at that man's face and I wanted to scream, but I was too afraid . . . of what he'd do to me. So I shut the door behind me. And I called the manager. He came up to see, then he called the police on 911."

"Ms. Gomez, the man you saw in the hotel room, lying on top of the girl in bed, is he in the courtroom today?"

"Yes," she said, with a voice that rang with assurance.

"Would you point him out for the jury?"

She pointed a finger at Lee, her face twisted with loathing. "Him."

Isaac Keet bowed his head. "No further questions."

As Keet walked back to the prosecution's counsel table, Judge Ashley said, "Ms. Bozarth, your witness."

I leaned in to Lee and whispered, "Anything in particular you want me to ask?"

He bent his head to my ear. "Leave her alone. Don't cross-examine her."

I shot him a look of surprise. "Why not?"

"There's nothing to be gained by it, and she's poisoned against me. Get her off the stand and out of here."

I understood his sentiment, but I had a point to make. Lee had been unconscious, unmoving, and therefore harmless when Juana Gomez saw him. I intended to make her admit it.

So I ignored my client. Picking up my notes, I walked around the defense table and leaned against the front of it. Lee poked me from behind and said "Don't" in a dangerous whisper. Too late.

"Ms. Gomez, describe the defendant's condition when you first saw him."

Her brow puckered. "Huh?"

I was taken aback. Her English had been strong during Keet's direct examination. "His condition. Didn't you say he appeared to be sleeping?"

"Appears? I don't understand."

I took a step closer. "Ma'am, you said in your testimony on direct examination that the man in the hotel room wasn't moving, his eyes were closed, and he didn't respond in any way. Isn't that correct?"

She was silent. After a second, she shrugged her shoulders.

I felt a wave of heat roll up my neck. Juana Gomez seemed determined to mess with me.

"Did he appear to be unconscious?"

"Conscience?" She shook her head. "That man have no conscience."

I heard Keet chuckle. Snapping my head toward the judge, I said, "Objection, Your Honor. I request the jury be asked to disregard."

"Sustained. Disregard the last answer, ladies and gentlemen."

I walked all the way to the witness stand and eyeballed the housekeeper. "Ms. Gomez. The man in the hotel room—he wasn't moving, barely breathing. So when you saw him, he wasn't harming anyone. Correct?"

No answer. I raised my voice.

"Isn't that right?"

In a sulky voice, she said, "Yeah. When I saw him."

"And when you made the noise, and he did awaken, what was his condition at that time?"

I wanted to paint a picture of Lee's vulnerable state, to set the stage for his incapacitation. We needed to establish that he was unable to do any harm. It was within my grasp, inches away, if I could just pull it out of Juana Gomez's mouth.

She cocked her head. "Conditions?"

"Yes, condition. How did he act? What did he do?"

"Oh, him." She sneered and turned to face the jury one last time. "He scream and cry like a little girl."

# CHAPTER 52

AS GOMEZ DISAPPEARED from the courtroom, Judge Ashley picked up his gavel.

"We'll break for lunch. Court is adjourned until one o'clock." He slammed the gavel on the bench, and Lee and I rose and stood while the judge departed into his chambers, the hem of his black robe flapping.

Lee turned on me and grabbed my upper arm. "Why didn't you do what I told you to do?"

I tried to snatch my arm away, but he held me fast. In a whisper I said, "I was trying to make a point."

His eyes were wide with fury. He pulled me closer, and the odor of his cologne engulfed me.

"Your cross-examination of the hotel maid was a disaster. She made you look like a fool. And she made me look like some kind of freak, some criminal."

With a mighty yank, I freed my arm. "You were in bed with a dead woman, Lee. That does look pretty bad."

His head jerked as if I'd struck him. He said, "It sounds to me like you harbor doubts about my innocence. Well, I have doubts about you, Ruby. About your competence. Your ability to represent me in this case. To provide effective assistance of counsel. I'm beginning to think my father was right."

The cologne made my eyes run, as well as my nose. I pulled my briefcase from its spot on the floor, pulled out a tissue and blew my nose.

Then I turned to Lee and said, "I've had a bellyful of your attitude."

I shoved the soggy tissue into the briefcase, followed by my legal pad, and closed it with a vicious zip. Then I looked up at him and said, "You want another lawyer? No problem, it's your privilege. If you want me to withdraw, I'd be delighted. I'll go into chambers and tell the judge, right this minute. Your call." I swiped at the allergic tears seeping out of my eyes.

Over Lee's shoulder I saw a figure loom: my law partner, Suzanne Greene. She reached up and grabbed Lee's left ear, then gave it a twist.

He howled. Pulling away from the assault and rubbing his ear, he turned to her and said, "Damn, Aunt Suze! That hurts."

"What have you done now? You've made your lawyer cry?" Though Lee stood a head taller than me, he had no advantage on Suzanne. At six feet tall, she stood nose to nose with Lee, and she outweighed him by seventy pounds.

Lee lifted his chin, straightened his tie. "Glad you could make it, Aunt Suzanne. My daddy was thinking you'd lost interest in the fate of your only nephew."

She squinted over the reading glasses that sat on the end of her nose. "Don't you try to turn this around on me. I walk into court and find you disrespecting your attorney, my law partner. How dare you carry on like that in a court of law? Are you trying to hang yourself?"

He dropped his voice. "Oh, Ruby's doing a fine job of that, with no help from me."

Suzanne reached for Lee's ear again, but when her hand rose, he stepped out of range. She paused and crossed her arms on her massive chest.

"Lee Greene, if you can't follow your attorney's lead and assist with the representation in a respectful fashion, then I believe you'd best go on back to Jackson and hire somebody else."

He glanced around the courtroom. It was empty, save for a gray-haired spectator napping on a far bench. "Where's my daddy? I'll have him make some calls. To the Jackson defense firm we've been thinking about."

Suzanne snorted. "You do that. You bring in some fancy-pants lawyer from Jackson. Stick him or her in court in Rosedale, in Williams County, where Ruby Bozarth is a rock star. The locals don't cater much to city slickers."

After a moment, he huffed a haughty chuckle. "So Ruby has dragged this trial to a hick town on the riverbank, and I'm stuck with her. Because of the hometown advantage." He dropped into his wooden chair at the counsel table and rubbed his eyes.

The courtroom door opened and I tensed, glancing over to see who might witness the battle at the defense table. When I saw a tall figure making his way toward me with a paper bag in one hand and a plastic cup in the other, my shoulders sagged with relief.

"Shorty! You should be at the diner, hon; it's gotta be packed today."

"I was worried about you. Why didn't you come over to eat lunch? You know I put a Reserved sign on your counter stool when you're in trial." He bent down and kissed my cheek, then set the bag on the table and handed the cup to me. "Sweet tea."

"Oh, Lord, honey—you're a saint." I took a long drag on the striped straw.

From his seat at the counsel table, Lee said, "Ruby, darling, introduce me to your friend. I don't believe I've had the pleasure."

I made the introductions as briefly as possible without being rude. To Suzanne, I said, "Suzanne and Lee, maybe y'all should go to the office and talk."

"Talk? About what?" Lee wore a hurt expression.

"You know. About what you want to do regarding your representation."

Lee laughed. "Now, Ruby, don't get moody on me. I've known you too long for that." To Shorty, he said, "She gets a little feisty sometimes."

Shorty's face was stony. He didn't respond.

In a warning tone, Suzanne said, "Lee, you'd best come along with me. Let Ruby have some lunch."

Lee ignored his aunt. He sighed and spoke to me in a wheedling tone, so sweet that butter wouldn't melt. "Ruby, honey, you know I wouldn't trust this case to anyone but you. You must have misread my meaning."

I was standing within arm's reach of his chair. He reached out to squeeze my calf.

"We're old, old friends…"

The sentence was cut off when Shorty reached across the table, grabbed Lee's striped necktie, and jerked him out of his chair.

As Lee clawed at his neck, Shorty gave the knot of the tie a twist. "Keep your hands away from her."

I watched with my mouth agape as Lee nodded, his face turning scarlet. When Shorty released him, Lee fell back against the railing. Shorty's eyes glittered with an unspoken threat. Lee raised his hands defensively and said, "I was just messing with you, man. Ruby and I are ancient history, everyone knows that. Our relationship is professional. Strictly business."

Suzanne took his elbow and ushered him away from the counsel table. Watching them go, I saw Lee loosen his necktie and try to smooth down the wrinkles in the silk fabric.

And I had a thought: maybe I'd just witnessed the real reason that Lee Greene began wearing bow ties.

# CHAPTER 53

I REACHED INSIDE the paper bag sitting on the counsel table and pulled out a fresh cheeseburger, still hot. As I took a wolfish bite, I moaned with pleasure.

Shorty said, "I left the onion off, since you're in trial." He glared at the courtroom door through which Suzanne and Lee had just exited. "Wish I'd layered them on."

Lodging the bite in my cheek like a chipmunk, I said, "This is so good. You're my hero, Shorty."

Shorty studied the courtroom for a long moment. Then he bent down and spoke into my ear. "I think you should bail on this one."

As I swallowed, I looked at him with surprise. "You're not serious."

"I'm serious as a heart attack. Got a read on that guy. I think he could be a sociopath."

"Oh, please. You're being dramatic." I sunk my teeth into the burger again.

Shorty turned his head away, running his fingers through his hair in a gesture I'd come to know well. Then his arm snaked around me. He pulled me to his chest.

"I worry about you. I don't like you having to be in such close company with Lee Greene. He's not our kind of people."

I felt his chin resting gently on the top of my head. Closing my eyes, I relished the embrace for a peaceful moment before I broke away.

"He's not a murderer, Shorty. He's the worst kind of jerk, but he wouldn't kill somebody."

"How do you know?"

I shrugged. "Gut instinct."

Shorty shook his head. He'd heard me raise my gut reaction as a rationale for all manner of decisions.

"Your instincts don't work where that douchebag is concerned." Shorty cocked an eye at me, adding, "He almost talked you into marrying him, remember?"

I sat on the surface of the counsel table and dug into the burger again. Chewing was a good dodge against tough questions.

I didn't believe that Lee killed that girl. But even if he had, it wouldn't cause me to drop my representation. Guilty people were as entitled to counsel as innocent folks.

Men who refused to cooperate with their lawyers—well, that was another matter. But maybe Suzanne could pull Lee back into line.

Shorty sat down beside me, his hip touching mine. "Damn, I almost forgot to bring this up. When will we have a minute to talk? I have a surprise for you."

To buy time, I sucked on my sweet tea. What had Shorty said that morning at the diner? He wanted to ask me something? Now he wanted to spring a surprise on me—but what kind of surprise? I didn't much like surprises—never had. And my gut told me that it involved our relationship. Did he seriously mean to advance our relationship—which was perfectly satisfactory, just as it stood—when I was up to my eyeballs in crazy?

Because I totally couldn't handle it. Not at the moment.

"Ruby," he said, but stopped when the courtroom door creaked open. The bailiff stepped inside, giving me a look of disapproval.

"This ain't no cafeteria," he said sternly.

The bailiff's announcement woke the sleeping spectator on the back bench of the courtroom gallery. The old-timer's head jerked up and around, as if to see what he'd missed.

The bailiff pointed an arthritic finger at me. "Ms. Bozarth, you can't eat in here. This here's a court of law. What are you thinking, sitting up on the table like it's a picnic bench?"

I ducked my head like a guilty child and dropped the remains of the burger into the bag.

The bailiff's lecture continued. "I'm doing the work of two men as it is, since they pulled Deputy Brockes out of here. Good old Potts volunteered to step in, but that judge from Vicksburg said no. I think Judge Ashley's half crazy."

Shorty spoke in a whisper. "Want to go out in the hallway and finish it?"

I shook my head. "Better hit the ladies' room and get ready for the afternoon round."

The bailiff called to me from the doorway. "Don't be leaving your trash in here. I'm not the janitor."

Shorty took the bag from the table. "I'll toss this for you. Talk to you later."

As I watched him go, I wondered again about the surprise he mentioned. What would I say if he pulled a small box from his pocket the next time we were together? How would I respond?

For a moment, I tried to envision it, to create a scenario in which I could make both of us happy. But we'd only been together for six months.

With a weary sigh, I slipped off the counsel table. I really did need to hit the john. I didn't have time to plot out the rest of my life, but it didn't really matter. Because when the time came, I knew just what I'd do.

Follow my gut.

# CHAPTER 54

AT FIVE THIRTY on Tuesday evening, I locked up the office and headed to my car. Cary Reynolds was waiting for me at his used-car lot in Vicksburg.

And my used car was waiting for me on the town square. As I approached my old Nissan, something looked off: the rear passenger tire was low. Too low to ignore.

Crouching on the pavement, I prodded it with a finger, thinking. It would be reckless to drive on the highway with a tire in that condition. I couldn't take a chance on being stranded in Vicksburg; I had to be in court at nine the next morning.

Fortunately, I had a friend in the business of car maintenance. I made a quick call, and ten minutes later I pulled into Roy's shop. Oscar Summers stood beside the gas pumps, waiting for me.

He beamed as I emerged from the car. Extending a calloused hand, he said, "Ruby, I'm glad to see you. Darrien's always asking after you."

I squeezed his hand and gave him a quick hug, breathing in his workingman's scent of motor oil. "How's Darrien doing? Is he all settled in at Ole Miss?"

"Yes, ma'am. I talked to him on Sunday. Sounds mighty happy. He's in a criminal procedure class. Says he raises his hand so much, he's afraid he's wearing the teacher out."

I smiled; Oscar's good spirits were contagious. "Darrien's going to set the bar over there, Oscar."

His eyes misted. "You tell Miss Greene how much we appreciate her getting that foundation scholarship for him."

"Yes, sir, I will."

Turning to the car, Oscar squatted on his haunches beside my back tire. He frowned at it. "I don't like the looks of this, Ruby."

I didn't much like it either. I watched with trepidation as Oscar stood and prowled around my vehicle, inspecting all four tires with a deepening scowl.

"What's the verdict, Oscar?"

He shook his head. "Ruby, you've got four bald tires. I can see the radials."

I could feel a lecture coming on, and I didn't have the time to hear it. "Can you patch the back tire up for me? So I can get going?"

"You need a new set."

"Yes, but Oscar, I've got someplace I gotta be. Can you patch it? Please?"

He gave me a stern look. "I'll give it a temporary plug, but it's only a Band-Aid. Are you just driving it around town?"

A convenient lie almost spilled out, but something about Oscar's grave face made me swallow it. "I've got to drive to Vicksburg tonight. To see a witness."

He slid into the driver's seat. "This won't take long. Wait inside the station. Tell Roy to give you a bottle of pop."

Inside the station, I found an extensive selection of tobacco products for sale—including nicotine gum. By the time my car was ready, I was chewing a wad of Nicorette, riding a nicotine high. So much for my resolution.

When Oscar pulled my Nissan out of the body shop, I ran to meet him.

"What do I owe you?"

"Nothing, no charge. Don't even ask."

I didn't dare argue. As I slipped behind the wheel, I said, "Oscar, you're a lifesaver. Looks like my old car is going to make it to Cary's Used Cars and Trux."

Oscar's eyes pinned me. Though I tried to shut the driver's door, he held it open with an iron grip. "What's that you say?"

"I'm meeting Cary Reynolds. He's in the car business; do you know him?"

He began to speak, then stopped mid-sentence, as if choosing his words carefully. But he just shut the car door and bent to look through the window.

"Be careful," he said.

# CHAPTER 55

THE OCTOBER SUN was setting as I reached the Vicksburg city limits.

I followed the GPS route, but when the directions led me to Cary Reynolds's business—Cary's Used Cars & Trux—I worried that, in spite of Reynolds's assurances to me over the phone, it might not be open. Though twilight approached, his sign wasn't lit.

The only structure on the car lot was a converted mobile home with a sign above the door identifying it as the office. The businesses nearby were run-down: a payday loan operation to the left, a pawnshop on the right that had bars on its windows, as did Cary's office. Seemed like a dicey neighborhood. I remembered Oscar's warning.

I stepped out of my vehicle and took a look around. Though the lot itself was trashy, Cary had some fancy cars parked near the office. A Mercedes convertible, a Jaguar, a Hummer. From the condition of the lot, I would have expected Cary's inventory to be broken-down junkers.

As I approached the office, I saw the shadowy figure of a man in uniform in the parking lot. I called out: "Hey! Is Cary inside?"

The uniformed man didn't turn around to answer but sidled around the side of the building, out of view.

Fortunately, the office door opened when I turned the knob. The office was lit by a single lamp overhanging a desk where a man sat with his cowboy boots propped up on the desktop. He looked up. "Yeah?"

"Mr. Reynolds?"

"That's me."

I extended my right hand. "So nice to finally meet in person. I'm Ruby Bozarth."

He set his boots on the floor and rose to meet my handshake. Like the high-end merchandise on the lot, Cary Reynolds was flashy. Tinted blond hair spiked with gel, a spray-tanned face, fancy alligator boots. Once I'd identified myself, he was all smiles.

"Now, don't you be calling me Mr. Reynolds; that's my daddy. You just call me Cary." He pulled a white plastic patio chair away from the wall and placed it in front of the metal desk. "Please sit on down, Ruby."

As I pulled out a legal pad, I said, "I thought I saw a cop on the lot when I pulled in. Is everything okay?"

He spoke in a confiding tone. "I hire a security guard to keep an eye on the cars at night. Don't want anyone taking a joyride."

Considering the neighborhood, his security measures made sense—but I didn't want to offend by saying so. I balanced my pad of paper on my knees and said, "Cary, I need for you to tell me everything you remember about the evening when you and Lee were together in Vicksburg."

"Haven't we gone through all this before?"

"I know," I said. I crossed my legs, trying to get comfortable in the patio chair. "But I need to be fresh on all the details."

He sighed, leaned back in his chair, and propped the boots on the desk again. "All right, then. All right all right all right." He winked. "Matthew McConaughey."

He seemed to be waiting for me to say something, so I obliged. "Love him."

"Yeah, Matt's cool. But about Lee—me and Lee were buddies at Ole Miss, frat brothers."

"And had you remained in touch?"

"Oh, not that much. He's busy, I'm busy. But I followed him on social media. He does a lot of Facebook and Instagram."

I kept a poker face. Lee Greene loved nothing better than posting selfies.

"So I knew Lee was coming to Vicksburg on business. I got in touch, said let me show you my town. We'll knock back some drinks, get dinner. For old times' sake."

I'd been scrawling down his answers, but I looked up and said, "Lee told me that your meeting was about business."

"Is that right?"

"Yeah. Lee said you wanted to hire him to do a start-up, to make your business a corporation, and that you wanted to talk about hiring him to file the paperwork and explain all the government regulations." I needed to make certain that their versions of events were consistent.

Cary scratched the stubble of a five o'clock shadow on his jaw. "Sure, right—it was a combination of business and plea-sure. We went to a bar, shot the shit, caught up on old college friends. Got some good advice on the corporate stuff. You know, I wanted to pay Lee for his time, but he wouldn't charge me a dime for it. He didn't even let me pick up the dinner tab."

That sounded typical. Lee loved to pick up a check. It gave

him the opportunity to show off his fancy American Express card.

"Since he wouldn't accept anything, I got an idea. I'd give him a present instead. A gift. I told Lee that I had something for him, but I needed to deliver it to his hotel."

"And?"

"And before too long, I showed up at Lee's hotel room with a bottle of twelve-year-old Scotch."

"The police report said it was Macallan Scotch."

"Yes, ma'am. And there was a bonus. We'd just sat down when a little hooker knocked on the door."

I kept my voice businesslike. "How did you locate a hooker in that brief space of time? And why?"

Cary shot me an "aw, shucks" grin. "I know where to look. I know Vicksburg pretty damn good. And I know Lee Greene really well."

I ignored the reference to Lee's preferences. "Let's talk about the Scotch. Where did you get it?"

"Liquor store, not far from the restaurant. In the Battlefield Shopping Center."

"Had it ever been opened?"

"No, ma'am. It was virgin, Ruby." He winked at me.

I pressed on. "When you came into the hotel room, did you both have a drink?"

"I got in there to his room at the Magnolia Inn, and we got some ice from the machine, and I poured one for Lee, one for myself. But I never got a chance to taste it. The call girl came in right about then, and she took the glass from my hand. She sat on Lee's lap and knocked that drink back."

"Did you pour another one?"

"No! I left, to give them privacy. I wanted to pay him back."

I finished my notes, then reached into my briefcase and

pulled a pink subpoena out of a file folder. Reaching across the desk, I handed it to him. "Cary, here's your subpoena for Lee's trial. I'll need you in court on Friday. You may have to sit around the courthouse hallway before you're called to the stand."

He tossed it onto a stack of loose papers. "You don't need to give me that. I guarantee I'll be at that trial. I owe him."

I shoved the pad into my bag and dug for my keys. "I went to Ole Miss, too. Graduated from undergrad about five years ago."

"Well, that makes you a few years older than me, I guess," he said, looking at me with surprise.

"Oh, I'm ancient. Twenty-seven. Got one foot in the grave."

He scratched his jaw again. "That right?"

"Were we on campus at the same time? Do you think we ever had a class together?"

He cleared his throat. "Probably not. I wasn't there that long. I dropped out and went into business on my own." He flashed the grin again. "You don't have to have a degree to be a kick-ass salesman."

"Just a degree in kick-ass."

He threw back his head and laughed. "Yes, ma'am. I've got a degree in that."

He followed me out of the office as I left, saying, "See you in court. You know I'll do whatever I can to help ol' Lee."

As I slid into my driver's seat, I said, "I'm glad to hear it. Your testimony could make all the difference."

But as I drove back to Rosedale, I puzzled over the information he'd shared, wishing I had asked more questions. The whole story about the hotel still didn't make sense. Lee had said from the outset that he couldn't remember anything after the first drink at the hotel. He only dimly recalled the prostitute coming to the room. He could remember that she was pretty, that she was black, that she was wearing red fishnet hose. But that's all.

I knew what the DA would claim in court: the young prostitute went into a coma and died during a sex act with Lee, with a toxic mix of alcohol and drugs in her system. The prosecution would tell the jury that the girl's drink was drugged, that she died from an overdose of Rohypnol—roofies, the "date rape drug."

Isaac Keet would contend it couldn't be self-inflicted. No one roofies herself.

But that raised another curious issue—one that I would introduce. The prostitute was there in a "professional" capacity. Who roofies a hooker?

# CHAPTER 56

IN MY OFFICE early the next morning, I paced in front of the storefront window, waiting for Suzanne to arrive. She couldn't stand me up for the second day in a row. There was too much at stake.

A car pulled into one of the parking spots directly in front of my building on the square. I pressed my hands to the glass and squinted; the sun had risen to the point where it blinded me from my vantage point.

But it wasn't Suzanne's car. A young man emerged from the vehicle and shuffled to my office door. His shoulders were slumped.

He tried the doorknob, but it was locked. I wasn't open for business. It wasn't even eight o'clock. He stepped over to the storefront and cupped his hands around his face to see inside. Then he rapped on the glass. Apparently, he'd spied me inside the building.

For a second, I considered sneaking off down the hallway to hide, but it wouldn't do to be impolite. My mama didn't raise me that way.

I unlocked the front door and cracked it open. Raising my

hand to block the glare of the morning sun, I now recognized the man. It was Deputy Brockes, dressed in jeans and a Crimson Tide sweatshirt.

"Morning, Deputy. What can I do for you?"

His face was unnaturally pale, making the circles under his eyes stand out in contrast. "I need to see Miss Greene."

He stepped forward, so I blocked the entrance. "She's not here, Deputy. We're not open yet." I tapped the letters painted on the door. "Our office hours are nine to five, usually. But we're in trial right now."

His head ducked. Recalling the scene in court the day before, I knew it hadn't been necessary to mention the trial. Looking at his unlined forehead, I wondered what role this young man could have played in the demise of my witness from Vicksburg.

"It's okay," he said. "I can wait."

I opened my mouth to protest, but then Suzanne's Lexus roared around the corner and zipped into the spot next to Brockes's car. The deputy ran up to the driver's side of the Lexus and stood beside the window as she rolled it down.

To Brockes, she said, "Looks like you beat me here."

"Thank you so much for seeing me, Miss Greene."

She unbuckled her seat belt and exited the car, pulling her enormous Dooney & Bourke briefcase along. "Come on in, hon, and let's talk."

I held the door open, glowering as Suzanne entered the office with Brockes at her heels. "Suzanne, we need a chance to confer before court."

She swept right past me. "Plenty of time for that, after I'm done with this young man."

The deputy dogged her tracks all the way to Suzanne's private office space. "Thanks so much, ma'am. Everybody says you're the best lawyer in this part of Mississippi, you know that?"

"That so?" Suzanne said as she waved the man into her office. Then she pulled the door shut with a solid click.

Shaking my head, I went to my own desk. I had a phone call to make. I looked through my handwritten notes, made on the night I'd first met Detective Guion in the sketchy bar in Vicksburg. I could swear he gave me a name: a man on the Vicksburg police force he trusted.

I scanned the notes with a sharp eye, but it took two reviews of my chicken scratch handwriting before I found the officer's name. I picked up my phone and dialed hastily, hoping I'd get a human on the other end, rather than a recording.

I was in luck. "Connect me with Officer Beau George, please," I said, and the receptionist connected me. A man's voice spoke in a gravelly drawl.

"This is George. I'm unavailable, but you can leave a message when you hear the tone."

Lord, yes, I'd leave a message: a desperate plea, begging him to return my call. I'd just ended the phone call and was sorting through the manila folders I needed for the second day of evidence when I heard the front door open. A man's voice called: "Hello? Anybody home?"

When I stuck my head into the lobby, I saw another deputy, this one in uniform. It was Potts, the cop who'd cuffed Brockes the day before.

A fist of impatience squeezed inside my chest. We'd hired a secretary to handle the incoming traffic, but she wouldn't arrive for another thirty minutes.

"We're not open, Deputy. Sorry, the door should be locked." I pointed at the glass exit, hoping he'd take the hint and depart. "Our hours are posted on the door."

He removed his hat and held it with both hands. "I'm looking for my partner, Brockes. Young fellow, early twenties, red hair. Have you see him?"

"Why are you looking for him?"

He advanced toward me. "I see that's his car out there, right in front of your office."

He walked past me, toward the door marked Suzanne Greene. I trotted behind. "Deputy? Excuse me? I told you, we're closed now."

Without breaking stride, he said, "If that boy is talking to a lawyer, I should be with him."

I thought, *Snoop Dogg*. I slipped in front of him and stood guard before Suzanne's door, with my arms crossed on my chest. There was no way I'd let a cop into a private legal conference concerning a criminal investigation.

"Deputy, you need to leave. Now."

He grabbed my arm and tugged me toward him. Startled, I broke free.

Potts raised his hands in a placating gesture. With a quaver in his voice, he said, "That boy is my partner; he's like a brother to me. He's just a kid, and he needs me. That boy don't know what to do on his own." He blinked, hard. "I got to get in there and help him out."

His speech was touching. But not persuasive. I patted his shoulder before I clenched my hand around his forearm and led him to the front door.

Without a trace of irony, I said to the deputy, "Suzanne Greene is the meanest lawyer in Mississippi. If you interrupt her conference, she'll snatch you bald."

He snorted. "I ain't afraid of no lawyer."

"Well, I am." I opened the door and gave him a not-so-gentle shove. "Because if Suzanne thinks I let you go back there, I'll be bald, too."

When he stepped outside, I shut the door and locked it.

# CHAPTER 57

THE DA HAD spent nearly an hour questioning the county coroner from Vicksburg. Keet led the coroner, Dr. Walker, through a summary of his medical background before eliciting testimony that described the autopsy and the condition of the deceased. Photographs of the dead girl had circulated through the jury box. Some of the jurors looked queasy.

Others looked somber. One man ran a hand over his face. Lee's fan club, consisting of two female jurors, no longer gave him the eye.

Isaac Keet stood at a podium near the jury box. He was wrapping up.

"Doctor, based upon your examination of Monae Prince, and your education, training, and experience, do you have an opinion as to the cause of death of the deceased?"

"I do, sir."

"And what is that opinion?"

"I believe that the deceased died as the result of ingesting an overdose of Rohypnol and alcohol."

"Thank you, Doctor. No further questions, Your Honor."

The judge pointed the gavel at me. "Ms. Bozarth?"

I moved quickly, hoping to break Keet's stride. Unlike the DA, I bypassed the podium and walked straight up to the witness stand, to shatter the notion of distance between us.

"Doctor, thank you for coming today."

He smiled, "You're welcome, Ms. Bozarth."

I made a show of rifling the pages of his report. "Doctor, you testified that the deceased was seventeen at the time of her death. Is that right?"

"I did."

"Why do you say she was seventeen?"

"Beg pardon, ma'am?"

"Her age. Upon what basis did you conclude that she was seventeen years old?"

He shifted in his seat and crossed his legs. "Well, there was information given to me by the police department."

"Ah." I nodded, smiling as if a lightbulb had come on. "So your testimony concerning her age wasn't a scientific determination, based upon your education and training."

"No." He uncrossed his legs. "Well, I could see she was young."

"Certainly. But as to her precise age: based on your examination, could she have been eighteen? Or nineteen? Or twenty-two?"

"I guess so. She could have been."

I shot the jury an expressive look before turning back to the witness.

"Doctor, the state has charged my client with causing death during an unnatural sex act."

"Objection." Keet stood at the prosecution table.

The judge tugged at the ear that held his hearing aid. "What grounds?"

"Defense counsel is making statements rather than asking a question."

Unruffled, I said to the judge, "Your Honor, have I misstated the charge?"

"You have not. Ask the witness a question, Ms. Bozarth."

"Doctor, was ejaculate found in the deceased's body?" I raised my brow, as if I didn't know the answer.

"It was not." His hands squeezed his knees. "That's not dispositive, you know. If a man wears a condom."

I cut him off. "Thank you, sir. And from your extensive review of police reports in this case, you are no doubt aware that no one observed the defendant engage in a sex act with the deceased. Correct?"

"Objection. Hearsay," Keet was saying, but the doctor talked over him, saying, "I observed tears around the anal opening of the deceased."

Now it was time to walk over to the jury box and lean on the railing. "Can you clinically tie those tears on the body of the deceased to my client, Mr. Lee Greene?"

"No. No, ma'am, I can't."

"Doctor, are you aware that professional call girls often entertain multiple clients over the course of an evening?"

Keet sprang from his chair, objecting that my question was outside the scope of testimony. He was right; it was. But I'd made my point.

With a triumphant nod, I picked up my papers. "No further questions."

Lee's eyes were approving as I slid into my seat. "Progress," he whispered.

I didn't have a moment to gloat. The DA had called his next witness, the Vicksburg police officer who had collected evidence at the scene of the crime.

Keet walked him through the crime scene. The officer described my client and the dead woman, naked in bed; the collection of hair from the hotel sheets, matching that of Lee Greene; the strewn clothing, his and hers, that was bagged and tagged; and Monae Prince's purse and the contents thereof.

Keet offered the various exhibits into evidence: clothes, bedding, hair samples, purse, contents.

"No objection," I said.

Keet's brows raised, and he gave me a look of mild surprise. "Your witness."

I walked over to Keet's counsel table and picked through the exhibits until I found what I was looking for: a Mississippi driver's license with a picture of the deceased. Strolling to the witness stand with a hint of a swagger, I handed the license to the witness.

"Officer Lake, I'm handing you State's Exhibit Twenty-two. Can you identify it, sir?"

He glanced down. "It's Monae Prince's driver's license."

"And where was her license found?"

"In her wallet, inside her purse." He pointed at Keet's table. "It's the brown handbag over there, with that fringe on it, I think you ladies call it."

*Sexist.* But I kept my voice polite. "And this is the license upon which you based your determination of her identity?"

A shade of confusion crossed his face. "Yes, ma'am, her license." He turned to the jury and said, "We never could locate next of kin."

"May I?" I extended my hand, and he returned the exhibit. I studied it and said, "Monae Prince, date of birth: September 6, 2000."

He shrugged, "If that's what it says. I didn't commit it to memory."

"So Monae was seventeen years old at the time of her death."

"Yes, ma'am, that much I know for certain. She was only seventeen."

I walked back to my table, where Lee held out a piece of paper. I took it from him and made a show of reading it, shaking my head.

My star witness, the Vicksburg vice cop, was dead. But he'd left a little treasure in my possession before he died.

I gave the paper to the court reporter, keeping my game face intact as she placed a sticker on it.

"Officer Lake, I hand you what has been marked for identification as Defendant's Exhibit One. Could you tell the jury what it is?"

"It's a printed copy of the license. Monae Prince's Mississippi driver's license. But the original was in her purse."

He attempted to return the sheet of paper. I took a step away from him.

"Is it identical to the state's exhibit?"

He looked at the paper again. "Monae Prince. Same photo."

"And the date of birth?"

As he bent over my exhibit, I saw a wave of color wash up his neck. "The date of birth is different. Well, date's the same, but the year says 1994." He glanced up. "But it's just a printed copy."

"That's true." In my hand, I held the plastic license, the state's exhibit; I returned it to him. "How long have you served in law enforcement?"

"Fourteen years."

"That's a long time." I shot the DA a look, and was tickled to see that he was poised on the edge of his seat. "I'll bet you can tell the difference between a real license and a fake ID. Tell the jury, Officer Lake: in your expert opinion, which license looks legitimate to you?"

He spent long moments studying the two exhibits. A muscle twitched in his cheek. I was gambling that he wouldn't lie under oath.

And I was right. With an apologetic glance at Keet, the officer said, "The state's exhibit appears to be fake."

I snatched up the plastic driver's license and held it high for the jury's benefit. "This one is fake?"

"Possibly." With a sheepish look, he corrected himself. "Probably."

"And defendant's exhibit?"

"It looks legit. I mean, it's a paper copy. But it looks like the real deal."

I faced the jury. "Then in your opinion, what was Monae Prince's age at the time of her death, Officer?"

He took a second to calculate. "Twenty-three."

I was on a roll. "Officer Lake, the state contends that an overdose of Rohypnol was in the deceased's system at the time of her death."

"Yes, ma'am."

"What is the street name for the drug, sir?"

"Roofie."

"And isn't it true that roofies are commonly known as a date rape drug?"

"True."

"So they're used for drugging people into having sex without their consent? Right?"

"Yes, ma'am. That's generally the use on the street."

I leaned against the jury box and cocked my head. "Officer, in your career in law enforcement, have you ever encountered a situation in which a prostitute was roofied by a client?"

"I've never seen it."

Score. I turned toward the counsel table, prepared to take my victory walk. But before I could say "No further questions," the officer spoke again.

"But whether she was a hooker or was seventeen or seventy, the girl is dead. And somebody killed her."

# CHAPTER 58

TWENTY-FOUR HOURS later, and the game was the same. I was still slugging it out with the DA and his witnesses.

I had to get my hands around the challenge: to create a reasonable doubt that would render the jury unable to return a guilty verdict against Lee. But to achieve it, I desperately needed the information my dead Vicksburg detective would have provided at trial. I was trying my best to establish those points through attacks on the state's witnesses, but my efforts were hit-and-miss. One step forward, two steps back.

During sleepless hours the night before, I'd decided I needed to visit the sheriff. My dead witness might have had a hard file or electronic file with him at the time of his death.

So when Judge Ashley declared a lunch break on Thursday, I sent Lee and his parents to Shorty's, along with Suzanne. And I headed for the Williams County sheriff's department.

As I walked around the town square, I rehearsed my pitch. The sheriff would be reluctant to part with evidence in a pending investigation. But if I knew it existed, I'd issue a subpoena duces tecum for the information and he'd have to bring it to court. It could be the shot in the arm my defense required.

I marched up to the uniformed woman at the reception counter. "Ruby Bozarth to see the sheriff, please."

The woman glanced at Sheriff Stark's office. The door was firmly shut. "He's tied up."

I gave her a brittle smile. "Thanks." I bypassed her, strode up to Stark's door, and walked on in without knocking.

Sheriff Stark sat behind his desk, which was littered with the remains of his lunch: chicken wings and fries. Deputy Potts sat on a folding chair at the sheriff's right hand, sucking on a chicken bone.

"Hey, Sheriff." I shut the door behind me. "Need to talk to you. In private."

Stark picked up a paper napkin and wiped sauce from his fingers. "Ruby Bozarth, you must've been brought up in a barn. Anyone ever teach you to knock?'

"Brought up in a barn. That's funny. Also true."

He wadded the orange-stained napkin and tossed it onto his desk. "Ruby, you've got one minute to say your piece before I have Deputy Potts escort you out of here."

It was an empty threat—probably. The sheriff and I had enjoyed a civil relationship since the outcome of the Jewel Shaw murder trial. But Potts dropped his chicken bone and scooted back his chair with a screech of metal. So I talked fast.

"Sheriff, I need information about the detective who was found dead on Monday night. He was coming to testify for the defense. What did he have in his possession? I need to subpoena it for trial."

The sheriff gave Potts a hooded glance, then said to me: "Not sure what you mean."

"In his car, on his person. Files, paperwork, computers, phone."

Sheriff Stark cleared his throat. "Can't say I'm happy to have a defense attorney meddling in an ongoing investigation of the murder of a lawman. It don't sit right. There's a brotherhood, Ruby."

"Blue brotherhood," Potts echoed.

I ignored Potts. *Snoop Doggy Dogg,* I thought again, wishing I could shove him outside like I'd done yesterday morning.

But my bad-girl persona wasn't getting the job done. With a sugary voice, I said: "Lord, Sheriff, I'd hate to do it, but if you won't share the information with me voluntarily, I'll have to get a court order. You know I'll do it. I'm a real pain."

I smiled like a contestant for the title of Miss Mississippi.

The sheriff bundled up the remains of his lunch and pitched it into the trash can. Maybe I'd ruined his appetite.

He said, "We'll cut to the chase—save you and the judge some time. The car was clean. Nothing in it but a suitcase."

I shook my head in disbelief. "Impossible."

"It's true."

"What about a phone?" In my dismay, I turned to Potts to support my position. "Everyone carries a phone."

Potts shrugged. "Everybody except him, I reckon."

Sheriff Stark said, "I thought it was peculiar, myself. But that Vicksburg detective had nothing on him. Potts, you was there when we searched. What did we turn up?"

"Nothing." Potts had resumed eating. "Just the body and the gun. Suitcase in his trunk." He dunked a wing in a plastic container of sauce.

The sheriff rose to his feet, a clear sign that the discussion was over. As he walked around his desk, he said, "Who knows what he was thinking. Those vice cops, they got a different procedure than men in uniform." To Potts, he said, "Did you know that dude, Potts? You worked patrol in Vicksburg."

Potts swallowed and said, "Not me."

I stepped out, deflated. The woman at the counter cut me a frosty glare that made me lift my chin and stand up straight.

As I headed out of the building, a thought nagged at me. About Deputy Potts.

He claimed to be a loyal comrade of young Deputy Brockes.

But was he rooting for Brockes? Or rooting around for the sheriff?

CHAPTER 59

I PUSHED MY way through the lunchtime crowd at Shorty's diner. Patrons blocked the center aisle, waiting for tables to empty out. Only one seat was open: a stool at the counter, bearing a RESERVED marker. I cast a longing eye at my usual spot but moved on to a table at the rear where the Greene family sat.

Suzanne removed her bag from the unoccupied chair at the table, and I dropped into the seat.

"I had to fight for that chair," she said. "Nearly came to blows with the old fart over there wearing the John Deere hat."

I twisted around to check out the man Suzanne described, hoping he wasn't a member of my jury. Lee's mother whispered, "Suzanne, please. I'm trying to eat."

Suzanne cut her eyes at her sister-in-law. "Who's stopping you?"

Mrs. Greene closed her eyes. With a strained voice, she said, "Your language."

Shorty walked up and placed a plate of meatloaf and mashed

potatoes in front of me. "Meatloaf special. I'll get you some sweet tea, Ruby." He looked at Lee. Lee glanced away.

I leaned across the table for the salt shaker. In a tone of false cheer, I said, "Pardon my boardinghouse reach. What've y'all been talking about?"

Lee Sr. cleared his throat. "The testimony. Whether we made any progress this morning."

"We're scoring some points. We've established that Monae wasn't a teenager, for one thing. I'm planting seeds about the sex act. They admitted that you might not have been her first customer that night."

Mr. Greene said, "None of this makes any sense. Why would the woman have a driver's license that made her appear younger than her age?"

His wife's voice was plaintive as she said, "When Lee was in college, some boys tried to get licenses that made them seem older. To buy liquor." Her hand snaked across the table and covered Lee's. "But not my boy."

Lee gave his mother a ghost of a smile.

Suzanne shrugged and said, "Could be she wanted to look younger so she could dodge a criminal charge for prostitution. Or maybe to appeal to the creeps who like young girls." She picked up the check and showed it to her brother. "You want me to pay this? I'm ready to go."

Lee Sr. sat stiff as a statue. "That's not necessary."

"Not a problem. I'll add it to your bill." With a grunt, she rose from her chair.

I jumped up. "Are you leaving?"

She nodded. "I've got a hearing set in Barnes County this afternoon."

As she muscled her way to the cash register, I followed at her heels. "Suzanne, you can't run out on me again. I need you."

"Honeybun, you're doing just fine. I kept an eye on you all morning long. You're hitting all the targets."

I grabbed her elbow. She paused, giving me a puzzled look. "What, Ruby?"

In a panicky undertone, I said, "Suzanne, I thought you'd have my back on this trial. There's so much at stake—and regardless of what you've concluded, things are not going according to plan."

She put an arm around my shoulders and squeezed, blocking the aisle. The man in the John Deere hat grumbled behind us, but Suzanne ignored him.

"I couldn't have prevented your witness from dying, honey. And as for the rest—you're handling it."

"Suzanne, I don't have your experience. The legal system—" I began, but she cut me off.

"There's more than one legal system in this country, Ruby. There's one for poor folks, but it doesn't work very well. They tend to get railroaded. And there's a different one for celebrities and people with so much money that they're above the law. That one doesn't work so hot either. They tend to get off scot-free."

I shook my head. Her lecture on class jurisprudence wasn't helping me.

"But there's another one: the system in which Lee Greene resides, where an honorable judge presides over a fair trial, decided by an unbiased jury. In this realm, justice will be done."

Frantic, I said, "I'm not reassured. That's not a guarantee of acquittal."

"If he's not acquitted in a fair trial, well—what does that tell you?"

My mouth fell open. What did she mean? Did Suzanne harbor doubts about Lee's innocence? Or was she clinging to a Disney fantasy of the jury system?

Because anything could happen in this trial. Anything.

Suzanne moved away, swiping her debit card at the register, chatting with the cashier. As I waited, I caught sight of a blond head in the crowd.

Cary Reynolds was making his way toward the back of the diner, waving enthusiastically. I turned and saw the target of Cary's greeting: my client.

"Oh, Lord, no," I said, and elbowed my way back to the Greenes' table. By the time I arrived, Cary was hanging over Lee's chair, shaking hands with his father.

Cary saw me and said, "Hey, it's Ruby Bozarth." Sliding an arm around my shoulders, he said, "I shoulda known Lee would hire a looker for his attorney. Smart and pretty."

Mr. and Mrs. Greene exchanged a glance. Their silence was deafening.

I edged away from Cary's arm. "Cary, I'm delighted to see you—we all are. Thanks so much for coming. But Lee really can't visit with you right now."

"What? My old brother?" He looked injured.

I tugged at his sleeve. "There's a policy: witnesses can't discuss their testimony during the trial."

"We weren't! I was just saying hello."

"I know, I know. But it's best to avoid even the appearance of impropriety."

I pulled him away from the Greenes and back into the diner crush. He looked over my head and gave a departing wave to the Greenes' table.

"If you say so. It's kind of crowded in here, anyway. Guess I'll go back across the street."

"Good idea." I watched him leave, to be certain he didn't change his mind and double back.

When I returned to Lee, his mother was talking into his ear. I heard her say, "I still don't recall ever seeing that boy."

Lee glanced over his shoulder, probably to see whether he could be overheard. In a low voice, he said, "Mama. He was a dropout."

"Oh," she said, sitting back in her chair. She pursed her lips.

Lee Sr. shook his head. "I could tell. That hair."

Standing over my plate, I took three bites of meatloaf in quick succession, ignoring the pointed stare of Lee's mother. I swallowed and said, "We need to head on back. It's almost one o'clock, so Judge Ashley will be starting up again. Cary Reynolds is already over at the courthouse."

Then it struck me. Today was Thursday.

I'd told Cary Reynolds to be in court on Friday. The subpoena I'd served made it clear: he was ordered to appear and testify on Friday.

What was Cary Reynolds doing in Rosedale on Thursday?

# CHAPTER 60

BACK INSIDE THE courtroom, the jurors shifted in their seats, as if they sensed an undercurrent of excitement. Judge Ashley said to the DA, "You may call your next witness."

Keet stood. "The state calls Cary Reynolds to the witness stand."

And the nugget of dread in my chest exploded like a grenade.

But I didn't let it show. My spine remained straight, my face noncommittal. Behind me, I heard Lee's mother gasp and cough. She leaned forward, whispering, "Lee? Honey? Isn't that your friend?"

Lee ignored her. I glanced at Mrs. Greene over my shoulder and narrowed my eyes at her. Her husband wrapped an arm around her shoulder, shushing her.

When Cary Reynolds's cowboy boots clicked past me, I looked up. He met my gaze. His face was unreadable.

After Reynolds was sworn in, he sat on the witness stand,

crossing his booted foot onto his knee. Isaac Keet smiled at him.

And Cary Reynolds smiled back.

Keet asked him to tell the jury about the evening of March twenty-second, when he'd met with Lee Greene in Vicksburg.

"I'd set up a meeting with Lee, to talk business. I'm a small businessman; I have a used-car lot in Vicksburg."

"What did you and the defendant do on that date?"

"Well, I thought we'd maybe get some dinner, talk over paperwork. But Lee wanted to get a taste of Vicksburg. The nightlife, I guess. So, we met up at a bar."

"And where exactly did you meet?"

"Roxy's."

I scratched a note onto my legal pad and shoved it toward Lee: *Bar was your idea?* Lee looked down, shook his head. But there was no time to confer; Cary was talking again.

"I'd printed out some paperwork that I'd emailed to Lee, thought I'd see if I had my ducks in a row, to file the articles of incorporation with the Mississippi Secretary of State's office. Lord, I couldn't hardly get ol' Lee to look at it. He was on a roll. Wanted to get shitface drunk, just like back in college."

With a sheepish face, Reynolds turned to the jury box. "Beg pardon, ladies. But it's a quote."

"How long did you stay at the bar?"

He tilted his head back as if trying to recall. "Two hours, maybe? He was doing some serious drinking. So I thought I'd best get some supper in him. I drove us to a barbeque place downtown. But I'll be danged if Lee didn't drink his dinner."

I shot a look at Lee. He was livid; the cords in his neck were visible.

"Then what happened?" the DA asked.

"Well, I drove him back to his hotel. I had got a gift for him: a thank-you, for meeting with me."

"What was the gift?"

"It was a bottle of Macallan. Twelve-year-old Scotch." In a rueful voice, he added: "Lee likes it."

Keet's voice was quiet, deadly. "What happened when you arrived at the hotel?"

Reynolds uncrossed his foot and set it down. "I handed him the box with the Scotch in it, said thanks a lot. He wanted me to come on up for a drink. I tried to beg off; I'm a workingman, needed to be at the car lot early the next day. But he wouldn't take no for an answer."

"So you accompanied the defendant to his hotel room."

"Yeah, I surely did. He was staying at the Magnolia. Nice place. I thought I'd best hustle him up to his room, see to it he didn't make a big commotion. I didn't want him to get kicked out."

I shifted my eyes to Isaac Keet. His face was stony. "And on that evening, y'all also obtained the services of a sex worker? A young woman named Monae Prince?"

Cary Reynolds laughed. It made a jarring noise in the quiet courtroom. "No, sir, Mr. Keet; that wasn't me. That was all Lee's idea. Not me, no siree." He edged forward on his seat and placed his elbows on his knees, like he was about to tell a secret. But his voice rang out loud and clear.

"Lee made that plan at the bar, didn't need any help from me. He spotted that little ol' gal outside Roxy's, made an appointment with her. He was thinking she looked 'barely legal.' He even said to me: you think that girl is underage? He said it like the idea gave him a thrill."

Reynolds paused. The courtroom was silent but for the sound of choking behind me. It was Mrs. Greene.

Cary Reynolds looked away from Isaac Keet. His eyes connected with mine. Cary pulled a rueful face and said, "Ruby, you know how Lee is."

Then I heard a rustle of fabric and a shout of alarm, as Lee's mother slid to the floor in a dead faint.

# CHAPTER 61

LEE'S MOTHER WAS puddled on the floor of the courtroom gallery. Lee jumped to his feet and bent over the railing. In an urgent whisper, he said, "Mama."

Her departure from the courtroom was swift. Mr. Greene hauled her to her feet and she stumbled out, with her husband supporting her on one side and the bailiff on the other. I pulled Lee back into his seat, but his eyes were glued to his mother's back as she made her way up the aisle with uncertain steps.

Judge Ashley cleared his throat. "Counsel? Do you require a recess at this time?"

Isaac Keet glanced my way. "I have no further questions of this witness."

I turned toward the witness stand and caught Cary Reynolds looking at me with a glint in his eye.

I snatched my legal pad off the counsel table and advanced on him. Reynolds leaned forward in his chair, crossing his arms against his chest like a man bent on destruction.

Looking at the tension straining his jaw, I was reminded of a pit bull. A pit bull could be a dangerous creature.

But he was no match for a junkyard dog.

"No recess, Your Honor," I said.

The judge nodded. "You may cross-examine."

"Mr. Reynolds, we have discussed your meeting with Lee Greene before, haven't we?"

"Yes, ma'am, Ruby." His body was tense, but his tone was friendly, familiar. "Couple of times."

"In fact, you gave me a statement over the phone on two separate occasions, and I discussed the case with you at your car lot in Vicksburg on Tuesday of this week, isn't that correct?"

"Sounds right. Probably so."

I raised my voice. "Was I or was I not at your office in Vicksburg on Tuesday?"

"You was—were. Yes, ma'am."

"And when we discussed the night in question, you never mentioned that my client was—and I quote—'shitface drunk.' Isn't that true?"

"Well, I said we went to a bar."

"Did you or did you not relate to me the extent of his intoxication?"

He leaned back in the seat on the witness stand and stretched out his legs. "Well, you're his lawyer. I figured you knew."

I heard a snicker behind me in the courtroom and had to restrain myself from turning to give the gallery a Medusa glare.

"You told me, in fact, that you conducted important business with my client. That Lee Greene gave you valuable legal advice, for which you were most grateful. Isn't that correct?"

He shrugged, apologetic. "I might have said something like that. I was trying to be polite."

I turned to the jury with a look of disbelief, then focused back on Reynolds. "Were you deliberately trying to mislead me on Tuesday night?"

"No! No, ma'am."

"Has your recollection of events changed or altered in forty-eight hours?"

"No, don't think so."

"Then you're misleading us now."

He gaped at me, shaking his head. "No, ma'am. Swear to God."

"Mr. Reynolds, you never told me that my client hired a prostitute, did you?"

"What?"

I walked up to the witness stand and gripped it with my right hand.

"You never said my client hired a prostitute. You said you did it."

"I don't think—" he began, but I cut him off.

"You hired Monae Prince. It was your idea, you brought her to the hotel as a gift for my client."

Reynolds didn't answer. Isaac Keet jumped to his feet. "Objection, Your Honor. The counsel for the defendant is badgering the witness, is not permitting him to answer."

The judge fiddled with his ear. "Sustained."

I stayed rooted to the spot; for an extended moment, Cary Reynolds and I engaged in a staring war. He blinked first.

In a calmer tone, I said, "Let me repeat the question, Mr. Reynolds. Did you tell me that you hired Monae Prince to come to Lee's room at the Magnolia Inn?"

"Never." The pit bull had disappeared; his voice oozed sincerity.

"May I remind you, sir, that you are under oath?"

As I asked the question, I heard a buzzing sound. At first, I thought it was coming from inside my head, but it grew louder, intensifying into an excruciating squeal. Three of the jurors clapped their hands over their ears.

Isaac Keet rose to his feet. "Judge Ashley."

Making an apologetic face, the judge pulled out the hearing aid and tinkered with it until the whine subsided and the room fell silent.

The judge looked at me. "Where were we? Do you need the court reporter to repeat the last question?"

Cary Reynolds spoke up. "No sir, Your Honor. I remember."

"You may answer."

Reynolds turned his face to me. I read the challenge in his eyes before he spoke.

"Yes, ma'am, I know I'm under oath. I swore I'd tell the truth, about that night in Vicksburg with Lee. And about the other night when we had our little chat. I'm under oath."

He coughed into his fist, then added. "But you ain't. Surely do wish you'd got it down in writing."

Reynolds's statement was accompanied by a smirk. The sight of his face caused a ball of fury to wedge in the center of my chest.

As I struggled for control of my anger, Judge Ashley said, "Ms. Bozarth? Any further questions of this witness?"

My voice sounded hoarse when I answered. "Not at this time, Your Honor."

"Redirect, Mr. Keet?"

"No, sir," the DA said.

"May this witness be excused?"

As Keet opened his mouth to speak, I jumped in. I'd regained my voice.

"No, Your Honor, he may not. Mr. Reynolds is under subpoena to appear tomorrow, and I want the opportunity to call him."

I fixed Reynolds with a junkyard glare as I added:

"As a hostile witness."

# CHAPTER

AS CARY REYNOLDS stepped down, Judge Ashley announced that he was adjourning court early due to a personal matter. While the judge spoke, Reynolds brushed by the counsel table, refusing to meet my eye. I tensed in my seat, eager for the judge to depart. I intended to waylay Reynolds and demand that he explain himself.

But Judge Ashley called the DA and me up to the bench to explain the reason for his early exit. As the judge spoke, mentioning something about his wife's medical appointment, I glanced over my shoulder and watched Cary Reynolds disappear from the courtroom.

By the time the judge had left the bench, my client was disappearing as well. I had to elbow through the courthouse spectators to catch up to Lee, slipping away at a brisk pace.

I chased Lee down the courthouse steps, calling his name, but he ignored me. I had to break into a run to catch up.

I managed to grab on to his suit jacket. He paused, then spun around. In an angry whisper, he said, "Why didn't you depose him?"

I was breathing hard; the past hour had been beyond stressful. "I tried to, twice—you know that. He bailed on us, had insurmountable conflicts both times."

Lee shook his head with a humorless laugh. "Right."

I kept my voice low as I said, "You said it would be fine. You told me a deposition wasn't crucial. You said that it was just as well because we wouldn't give Isaac Keet a shot at him before trial."

I was nose to nose with Lee, but he wouldn't meet my eye. A suspicion took hold in my brain.

He sighed, with a weary sound. Looking up at the courthouse clock, he said, "I wish I were dead."

"Stop it. Don't say that to me."

"It would be better than this. Better to just disappear. I can't take any more of this."

He still wouldn't make eye contact.

I knew Lee well. Well enough to know he was less likely to contemplate suicide than anyone on this side of the Mississippi River.

And he was entirely likely to deceive me when he thought it was in his best interest.

I pointed at a stone bench on the courthouse lawn. "We're gonna stroll over there and have a talk, Lee."

I took his arm and he followed my lead, walking like an automaton. Once we were planted on the bench, I took a careful look around to make sure no one was within earshot.

Then I lit into him.

"It's high time you told me the truth about your relationship with Cary Reynolds."

Lee looked down, where my fist was still clutching his arm.

In an offhand voice, he said, "You're missing a button. On your jacket."

It distracted me for a moment. I looked down at my cuff; as Lee said, a bare thread dangled where a navy button used to be. On my brand-new suit.

But if I was still Raggedy Ruby, I was also the HBIC. I reached over and jerked a brass button from his chest, then threw it across the courthouse lawn. "You've lost a button, too. So what? Don't you dare dodge me, Lee. What happened with Cary Reynolds?"

His head dropped, and he didn't say anything for a moment. Then he spoke in a halting voice.

"It was the semiformal. At the fraternity. Sophomore year."

He paused. To prompt him, I said, "Cary Reynolds's sophomore year."

He shot me an impatient look. "My sophomore year. Cary was a pledge, a freshman."

I waited for him to elaborate. What could happen at a dance that would be so terrible? Then I had an unpleasant suspicion. "Was it hazing? The university doesn't allow it, not these days."

He laughed, but it was a hollow sound. "Oh, Ruby. There are so many things you'll never understand."

I didn't argue. "Okay. Tell me about it."

He rubbed his thighs with the palms of his hands, which left a damp spot on the fabric. "Cary was all psyched about the dance. I asked if he needed me to fix him up—because I was his pledge father. He told me he was going to bring his old high school girlfriend from Vicksburg. Said she was a freshman at Ole Miss."

"So what was the problem? I know you, Lee—you're about to tell me she didn't measure up. Not pretty enough?""

He grimaced. "She was black."

I pulled a face of disbelief. "Oh, my God."

"Well, she was."

"And that was a problem?"

He looked away, defensive. "Do you want to hear this? Or do you want to preach at me?"

He had fallen silent again. I nudged him. "And?"

He looked chagrined when he spoke. "When they saw Cary's date, the brothers were appalled. They said he had to get her out, that if he was interested in becoming a member of the fraternity, he'd never bring a black girl into the house again."

I tried to keep my face impassive. Lee was my client, not Cary. But I couldn't stop myself from asking: "And you went along with that? You didn't stand up for him?"

"You don't know what it's like. The peer pressure in an organization like that."

I shook my head. "Oh, Lord."

He lowered his voice to the barest whisper. I had to bend my head to hear.

"The brothers pulled me aside, said it was up to me to drive the two of them home and make sure they didn't return. I dropped Cary off first; his dorm was close to Greektown. When I pulled into his date's parking lot, she was crying in the backseat."

Oh, hell. A feeling of dread came over me. I had a pretty good idea what was coming next.

"I got into the backseat with her. Seduced her, I guess you'd say."

I made a snort of disapproval, and he turned on me with burning eyes.

"It was consensual."

I shook my head; my face wore an expression I didn't try to hide. "You kicked them out and screwed his date? You're shitting me."

"Oh, Ruby, you're so crass."

I didn't take the bait. He was going to finish telling the tale, regardless of the number of slights he launched in my direction.

When I didn't respond, he sighed and went on. "I'm really not the villain of this tale. The girl told Cary about it—God knows why."

"How did he react?"

He made a face of distaste. "He beat the tar out of her. Somebody reported it, and Cary was kicked out of the university. Which apparently was the end of his academic career."

Lee let out another breath, the sound of a long-held confession finally released. I waited, wondering whether there was another horrific chapter to the episode, but none came.

I finally said, "But what about the girl? What happened to her?"

He looked at me with surprise. "Good Lord—how would I know? I never saw her again." He paused. "I don't even remember her name."

Recalling the conversation at lunch, when Lee described Reynolds as a "dropout," I felt that I should have known there was more to the story.

But I had a last question. "You knew Cary Reynolds had good reason to hold a grudge against you. So why on earth did you agree to meet up with him in Vicksburg?"

He huffed out another breath that sounded like a groan. "I know you like to think I'm a total ass. But how things went down with Cary . . . it's bothered me for years. I thought I could make amends by doing him a favor, giving free representation. It could be payback. You know?"

Oh, I knew. What transpired in court today was payback, all right. Just not the kind Lee had predicted.

CHAPTER 63

LEE WENT IN search of his parents, leaving me alone on the bench. As he walked away, I unearthed a nugget of Nicorette and chewed down on it.

Lost in thought, I stared at the patchy grass and kicked at a clump of it with the toe of my shoe.

Cary Reynolds had transformed from a supportive defense tool into a poison pup, but at least I knew why. He had an ax to grind because he was bearing an old grudge. In my head, I pictured him returning to the witness stand, and tried to calculate how I might undo the damage without opening the door to further injury. If I opened the door on the reason for his bias against Lee, it would muddy my client as well as Cary Reynolds.

When my cell phone hummed, I was tempted to ignore it. I was in no mood for conversation. But I pulled it out of my pocket just before it went to voice mail, and though it was from an "unknown caller," I answered.

"This is Ruby Bozarth."

"Yeah, this is Officer George, with the Vicksburg PD. I've been trying to reach you all afternoon. I got your message."

I sat up straight. "Oh, thank God."

"Did you get my message?"

"No, I'm sorry, Officer George. I've been in court all day. You worked undercover in Vicksburg, right? With Detective Guion?"

Since Tuesday, when I'd learned about the death of my Vicksburg cop, I had tried repeatedly to reach his coworker, without success. I was so happy to hear him on the phone, I almost swallowed my gum.

In a voice pitched so low I had to strain to hear it, he asked, "How'd you get my name?"

"Detective Guion mentioned you, said you were a good cop. That he trusted you. I'd really like to talk to you. Can I meet you somewhere?"

He hesitated. "I'm beat. I'm on a crazy investigation, haven't hardly slept in two days."

I stood, pacing in front of the bench. "It's really important. We can meet anywhere you like, whatever is convenient for you. But I have to talk to you, and I want to do it in person."

He sighed into the phone. "Okay. I gotta eat something, anyway. You know the Seven Gables truck stop? It's on the highway, outside the Vicksburg city limits."

I didn't know the place, but I said, "Sure. I'll meet you there. Six o'clock?"

"Okay."

When he ended the call, I took off for my car at a run.

# CHAPTER 64

WHEN I REACHED the truck stop, I walked into the adjoining restaurant, taking a careful look around. I hadn't asked him for a description, figuring I could spot a cop. But walking through the tables of customers, I didn't see anyone who looked like a law enforcement officer.

As I cruised by a booth in the back, a shaggy-haired man in a camouflage jacket nodded at me. I paused by his table. He pointed to the opposite side of the booth and said, "Sit down, Ruby."

I slid into the vinyl seat across from him. "You had me fooled for a minute."

"That's the idea." He leaned forward and spoke in a low voice. "I'm undercover. Don't blow it."

"Right." I dropped my voice to a whisper. "I represent Lee Greene. He's on trial for the murder of Monae Prince last spring."

When the cop didn't say anything, I went on. "Your friend Guion was supposed to testify at the trial."

He blinked. "Got him killed."

I waited for him to elaborate, but he was mute. So I said, "Really? You think?"

"Monae was snitching for him."

"Yeah. I know that. He was going to testify at trial about her criminal background. Her prostitution and drug use. But—obviously—Monae is dead. So why would talking about her put Detective Guion in danger?"

The officer rubbed his face with his hand. He had a three-day growth of whiskers. "Monae knew too much."

Again, I waited in vain for him to say more. When he remained silent, I prodded. "Too much about what?"

He looked like he was trying to decide whether to answer me. Finally, he shook his head and squeezed his eyes shut for a moment. When he opened them, he said, "What Monae told him was bigger than prostitution. It was a major drug trade, and a big meth ring. So much money involved, there was a money-laundering operation to cover up the illegal funds."

"Wow. I didn't know all that. He didn't tell me." I reached into my bag for a legal pad, but the officer stopped me with a warning shake of his head.

So I whispered again. "This insight into Monae's life could have a crucial impact on my trial. I need to establish it in court. Can you testify? Tomorrow? Or next week?"

"No."

I sat up straight in the booth, attempting to look intimidating. "If you are under subpoena, you'll have to appear. You know that."

His voice was hoarse when he spoke. "I can't testify because I don't have the personal involvement. There's nothing I could say that would get into evidence. Never worked with the snitch, never even met her. Guion kept her under wraps. And he kept the information close to his chest."

"But he must have submitted reports in writing. Someone has to know about this, someone who can help me."

"He was after a major player. And the guy had connections. That's the worst part. Someone inside the department was on this dude's payroll. Guion didn't trust anybody with the information. He was afraid of a leak."

I slumped in my seat. "No hard file I can access, maybe?"

"Nothing." He picked up a coffee mug and wrapped both hands around it. "Nothing at all."

Shortly after that, the cop left the booth. As I watched his camouflage jacket disappear through the door, I was so frustrated I wanted to spit. The testimony I needed to defend Lee was buried with Detective Guion. Literally.

# CHAPTER 65

SO, IT WAS back to Plan B: Cary Reynolds. Somehow, I had to back him down from the damning testimony he'd given in court. I turned to the window and looked down the highway toward Vicksburg. I wasn't all that far from his car lot. It occurred to me: what if I surprised him in his office?

I popped a piece of gum, and adrenaline started to hum in my veins. That was just what I needed to do. Time for a smackdown.

Pulling out my phone, I punched in the address of Cary's business. As I scanned the route on the phone screen, I debated whether I should reveal my knowledge regarding his bad blood with Lee. It might shake the truth out of him, but I didn't want to give him time to think up a new way to lash out when he returned to the witness stand.

While I drained the dregs of my coffee cup, I toyed with the phone, reviewing Cary's social media pages to see if he'd posted anything new that might clue me in to his state of mind.

Nothing on his Twitter account, but he didn't utilize it often, aside from some game-day tweets. I went to his Facebook page and saw that he'd posted a picture of a pulled-pork sandwich that he'd eaten the previous week. No help there. Prior to the sandwich, he'd shared some beach pics from Gulf Shores, but they were old.

Cary also had a business page on Facebook for Cary's Used Cars & Trux. I hit that next. I'd examined it several weeks before, and it looked the same. Clearly, he didn't update it often, and the page only went back a few years. But as I gave it a second perusal, I saw something that made me look twice.

Four years back in the timeline, there were photos to mark the grand opening of Cary's Used Cars & Trux. In one of the pictures, a pretty young woman held a banner that read: GRAND OPENING.

The young woman looked a lot like Monae Prince.

I enlarged the picture on my screen to examine it more closely. True, I'd never seen Monae during her lifetime, and the only pictures I'd had access to were crime scene photos and the driver's license. But the smile on the driver's license was the same: dimples in both cheeks and a slight gap between her two front teeth. The more I looked, the more certain I became: Monae was the banner girl for Cary Reynolds's grand opening.

So what the hell was up with that?

I walked out of the truck stop diner to my car.

The rear tire was flat as a pancake.

# CHAPTER 66

I KNOW HOW to change a tire. My mama taught me the ropes when I was a teenager. The used cars she could afford were notoriously unreliable.

I stripped off my jacket to keep it clean and rolled up the sleeves of my white blouse. The sun had set, but the lights in the parking lot provided fair illumination.

To get to the jack, I had to pull out the spare. When I dropped the spare tire onto the pavement, I knew I had a problem. The spare was flat, too.

I kicked the tire, which didn't make me feel better and didn't help the tire any. Then I cussed at it, loudly enough that a man walking to his nearby car let out a shrill whistle.

A trucker saw my plight and jumped out of his rig.

"Can I give you a hand, ma'am?"

"Thanks, but no. I don't think your tires would fit my old Nissan."

I sat in the car and called Shorty first. When it went to voice mail, I literally crossed my fingers and called Suzanne.

Forty-five minutes later, her Lexus tore into the lot, spraying gravel in its wake. I grabbed my briefcase and ran to the passenger side.

"Suzanne, I'm so sorry about this," I began, but she cut me off.

"Don't even get started with that. This is why you have a partner. To help you when you're stranded—literally or figuratively." She put the car in drive. "Where are we headed?"

"Well, I'd planned to drive on down to Vicksburg to see that frat brother of Lee's, but I expect you need to get home."

She turned the car onto the highway, heading to Vicksburg, rather than Rosedale. "I'm at your disposal, little sister. Did you get your car towed?"

I'd talked to a lady inside the truck stop who gave me a lead on an automotive repair shop in the area, but they couldn't help me until the next day. So I was without wheels.

Suzanne drove to Vicksburg in record time, passing so many vehicles that I worried she'd get pulled over. I offered to serve as navigator, but her high-tech Lexus didn't require my assistance. As we neared the car lot, Suzanne took in the neighborhood and whistled through her teeth.

"What a dump," she said in a clipped Yankee accent. Then she looked at me and grinned. "Bette Davis."

"Beg pardon?" I said. I didn't know a friend of hers named Betty.

Suzanne sighed with resignation, shaking her head. I pointed out the CARY'S USED CARS & TRUX sign, and she wheeled in and pulled up to the office, putting the car in park.

I grabbed my briefcase, but the engine continued to idle. "You coming, Suzanne?"

She grimaced. "I don't mean to bail on you, sugar. But I haven't eaten a bite of food since noon. I've got the weak tremblies." She held out her hand; it did have a slight tremor. "My blood sugar is dipping. If I don't get something to eat pretty quick, I'm going to collapse."

Opening the passenger door, I said, "Not a problem. Should I call you when I'm done here?"

"Oh, honey, I'll be right back. I'm just going to find me a hamburger stand. Shouldn't take me all that long."

I walked in the evening gloom toward the office. To be downright honest, I longed to have Suzanne at my back, but I also needed to put on my big-girl pants. Suzanne had already saved the day when she rescued me at the truck stop. Squaring my shoulders, I approached the door.

When I walked into Cary Reynolds's office, he looked up from his desk with genuine surprise.

I spoke before he had a chance. "Sorry I didn't call for an appointment. I was in the neighborhood."

He stuck out his hand. And had the nerve to smile at me. "Nice to see you, Ruby."

I ignored the extended hand. I picked up one of the plastic chairs and placed it directly in front of Cary's desk. Without waiting for an invitation, I sat.

"Cary, I wanted to talk to you about your testimony today. You said some things that took me by surprise."

"Is that right?"

I kept a poker face. He knew he'd turned tail today. "So, can we talk?"

"All right."

In my head, I heard his Matthew McConaughey: All right all right all right. I pulled out my iPhone. "Okay if I record this?"

He gave me an affronted look. "Do you really think that's necessary?"

I gave him a wink. "Fool me twice."

"Doesn't seem like a friendly way to hold a conversation."

I took that as a yes and pushed the button. "So, Cary—what happened to you in court today?"

Cary sighed and scratched the back of his neck. "Gotta say, that Keet dude is pretty intimidating. Can't deny."

"So, did the DA tell you to testify that Lee Greene hired Monae? Or was it your idea?"

"I don't think I said that."

"Pretty sure you said exactly that, on the stand this afternoon. Cary, I know that it's tough being a witness. Sometimes people shift the facts if they're embarrassed. But Lee Greene's life is at stake here."

"No—you're not letting me explain. I never said that other. I never told you that I hired that hooker."

I blinked and fell silent. He had the gall to lie to my face. Maybe I should drop the bomb.

When I found my voice, I said, "Cary, I know you probably hold a grudge against Lee." I tried to soften my tone. "I know he done you dirt, back when you were both in undergrad. That deal that went down at the fraternity dance. Lee disrespected you, had sex with your date. But that doesn't justify committing perjury at his murder trial."

"You've been nosing around, it sounds like."

"I have. I hate surprises. Speaking of surprises," and I scooted the chair closer to the desk, "I was shocked to see that you were acquainted with the murder victim. Monae Prince."

"That's crazy."

"Yeah, I thought so, too. But funny thing—she's on your Facebook page."

He looked away, shaking his head. "Don't think so."

I leaned back in the chair, tipping it onto its plastic legs. I hoped it wouldn't collapse.

"Looks like Monae to me. I took a screenshot. Want me to send it to you?"

He shrugged, frowning. "Ma'am, you've been working too hard. You're all mixed up."

A narrow hallway led to a back door; I heard it open. A voice called out, "Hey, Cary."

"In here." Cary smiled at me. "My security guard."

As heavy footsteps moved our way, I said, "You hire someone to watch those cars every night? Couldn't you just set up a camera?"

Cary chuckled. Slitting his eyes, he said, "You've got all kinds of ideas, don't you?"

The uniformed guard stuck his head into the room. "Cary, everything okay?"

When I saw him, my mouth fell open. I shut it so fast that my teeth clacked.

It was a deputy from the Williams County sheriff's department. Deputy Potts.

# CHAPTER 67

CARY REYNOLDS FLAGGED an arm in invitation. "Come on in here, Potts. We got company. I'll introduce you."

Potts cut his eyes at me then looked away. A copy machine stood inside the doorway. He leaned against it and ran a finger along the buttons.

I said, "We've met."

Cary Reynolds turned to me with a quizzical look. "That right?"

I glanced over at Potts, deliberately casual. "Sure. At the courthouse in Rosedale. And the sheriff's office. Plus, my law partner is representing a good buddy of the deputy."

Reynolds's face was a blank. "What buddy is that?"

"A young guy named Brockes. He was Deputy Potts's partner. Until this week. Brockes has been suspended from the sheriff's department, pending the outcome of an investigation."

Potts's eyes shifted. The tension in the room was mounting, but Cary Reynolds seemed unaffected. He whistled and said,

"Seems like things are hopping in your community. Murder trials, murder investigations, I don't know what all."

I nodded. "The sheriff's department has been so busy lately, I'm amazed that Deputy Potts has the time to moonlight at a car lot so far from Rosedale."

Potts made eye contact with Reynolds. There was a moment of silence. To break it, I said, "How long have you been with our sheriff's department, Deputy Potts? I don't recall seeing you around when I started my practice in Rosedale."

Potts just stared at me. His gaze made me uncomfortable. I crossed my legs and made a show of looking inside my briefcase. And then I recalled something I'd heard earlier that day.

I twisted in my seat and fixed Potts with a look. "Sheriff Stark said you used to work in Vicksburg, didn't he? For the police department. When was that? It would have to be way less than a year ago. Isn't that right, Deputy?"

He responded with a bare movement of his head.

I set the briefcase back on the floor. "What does Sheriff Stark think of you running over here in his uniform to work at Cary's business?"

Potts's voice was tight as he said, "What I do on my time is my business."

Behind his desk, Cary Reynolds took a deep breath and rubbed his hands together. "I'm afraid I'm being a bad host. How about a drink?"

I shook my head. "Not for me, thanks."

"Oh, come on now. A friendly drink never hurt anybody." He opened a drawer of his desk and pulled out a bottle, half full of amber liquid. I could see the label: Macallan Scotch.

A miniature refrigerator sat in the corner, within reach of his chair. Reynolds picked up a sleeve of disposable cups in clear plastic that sat atop the refrigerator. He pulled out two cups.

Over his shoulder, he said to Potts, "I'd best leave you out of this round, bro, since you're in uniform."

"Leave me out, too," I said. "I appreciate your hospitality, but hey—I'm working."

He turned and stared at me—and not in a friendly way. "You come barging in here tonight, without so much as a by-your-leave. Put out a phone to record what I say."

He opened the door to the mini-fridge and removed a water bottle. He set the water and the empty cups on his desk.

Pinning me with his gaze, he said, "If you want to talk with me, you'll do me the courtesy of taking a drink with me. Otherwise, you can pack up and hit the door."

Well, I wasn't ready to leave. We hadn't resolved the inconsistencies in his testimony. And my ride was at a hamburger stand, somewhere in the city of Vicksburg. I glanced at the office door, wishing that Suzanne would hurry on back to give me a hand.

With a sigh, I gave in. "All right. Just one. Don't make it very strong, okay?"

# CHAPTER 68

HE SMILED, RESTORED to good humor. "No problem, Miss Ruby. I know how to mix a lady a drink." He poured a finger of Scotch into one of the glasses, then filled it to the brim from the bottle of water. He handed me the cup and said, "There you go, weak as tea. Sorry I don't have any ice. But the water's good and cold."

I took a sip and refrained from making a face. I've never cared for Scotch, but it didn't seem polite to ask if he had anything else.

Reynolds poured a generous measure of Scotch into the other cup without watering it down. He raised it. "Cheers."

I tipped my drink to his and we both swallowed. He raised his glass again. "Here's to old friends." I couldn't refuse that toast, so I held my breath as I swallowed a third mouthful, thinking that all brown liquor tasted like a rusty nail to me. But I managed a smile.

Cary threw back his head and laughed. "Now you're acting like an Ole Miss gal."

Potts chuckled deep in his throat. "That's right. Y'all are having a party here."

Cary stared at the cup in my hand, then his gaze shifted to my face. I was glad I wasn't driving. I was already feeling a little buzz.

Reynolds picked up the open Macallan bottle. Nodding at my cup, he said, "Want me to sweeten that for you?"

"Lord, no. Thank you."

"Oh, come on. Be sociable, now."

I heard a high-pitched giggle, and was astonished to realize that I was the source of the sound. I hadn't giggled since grade school and wasn't often guilty of it back then.

Cary walked around the desk, took the drink from my hand and refilled it. As he set it down on the desk and took a seat, he said, "Oh, come on. It's just got a spoonful of booze in it. No way it'll get your blood alcohol too high. Isn't that right, Deputy? Is that what you're worried about, Ruby?"

I wasn't worried about my blood alcohol, but something was nagging at me. Something I needed to do.

It struck me: Cary's testimony. I was supposed to be getting him to back away from the statements he'd made on the witness stand and admit to his bias against Lee. I needed to get my head back on task. My forehead wrinkled as I asked: "What were we talking about?"

His brow rose. "Ma'am?"

"About Monae."

He huffed a laugh as he nudged the plastic cup closer to me. "You're like a dog after a bone, ain't you?"

Potts left his position by the copy machine and walked up to Cary's desk, setting a hip on it. He picked up the Scotch bottle and took a swig from the neck. "Can't beat Macallan."

Cary swiveled in his seat, giving Potts a look of annoyance. "Get your ass off my desk."

Potts backed off, wiping his mouth with his hand. "You ready for me to make the deposit?"

"Not yet."

"It's a sizable amount."

"Potts. We got company. We're drinking here." Reynolds propped his boots on the desk in the very spot Potts had vacated. In a confiding tone, he said, "Yeah—Monae. I loved that girl, I really did. Even after she boned old Lee Greene, I forgave her. But she had a flaw. No loyalty." He winked at me. "A fatal flaw."

Potts emitted a warning grunt, but Cary flailed a careless arm in response. I glanced over at Potts. He was watching us with an eagle eye. It should've made me nervous, but I didn't feel a bit anxious. My muscles had relaxed. All the tension in my shoulders had disappeared.

# CHAPTER 69

POTTS AND CARY kept talking about money, but I quit following the thread of the conversation. Turning to Cary, I meant to ask something, but my eyes lost focus when I looked at him. I blinked and rubbed my eyes, but it didn't help.

"I don't feel good," I said. My voice sounded far away, my speech was slurred.

Cary gave me a tight smile. Though I was woozy, I heard him say, "What are we going to do with you?"

He drained his Scotch and set the glass down. "Poor little old thing, can't hold your liquor. I believe we'd best take your car keys away."

I clutched my bag in a defensive move, but I had enough recall to say, "My car's not here."

The information seemed to startle him. Returning his boots to the floor, he wheeled his chair over to the window and lifted one of the plastic blinds.

"Damn. How'd you get here?"

I didn't answer. I was trying to remember how I got there.

"Shit." Cary turned to Potts. "Go on out back and start up the van."

Potts said, "You don't need any help in here?"

"Oh, I think I can take care of a lady. We need to get moving."

I saw Potts shake his head, but then he walked down the hall-way. The back door banged when it closed.

I squeezed my eyes shut. When I opened them, I had double vision. Two Cary Reynoldses were staring at me.

I whispered, "Oh, Lord."

Reynolds didn't reply. He shook a set of keys from his pocket and picked a key from the ring.

"I think I'm sick."

He looked at me and smiled, shaking the key ring.

As my head rolled on my neck, I saw the front door fly open. Two Suzanne Greenes stood in the doorway.

Then I remembered. That's how I got there. Suzanne drove me.

Her voice rang out so loud I wanted to cover my ears as she said, "What the hell is going on here?"

I said, "I am drunk as fuck." Then I laughed again, because it's not something I'd usually say.

Cary froze behind his desk, still holding that little key be-tween his fingers. He didn't look happy as he demanded, "Who are you?"

"It's Suzanne. She's my *podner*." I tried to straighten up in my seat, but I felt myself slipping sideways instead. "She's gonna take me home and put me to bed."

Suzanne took another look at me and commenced digging in her big brown bag. "I'm calling 911."

Cary stuck the key in his desk drawer and jerked it open. "You ain't calling nobody. Y'all are going out the back and get-ting in the van."

He thrust his arm in the desk drawer. When he pulled it out, he was holding a handgun. I thought I must be dreaming. Who brings a gun to a party?

Suzanne stood still as a statue, her hand deep inside the brown bag hanging off her elbow.

When Cary said, "You drop that bag on the floor. You won't be bringing it along," she followed his order.

She dropped the bag. I watched it fall to the floor. It tipped onto its side, and her cell phone spilled out, close to my shoe.

But when I looked up, she held something in front of her, clutching it with both hands.

Suzanne and Cary shouted at the same time, but I couldn't make out what they said. Because there were fireworks. Lights flashing, rockets going off.

That's when I slid out of the chair and passed out.

# CHAPTER 70

WHEN MY EYES opened, I focused on the pattern of ceiling tiles overhead, trying to remember where I was.

I was lying on a narrow mattress, covered with a sheet. My head was fuzzy. And my stomach hurt. A blue nylon curtain surrounded me. The curtain was ripped aside so abruptly that it frightened me, and I nearly rolled off the bed.

Before I could escape, I was snatched up into a fierce hug that smelled of tobacco and Estée Lauder. My eyes closed as I sagged into Suzanne's embrace.

"They said you were coming around, honey." She released me and stood back, examining me over her glasses. "How are you feeling?"

"Not great."

Suzanne hugged me again and kissed my cheek. The gesture made me tear up. I hadn't experienced a hug and kiss like that since my mama passed. Suzanne grabbed a stool in the corner, rolled it next to my bedside, and sat down.

She stroked my hair. It eased the ache in my head. "Well, they pumped your stomach. I expect that took the sap out of you."

My head was clearing. As the clouds parted, I grasped the reason that I was in a hospital bed. My nerves jangled with delayed fight-or-flight instinct.

"Good Lord, Suzanne. What happened?"

"Do you recall anything? The police tried to take a statement from you, but you were too woozy."

The scene came back to me. Sitting in Cary Reynolds's office. Drinking a weak Scotch and water. Getting blind drunk from one drink.

Not drunk. I don't pass out from one drink.

"Did he drug me?"

She took my hand in a warm grasp. "Slipped you a mickey, honey."

"Oh, my God." My frazzled brain struggled to piece it together. He didn't slip a pill into the glass; I would have seen that. Was it in the Scotch? But Cary drank the Scotch, too. And Potts.

My heart started to hammer in my chest. "Suzanne, that deputy was there. The one from Rosedale. Potts."

"Yeah—originally from Vicksburg, till he left about six months ago, the police tell me. I'm guessing that the late Detective Guion had caught on to Potts's employment sideline. He's in custody. The police got him, running down the highway, holding a big old bag of cash. There was a van running in the back. With the back open. For you, I reckon."

My head was pounding again. I rubbed my forehead, trying to remember. "Potts was there. Reynolds sent him out back. I had a drink. That's all I remember."

"Nothing else?"

A vision floated up: Suzanne in the doorway. Pulling something from her purse. I sat up so fast my head began to spin.

"Suzanne. Did you have a gun?"

"Yes, sugar. It's all legal. I have a concealed-carry permit."

My throat was dry, but I tried to swallow before asking, "Did you kill Cary Reynolds?"

She reached out and patted the sheet where it covered my knee. "No, honey. I got him in the chest, but he's still breathing. Worthless son of a bitch."

I lay back on the hard mattress as I tried to absorb Suzanne's revelations. "Was I in danger?"

"What do you think?" Suzanne rummaged in her bag, pulled out a flowered handkerchief, and wiped her glasses with it.

She said, "When I walked in there, you were sliding out of that little chair. Why, I hadn't left you there for twenty minutes. I knew he'd done a number on you when I set eyes on you. And when I barged in, he reached for a gun in his desk drawer. But I had my Smith and Wesson."

I was reeling. Reynolds had drugged me. Suzanne came to my rescue and shot him. I was still processing when the metal rings on the blue curtain jingled again. A woman dressed in scrubs gave me a genuine smile. "You're awake."

"Yeah. Trying to get my head to wake up." I pulled the sheet up to my neck, as bashful as if I'd ended up in the ER due to intentional overindulgence.

She ripped the Velcro of a blood pressure cuff and wrapped it around my arm. "I'm going to take your vitals. Then a police officer would like to talk to you. Are you up for that?"

My stomach twisted, but I ignored it. "Sure."

The nurse slipped a plastic clip onto my fingertip. I lay back, quiet, until Suzanne announced that she was stepping out.

As she hooked her bag over her shoulder, the vision of the prior night returned.

"Suzanne! How do you know what to do with a handgun?"

She returned to my bedside, ignoring the nurse's warning look, and tucked the sheet around me with a gentle hand. "My daddy taught me how to shoot. It's a Greene family tradition."

Giving the sheet a final pat, she added, "He taught me how to drink, too. Always take it neat. You and my nephew could stand to take a lesson from him."

As she swept through the curtain, my weary brain finally made the connection.

Lee Greene's memory loss. My incapacity. Monae Prince's death. It was in the water.

# CHAPTER 71

AT NOON ON Friday, I was back in the Ben Franklin, poring over reports. I'd received a fortuitous email from Judge Ashley that morning; his wife required follow-up tests, so he informed Isaac Keet and me that the Greene trial would be delayed until Monday morning.

I should have taken the opportunity to sleep, but I was too wired. After I was released from the ER in Vicksburg, Suzanne and I spent the wee hours of Friday morning at the Vicksburg police department, providing witness statements to the detective division. The police indicated that Suzanne's use of her firearm was justifiable self-defense; moreover, while we were at the PD, the cops were performing a search of Cary Reynolds's car lot. I was wild to know what the search revealed, and kept my phone near at hand.

An unwrapped Clif Bar sat on my desk. The sight of it made me want to gag. I needed something soft on my stomach. A scrambled egg, maybe. Or grits.

The vision of a dish of grits made me reach for my phone for the umpteenth time. Still no word from Shorty, though I had called and texted repeatedly.

"Some boyfriend," I muttered, petulant.

I tossed the phone in my bag and left the office. If he wasn't answering the phone, I'd hunt him down at the diner. I was so intent on my injured feelings that I didn't notice that the neon bulbs that ordinarily greeted me were turned off.

And when I reached the entrance, I saw that inside the glass door was a sign that was never displayed at noon: SORRY! WE'RE CLOSED!

My disappointment was so profound that tears blurred my vision. I blinked them back, wondering when I'd become such a crybaby. I tried the door, but the dead bolt held it fast. Pounding my fist on the glass didn't raise anyone.

I turned to walk back to the Ben Franklin, moving in slow motion. Then I noticed Shorty's car, parked on a side street beside the alley that ran behind the diner.

Picking up my pace, I headed for the alley. When I pushed the screen door that led into the kitchen, it opened wide. "Shorty? You in here?"

He appeared, wearing a smile. At the sight of him, I jumped over the threshold, grabbed him, and held on tight. Then I started to bawl.

"What?" He tried to lift my chin with his hand, but I buried my face in his shoulder. "Ruby, honey. What's wrong?"

When I was able to speak, my voice came out in a whine. "Where were you?"

"Arkansas."

I swiped at my nose, which was running—not a glamorous sight. "But I tried to call you."

He groaned, stepping over to a stainless-steel counter where a roll of paper towels sat. He ripped a towel off and handed it to me, saying, "I forgot my charger. My phone is dead."

I blew into the towel. It was scratchy, but I was grateful to have it. "You could've picked one up at a gas station."

"Yeah. I could've. But I was only gone overnight. What happened?"

With an immature "they'll feel bad when I'm dead" reaction, I took a perverse pleasure in responding. I gave a little shrug and said, "I got roofied."

He stared at me. "You're serious."

"Yeah." I let out a small sigh.

His jaw began to twitch. He spun around, grasping the counter where the pots and pans were stacked. With a swift movement of his arm, he sent them crashing onto the tile floor.

I jumped back. "Jesus!"

He turned to face me again, his eyes burning. "I'll kill the son of a bitch. Where is he?"

I shook my head, stupefied; this was a side of my mild-mannered lover that I'd never seen. "He's in the hospital. I think. Or the jail. Probably the hospital."

"Then I'm going over there." He ripped off his apron and flung it to the floor, and pushed the screen door so violently I feared it would come off its hinges.

I ran to the door. Through the screen, I shouted, "What are you doing?"

He faced me. He was breathing hard. "I'm going to find Lee Greene and kick his fucking ass."

# CHAPTER 72

MY REACTION WAS delayed. He was storming out into the alley as I called out to him. "Shorty, no! Lee Greene didn't roofie me. Cary Reynolds roofied me."

He turned, his brow furrowed. "Who?"

I heaved a huge sigh and gave the screen door a push. "Get on back in here. We've got some catching up to do."

As he stepped back into the kitchen, I leaned against the counter, kicking a stray saucepan out of my way. "I'm not helping you pick that mess up, baby. I am wore slick."

"How did you get roofied?"

"I ran up to Vicksburg last night to talk to a turncoat witness, and I'll be damned if he didn't try to do me in."

Shorty shook his head, looking shocked. "I can't believe it. When you needed me, I wasn't around to help. Good God, Ruby. I am so sorry."

"Shoot—it's not like you could've predicted it. So why'd you run off to Arkansas without saying a thing about it?"

"It's a surprise. For you."

I squeezed my eyes shut, shook my head with a silent "no." Surely, we weren't back to that debate again. Shorty's timing was worse than terrible. Couldn't he see that I was at the end of my rope? I tried to send him a silent message: *Don't pull out a ring box. Just don't.*

"I drove all the way to Little Rock to pick up your surprise. And, by God, here she comes."

My eyes popped open. Here who comes?

Through the screen panel in the door, I could see a gray-haired figure bearing a brown paper grocery sack. She said, "Shorty, your daddy is spinning in his grave. I guarantee, he never in his life ran out of baking powder at the diner."

Shorty pushed the door open, saying, "Mama, Ruby's here."

She shoved the grocery sack into Shorty's hands and said, "Well, isn't this a pleasure."

My weak stomach twisted. Meeting my boyfriend's mother without prior notice? That rocked me back on my heels. I wished I'd had the chance to brush my teeth, at least.

But Shorty's mother was smiling like she'd just won the lottery. She extended her hand. "Ruby, I'm Cassie. And I've been dying to meet you."

When I took her hand, I had to look up. She was almost as tall as her son. I'd swear that Cassie was six foot two. I gave her hand a squeeze. "Pleased to meet you, ma'am. Your son has told me such wonderful things about you."

She reached out and patted his cheek. "Shorty's a good boy. Drove all the way to Little Rock to bring me back to Rosedale to meet you." She looked chagrined. "I just can't do that highway driving. Makes me a nervous wreck."

We fell silent. I struggled to think of something to say.

Cassie clapped her hands together. "I've met the famous Ruby

Bozarth at last. This calls for a celebration. Shorty, where did this mess come from? Pick it up, for goodness' sake. I'm going to fry y'all some chicken."

A vision of golden fried chicken swam before my eyes. And suddenly, I was gloriously hungry.

As Cassie tied an apron over her clothing, Shorty bent to pick up the pans scattered on the floor.

"Mama's showing off for you. She knows her chicken's better than mine." He stood and whispered in my ear. "She wants you to like her."

She wanted me to like her. Well, that was refreshing.

And Cassie had nothing to fear. I liked her already. How could I not?

She was just like Shorty.

# CHAPTER 73

THE FOLLOWING TUESDAY afternoon, I stood beside Isaac Keet near my counsel table. The courtroom was deserted but for the two of us.

I held a compact in my hand, which shook slightly as I dabbed on a coat of lipstick.

"You look fine," Isaac said.

To my surprise, I did look pretty fresh, considering we had just made our closing arguments to the jury that afternoon. My suit was unwrinkled, all buttons accounted for. My blouse was crisp. My hair wasn't hanging in my face.

My gut, on the other hand, was queasy. Despite Cassie and Shorty's cooking, I hadn't felt 100 percent right since my stomach was pumped at the hospital. And today I was high on adrenaline due to our jury instruction conference and the closing before the jury. It made me jumpy and slightly nauseated.

It didn't help that I had a wad of nicotine gum lodged in my jaw. I intended to give it up. Right after the Lee Greene trial was put to bed.

When I returned the compact to my briefcase, my hand trembled so violently that I nearly dropped it.

Keet reached out and squeezed my shoulder. "You nervous, Ruby?"

Folding my hands together to still them, I lied. "Nothing to be nervous about. The jury hasn't even been deliberating for an hour yet."

He turned and checked the big clock on the courtroom wall. "They've been out for over an hour."

I shrugged, trying to look confident. "It takes that long to read through the instructions and vote for a foreman."

"Well, you're right about that." He stepped away from the table and stretched his arms over his head. "I'm worn out, too, I gotta confess. Quite a weekend."

"No shit." Without irony, I added, "I kept the Vicksburg PD working overtime."

He nodded soberly. "Now that you've cracked the crime ring and the money-laundering scheme, they may want to present you with the key to the city."

A moment of silent agreement hung between us. I broke it, with a touch of resentment in my voice.

"You could've just dismissed the charge."

He swung around, facing me with a look of reproach.

"Don't you complain to me, Ruby. I laid down on the floor in this case. When you rolled in with your law partner and your wild new evidence, I didn't object to your evidence or your exhibits. Not even the smoking gun the jury's got in the jury room with them right this minute."

I turned my head to the jury room, wishing I were a fly

on the wall inside. "Wonder why they asked to see that exhibit."

He huffed a rueful laugh, shaking his head. "It's a ticking bomb, that's for sure. Don't know why they needed the judge to send it to the jury room. Guess we'll see soon enough."

The big entrance to the courtroom opened with a mighty creak. In walked the bailiff, accompanied by a uniformed deputy. I was happy to see that the uniformed man was young Deputy Brockes, back on the job. His uniform hung even looser on him than it had the week before, as if he'd been on a long fast. But his freckled face was bright again.

Brockes and the bailiff carried trays loaded with coffee in foam cups and cold drinks. As the two men bore the trays toward the jury room, Keet nudged me.

"See? We still have a wait ahead. They can't return a verdict before they get something to drink. They may even hold out for a meal."

As the bailiff knocked on the door of the jury room, Deputy Brockes turned and faced us. I made eye contact with him. He gave me a nod, and a bashful smile lit his face.

In a low voice, Keet said, "The bailiff has his helper back. Remember when the sheriff offered Judge Ashley Deputy Potts in Brockes's place?"

"I sure do."

"I should've paid attention to that. Ashley is a sharp old dog. If he suspected Potts was dirty, that should have sent a message to me."

I shot Keet a glance. If my face was smug, well, I couldn't help myself.

He went on. "Judge Ashley's got a sharp eye."

I couldn't resist: "And a deaf ear."

He laughed but said in a bantering tone, "Watch yourself, girl. Someday you'll be old and gray like the rest of us."

The door to the jury room opened, and the bailiff walked back out, his empty tray smacking the door frame.

"Go get your client, Miss Bozarth; I'll get the judge. They've got a verdict."

# CHAPTER 74

LEE GREENE AND I stood shoulder to shoulder at the defense table as the jury filed into the jury box. My client's chest rose and fell so rapidly that his breathing made his power tie dance. Behind us, I could sense the panic emanating from Lee's mother. I'd swear I could hear her teeth rattle.

I focused my attention on the men and women in the jury box. My brow wrinkled as I studied them. Something looked off.

But when I saw that the verdict form was in the hands of a woman who'd been one of Lee's most ardent admirers, my shoulders relaxed.

As the judge said, "Ms. Foreman, do you have a verdict?" I made eye contact with Lee and gave him a ghost of a smile. He nodded in understanding. The foreman of the jury was on our side.

The woman held up her sheet of paper and said, "We do, Your Honor."

The bailiff was peering into the jury room. He turned to the judge with an expression of dismay. He sprinted to the bench with more speed than I thought the old guy could muster and whispered into the judge's ear.

The judge shook his head and fiddled with his hearing device. The whine that pierced my ears made me shudder involuntarily.

Looking from the judge to the jury, I finally realized what I'd missed. One of the spots in the jury box was unoccupied; there was an empty chair in the middle of the first row. I counted heads to be certain: eleven. A juror was missing.

When the whine from the hearing aid subsided, Judge Ashley said, "What's wrong with the remaining member of the jury?"

The woman holding the verdict form answered. "He's in there, Judge." She held up the sheet of paper in her hand. "We all voted before it happened."

Judge Ashley shut his eyes and shook his head. Then he said to the bailiff, "Get in there and get him into the jury box."

The bailiff disappeared into the jury room, and Deputy Brockes ran to join him.

Lee elbowed me. Under his breath, he said, "What the hell?"

I met his eye and a wave of panic engulfed me. We had come so far, and our evidence was compelling. Why was there a holdout?

The events of the past few days had even been a game changer for the prosecution. After the shooting of Cary Reynolds and subsequent arrests of Reynolds and Potts, Keet bent over backward to let the jury see what the defense wanted to reveal. I was certain that we had created a reasonable doubt for the jury. Dead certain.

But only eleven jurors walked out of that room. The verdict in a criminal case had to be unanimous.

I was counsel for the defendant; I was responsible for presenting and arguing our case. Had the points in my closing argument not been convincing enough? If there was a hung jury, Lee's case would not be resolved. And it would be all my fault.

# CHAPTER 75

IN MY HEAD, I was reviewing the matters I'd driven home in my argument—maybe I hadn't been clear. Behind me, Suzanne was sitting beside Lee's parents. They were whispering, but I could hear Suzanne's response.

"Y'all just settle down. We'll know in a minute."

She fell silent as the bailiff and Deputy Brockes walked out of the jury room with the last juror. I was desperate to see what was happening, but Lee was blocking my view. To get a good look, I leaned so far over the counsel table that I was in danger of flashing my panties for the whole courthouse.

When I saw the juror, I forgot to worry about my underwear. Brockes and the bailiff were straining to hold the man up. His head dangled from his neck, and his feet dragged on the tile floor.

The judge's voice boomed from the bench, causing me to jump. "Which one is he? Which juror?"

The bailiff answered. "This one's Morris. He's number three."

I snickered. Lee looked at me, shocked. I covered my mouth; this was no time to explain my inappropriate reaction.

But my eyes strayed to that empty chair in the front row of the jury box. Lord, have mercy: what were the odds? Juror number three. Again.

Judge Ashley said, "Is juror number three sick? Did he fall ill?"

The jury foreman leaned forward, grasping the railing. She said, "He wanted to try it. The defendant's exhibit, that water bottle."

Judge Ashley stared at her with shock. "What's that, ma'am?"

She nodded and lifted her shoulders. "The water in the bottle. He didn't believe it could knock out a grown man. He said he didn't buy Ms. Bozarth's scientific evidence." She paused, then added, "That's a quote."

Judge Ashley took off his glasses and rubbed his eyes.

The foreman continued: "Even when we said to him that Ms. Bozarth called a real scientist who tested it to the stand. And that scientist swore under oath and testified what was in that water bottle and what it could do to anybody who drank it. But that polecat said he'd have to see it to believe it." She glanced over at the slumped figure of the twelfth juror and snorted.

The judge tapped the gavel on the bench. "Read your verdict, Ms. Foreman."

She stood up straight and shot a look at Lee, then turned her eyes to the verdict form.

"We, the undersigned, find the defendant, Lee Greene, not guilty."

Lee's head dropped back on his neck as a smattering of applause broke out in the courtroom gallery. Lee's mother lunged over the railing, hugging him from behind. I edged away, to give him room to turn around and share the moment with his parents.

Suzanne flew out of the gallery and came to my side. She gave me a hearty kiss, no doubt leaving a red print of lipstick on my cheek.

She cupped my cheek with her hand and looked at me with pride shining in her eyes. "You saved the farm, girl." Dropping her voice, she added. "Not to mention my bad-boy nephew."

I gave her a quick hug. "And you saved my skin. I still get shaky when I think of what Reynolds and Potts had in store for me."

"I guess I never mentioned. I always carry heat."

The idea of Suzanne toting a deadly weapon was frightening in principle. But it had come in handy five nights before.

Lee broke away from his parents. He walked up to me, took my hand, and squeezed it.

"Ruby, we're celebrating. Join us for dinner. Please."

He gave me a smile that had a glimmer of the old Lee Greene charm. But when his mother called to him, he moved away to answer her.

Suzanne said, "Come on out and eat with us. Let the Greene family suck up to you for an evening."

Having the Greenes court me would have been a novel experience. But I no longer had an appetite for it. I dodged the invitation, saying, "Nobody's eating anything until Lee does his victory dance for the press. The reporters are probably running across the courthouse lawn right this minute."

"You're right." A stray lock of hair had fallen over my cheek; Suzanne reached out to tuck it behind my ear. "Smile for the cameras, honey."

# CHAPTER 76

AFTER LEE AND I fielded all of the reporters' questions, they packed up their equipment and drifted to the vans parked on the courthouse square. Lee heaved a sigh.

"It's over," he said.

I flashed a smile at him. "Well, almost. You'll need to pay the remainder of your attorney's fee."

"Gladly." He pulled the fountain pen from his jacket and used it to point at my office. "Let's go wrap that up right now."

I flushed. "I was just teasing, Lee. We'll send it in the mail, with an accounting of my hours."

"No, ma'am." He took my elbow, propelling me down the sidewalk. "I'm no charity case. This is a debt I'm happy to pay right away." Over his shoulder, he said to Lee Sr., "Daddy, tell Mama we'll meet y'all at the club."

Once inside the Ben Franklin, I pulled up the file on the computer and did a quick calculation of the time I'd spent in the past week. While my hands were busy on the keyboard, Lee paced the office.

A cardboard box sat in the corner. I'd written *Goodwill* on the side of the box with a Sharpie. Lee lifted the top flaps and looked inside.

"What's this?"

Swiveling in my chair to face him, I said, "It's some stuff of mine that I'm donating. Since I bought some new clothes and got a new set of pots and pans, I'm getting rid of my old college stuff."

He lifted a gray jacket that was folded on top and shook it out.

"What in God's name is this? Merciful heavens."

Lifting my chin, I said, "A suit."

"I can see it's a suit. How did such a rag make its way into your possession?"

"I bought it. At Goodwill." With an edge in my voice, I added, "Tried my first case in that suit."

He chuckled as he dropped it back into the box. I saw him pull a monogrammed handkerchief from his pocket. He wiped his hands as he dropped into the seat facing my desk.

"That's the thing about you that always fascinated me, Ruby. You were such a diamond in the rough. I could always see the possibilities, how you could someday shed that humble outer layer and shine."

My voice was flat. "Thanks. Wow."

He tucked his handkerchief away and crossed his legs. "Don't get huffy, darlin'. I'm serious. You are a rare jewel. I could always see it, even though my parents were blind to your charms."

"Well, that's something we can all agree on." I hit the Print button, and pages began to crank out of the printer. I gave the bill a careful review, then handed it across the desk.

He pulled a checkbook from an inner pocket of his suit coat. Without a glance at the particulars, he wrote a check, signing his name with a flourish.

I pressed my lips together to hide my glee as I locked the check in my desk. The amount was substantial. A vision of a new set of tires danced in my head.

"You've won them over," he said. I looked up. He was smiling, looking at me with unmasked admiration.

"What's that?" I said.

"My mama and daddy. They see you in a new light. Mama said so last night. She wished she'd been more welcoming a year ago, made you feel like a part of the family."

There was some satisfaction in hearing about his parents' change of heart, but I was eager to get to the Firestone shop. I was tired of limping around on a patched tire. "That's real sweet, Lee. You tell her I said so."

I walked around the desk, hoping to signal an end to the conversation. But Lee grabbed my hand and pulled me into the chair beside his.

"You tell her. We're celebrating tonight; Daddy got a table at the country club. We'll order a bottle of Dom. Remember the first time you tasted Dom Pérignon? The night we got engaged?"

"It's the only time I've ever tasted it," I said.

He laughed, as if I were trying to be witty. He reached into the side pocket of his coat and placed a box on my desk.

A small black velvet box. I thought, *Oh, shit.*

# CHAPTER 77

I DIDN'T SAY anything. Just looked at him with disbelief.

"Aren't you going to open it?" he said.

I folded my hands in my lap. "Lee."

He ignored me, lifting the box from its spot on the desk and pulling back the lid.

I recognized it, all right. It was the engagement ring he'd given me, back in law school. The one I'd thrown in his face when I caught him cheating on me in a bathroom stall.

I tried to keep my voice light. "You can't turn back the clock, Lee."

"I don't want to go back. I want to go forward." He set the open box back on the desk, in a beam of sunlight from the window. The stone sent out a shard of light. My eyes were drawn to it, lured by the rainbow of facets.

I reached for the velvet box. And I snapped the lid shut.

"Lee, you flatter me. But I have a man in my life right now; you know that."

He gave me a side-eye glance through lowered lids. "Shorty Morgan? The fry cook? Oh, Ruby. Be serious."

He reached for my hand and held it in his. I was startled to feel how cold his fingers were.

Lee said, "The only real impediment to our future was my parents' failure to accept you. Now that they have, they'll pave the way for us. You'll get back the job with the law firm in Jackson; you can leave this shabby little office behind. You'll love my loft in the city. And I know you were never much of a joiner, but Mama can fix all of that. She'll get you into the Junior League."

I laughed aloud; I couldn't help it. Incredulous, Lee said, "Do you hear what I'm saying? What I'm offering you?"

With a struggle, I pulled a straight face. "Lee, thanks for your offer. But I can't accept this ring."

I tried to pull my hand from his grasp, but he held on to my fingers. "You don't need to wear it on your finger. I understand that; it's too soon. Get it reset—as a pendant, maybe. I'll buy another ring when you're ready."

I met his gaze. His eyes were a startling blue, and he looked at me with such intensity that it lent sincerity to his plea. A woman could get lost in his blue eyes. If she didn't know him like I did.

With my free hand, I nudged the velvet box closer to him. "Save the ring for the right woman, Lee. I know you'll find her."

He stood abruptly, shoved the box in his jacket, and turned to go. "I don't suppose you'll be joining us at the club for dinner."

"No. I'd best not."

He left my office without a backward glance. Relieved to hear the front door slam shut, I let my shoulders relax.

Returning to my desk, I emptied my briefcase, pulling out my folders and legal pads and stacking them. I'd file them later.

The briefcase sat in my lap, still almost as shiny as the day

Lee had presented it to me in a big box tied with a red ribbon. I inspected it. There was a scuff mark on one side, but it wiped clean when I rubbed it with my fingers.

Inside, I had a fistful of change, four or five pens, a wad of Kleenex, and a box of Nicorette. I took a piece of gum from the box and chewed down.

And inspiration struck. I knew just what to do.

I turned the bag upside down and shook it. The coins and pens tumbled onto my desk, followed by the tissues. I took care to shut the nicotine gum in the top drawer of my desk.

Then I stood up and tossed the Coach briefcase into the Goodwill box, right on top of my secondhand jacket. With an effort, I hefted the box in my arms and headed out.

It was going to be a red-letter day at Goodwill. And a good day for me.

# ACKNOWLEDGMENTS

Some people provided excellent assistance as we shaped Ruby's courtroom practice and the cases she encountered. Special thanks go to John Appelquist and Susan Appelquist for their wise counsel and legal expertise; to Dr. Patti Ross Salinas for sharing her knowledge of criminology; and to Dr. Manuel Salinas for explaining the medical issues involved in the story line in a way the layperson can understand.

# ABOUT THE AUTHORS

JAMES PATTERSON received the Literarian Award for Outstanding Service to the American Literary Community from the National Book Foundation. He holds the Guinness World Record for the most #1 *New York Times* bestsellers, and his books have sold more than 375 million copies worldwide. A tireless champion of the power of books and reading, Patterson created a children's book imprint, JIMMY Patterson, whose mission is simple: "We want every kid who finishes a JIMMY Book to say, 'PLEASE GIVE ME ANOTHER BOOK.'" He has donated more than one million books to students and soldiers and funds over four hundred Teacher Education Scholarships at twenty-four colleges and universities. He has also donated millions of dollars to independent bookstores and school libraries. Patterson invests proceeds from the sales of JIMMY Patterson Books in pro-reading initiatives.

NANCY ALLEN practiced law for fifteen years in her native Ozarks and is now a law instructor at Missouri State University. She is also the author of the Ozarks Mystery series.

# BOOKS BY JAMES PATTERSON

## FEATURING ALEX CROSS

*The People vs. Alex Cross* • *Cross the Line* • *Cross Justice* • *Hope to Die* • *Cross My Heart* • *Alex Cross, Run* • *Merry Christmas, Alex Cross* • *Kill Alex Cross* • *Cross Fire* • *I, Alex Cross* • *Alex Cross's Trial* (with Richard DiLallo) • *Cross Country* • *Double Cross* • *Cross* (also published as *Alex Cross*) • *Mary, Mary* • *London Bridges* • *The Big Bad Wolf* • *Four Blind Mice* • *Violets Are Blue* • *Roses Are Red* • *Pop Goes the Weasel* • *Cat & Mouse* • *Jack & Jill* • *Kiss the Girls* • *Along Came a Spider*

## THE WOMEN'S MURDER CLUB

*The 17th Suspect* (with Maxine Paetro) • *16th Seduction* (with Maxine Paetro) • *15th Affair* (with Maxine Paetro) • *14th Deadly Sin* (with Maxine Paetro) • *Unlucky 13* (with Maxine Paetro) • *12th of Never* (with Maxine Paetro) • *11th Hour* (with Maxine Paetro) • *10th Anniversary* (with Maxine Paetro) • *The 9th Judgment* (with Maxine Paetro) • *The 8th Confession* (with Maxine Paetro) • *7th Heaven* (with Maxine Paetro) • *The 6th Target* (with Maxine Paetro) • *The 5th Horseman* (with Maxine Paetro) • *4th of July* (with Maxine Paetro) • *3rd Degree* (with Andrew Gross) • *2nd Chance* (with Andrew Gross) • *1st to Die*

## FEATURING MICHAEL BENNETT

*Haunted* (with James O. Born) • *Bullseye* (with Michael Ledwidge) • *Alert* (with Michael Ledwidge) • *Burn* (with Michael

Ledwidge) • *Gone* (with Michael Ledwidge) • *I, Michael Bennett* (with Michael Ledwidge) • *Tick Tock* (with Michael Ledwidge) • *Worst Case* (with Michael Ledwidge) • *Run for Your Life* (with Michael Ledwidge) • *Step on a Crack* (with Michael Ledwidge)

## THE PRIVATE NOVELS

*Princess: A Private Novel* (with Rees Jones) • *Count to Ten: A Private Novel* (with Ashwin Sanghi) • *Missing: A Private Novel* (with Kathryn Fox) • *The Games* (with Mark Sullivan) • *Private Paris* (with Mark Sullivan) • *Private Vegas* (with Maxine Paetro) • *Private India: City on Fire* (with Ashwin Sanghi) • *Private Down Under* (with Michael White) • *Private L.A.* (with Mark Sullivan) • *Private Berlin* (with Mark Sullivan) • *Private London* (with Mark Pearson) • *Private Games* (with Mark Sullivan) • *Private: #1 Suspect* (with Maxine Paetro) • *Private* (with Maxine Paetro)

## NYPD RED NOVELS

*Red Alert* (with Marshall Karp) • *NYPD Red 4* (with Marshall Karp) • *NYPD Red 3* (with Marshall Karp) • *NYPD Red 2* (with Marshall Karp) • *NYPD Red* (with Marshall Karp)

## SUMMER NOVELS

*Second Honeymoon* (with Howard Roughan) • *Now You See Her* (with Michael Ledwidge) • *Swimsuit* (with Maxine Paetro) • *Sail* (with Howard Roughan) • *Beach Road* (with Peter de Jonge) • *Lifeguard* (with Andrew Gross) • *Honeymoon* (with Howard Roughan) • *The Beach House* (with Peter de Jonge)

## STAND-ALONE BOOKS

*Juror #3* (with Nancy Allen) • *Texas Ranger* (with Andrew Bourelle) • *Triple Homicide: From the Case Files of Alex Cross, Michael Bennett, and the Women's Murder Club* (thriller omnibus) • *Murder in Paradise* (thriller omnibus) • *The President Is Missing* by Bill Clinton and James Patterson • *Fifty Fifty* (with Candice Fox) • *Murder Beyond the Grave* (Murder Is Forever book 3) • *The Patriot* (with Alex Abramovich and Mike Harvkey) • *Murder, Interrupted* (Murder Is Forever book 2) • *Home Sweet Murder* (Murder Is Forever book 1) • *The Family Lawyer* (thriller omnibus) • *The Store* (with Richard DiLallo) • *The Moores Are Missing* (thriller omnibus) • *Murder Games* (with Howard Roughan) • *Penguins of America* (with Jack Patterson and Florence Yue) • *Two from the Heart* (with Frank Costantini, Emily Raymond, and Brian Sitts) • *The Black Book* (with David Ellis) • *Humans, Bow Down* (with Emily Raymond) • *Never Never* (with Candice Fox) • *Woman of God* (with Maxine Paetro) • *Filthy Rich* (with John Connolly and Timothy Malloy) • *The Murder House* (with David Ellis) • *Truth or Die* (with Howard Roughan) • *Miracle at Augusta* (with Peter de Jonge) • *Invisible* (with David Ellis) • *First Love* (with Emily Raymond) • *Mistress* (with David Ellis) • *Zoo* (with Michael Ledwidge) • *Guilty Wives* (with David Ellis) • *The Christmas Wedding* (with Richard DiLallo) • *Kill Me If You Can* (with Marshall Karp) • *Toys* (with Neil McMahon) • *Don't Blink* (with Howard Roughan) • *The Postcard Killers* (with Liza Marklund) • *The Murder of King Tut* (with Martin Dugard) • *Against Medical Advice* (with Hal Friedman) • *Sundays at Tiffany's* (with Gabrielle Charbonnet) • *You've Been Warned* (with Howard Roughan) • *The Quickie* (with Michael Ledwidge) • *Judge & Jury* (with Andrew Gross) • *Sam's Letters to Jennifer* • *The Lake House* • *The Jester* (with Andrew

Gross) • *Suzanne's Diary for Nicholas* • *Cradle and All* • *When the Wind Blows* • *Miracle on the 17th Green* (with Peter de Jonge) • *Hide & Seek* • *The Midnight Club* • *Black Friday* (originally published as *Black Market*) • *See How They Run* (originally published as *The Jericho Commandment*) • *Season of the Machete* • *The Thomas Berryman Number*

## BOOKS FOR READERS OF ALL AGES

### Maximum Ride

*Maximum Ride Forever* • *Nevermore: The Final Maximum Ride Adventure* • *Angel: A Maximum Ride Novel* • *Fang: A Maximum Ride Novel* • *Max: A Maximum Ride Novel* • *The Final Warning: A Maximum Ride Novel* • *Saving the World and Other Extreme Sports: A Maximum Ride Novel* • *School's Out—Forever: A Maximum Ride Novel* • *The Angel Experiment: A Maximum Ride Novel*

### Daniel X

*Daniel X: Lights Out* (with Chris Grabenstein) • *Daniel X: Armageddon* (with Chris Grabenstein) • *Daniel X: Game Over* (with Ned Rust) • *Daniel X: Demons & Druids* (with Adam Sadler) • *Daniel X: Watch the Skies* (with Ned Rust) • *The Dangerous Days of Daniel X* (with Michael Ledwidge)

### Witch & Wizard

*Witch & Wizard: The Lost* (with Emily Raymond) • *Witch & Wizard: The Kiss* (with Jill Dembowski) • *Witch & Wizard: The Fire* (with Jill Dembowski) • *Witch & Wizard: The Gift* (with Ned Rust) • *Witch & Wizard* (with Gabrielle Charbonnet)

## Middle School

*Middle School: From Hero to Zero* (with Chris Tebbetts, illustrated by Laura Park) • *Middle School: Escape to Australia* (with Martin Chatterton, illustrated by Daniel Griffo) • *Middle School: Dog's Best Friend* (with Chris Tebbetts, illustrated by Jomike Tejido) • *Middle School: Just My Rotten Luck* (with Chris Tebbetts, illustrated by Laura Park) • *Middle School: Save Rafe* (with Chris Tebbetts, illustrated by Laura Park) • *Middle School: Ultimate Showdown* (with Julia Bergen, illustrated by Alec Longstreth) • *Middle School: How I Survived Bullies, Broccoli, and Snake Hill* (with Chris Tebbetts, illustrated by Laura Park) • *Middle School: Big Fat Liar* (with Lisa Papademetriou, illustrated by Neil Swaab) • *Middle School: Get Me Out of Here!* (with Chris Tebbetts, illustrated by Laura Park) • *Middle School, The Worst Years of My Life* (with Chris Tebbetts, illustrated by Laura Park)

## Confessions

*Confessions: The Murder of an Angel* (with Maxine Paetro) • *Confessions: The Paris Mysteries* (with Maxine Paetro) • *Confessions: The Private School Murders* (with Maxine Paetro) • *Confessions of a Murder Suspect* (with Maxine Paetro)

## I Funny

*The Nerdiest, Wimpiest, Dorkiest I Funny Ever* (with Chris Grabenstein) • *I Funny: School of Laughs* (with Chris Grabenstein, illustrated by Jomike Tejido) • *I Funny TV* (with Chris Grabenstein, illustrated by Laura Park) • *I Totally Funniest* (with Chris Grabenstein, illustrated by Laura Park) • *I Even Funnier* (with Chris Grabenstein, illustrated by Laura Park) • *I Funny: A Middle School Story* (with Chris Grabenstein, illustrated by Laura Park)

## Treasure Hunters

*Treasure Hunters: Quest for the City of Gold* (with Chris Grabenstein, illustrated by Juliana Neufeld) • *Treasure Hunters: Peril at the Top of the World* (with Chris Grabenstein, illustrated by Juliana Neufeld) • *Treasure Hunters: Secret of the Forbidden City* (with Chris Grabenstein, illustrated by Juliana Neufeld) • *Treasure Hunters: Danger Down the Nile* (with Chris Grabenstein, illustrated by Juliana Neufeld) • *Treasure Hunters* (with Chris Grabenstein, illustrated by Juliana Neufeld)

## House of Robots

*House of Robots: Robot Revolution* (with Chris Grabenstein, illustrated by Juliana Neufeld) • *House of Robots: Robots Go Wild!* (with Chris Grabenstein, illustrated by Juliana Neufeld) • *House of Robots* (with Chris Grabenstein, illustrated by Juliana Neufeld)

## Other Books for Readers of All Ages

*Cuddly Critters for Little Geniuses* (with Susan Patterson, illustrated by Hsinping Pan) • *Unbelievably Boring Bart* (with Duane Swierczynski) • *Not So Normal Norbert* (with Joey Green) • *Jacky Ha-Ha: My Life Is a Joke* (with Chris Grabenstein, illustrated by Kerascoët) • *Give Thank You a Try* • *The Injustice* (with Emily Raymond; also published as *Expelled*) • *The Candies Save Christmas* (illustrated by Andy Elkerton) • *Big Words for Little Geniuses* (with Susan Patterson, illustrated by Hsinping Pan) • *Laugh Out Loud* (with Chris Grabenstein, illustrated by Jeff Ebbeler) • *Pottymouth and Stoopid* (with Chris Grabenstein, illustrated by Stephen Gilpin) • *Crazy House* (with Gabrielle Charbonnet) • *Word of Mouse* (with Chris Grabenstein, illustrated by Joe Sutphin) • *Give Please a Chance* (with Bill O'Reilly) • *Cradle and All* (teen edition) • *Jacky Ha-Ha* (with

Chris Grabenstein, illustrated by Kerascoët) • *Public School Superhero* (with Chris Tebbetts, illustrated by Cory Thomas) • *Homeroom Diaries* (with Lisa Papademetriou, illustrated by Keino) • *Med Head* (with Hal Friedman) • *santaKid* (illustrated by Michael Garland)

For previews of upcoming books and information about the author, visit JamesPatterson.com or find him on Facebook, Twitter, or Instagram.